BEYOND
ALL
DOUBT

BEYOND ALL DOUBT

A NOVEL

HILTON REED

CROOKED LANE

NEW YORK

Published in the United States by Crooked Lane Books, an imprint of The Quick Brown Fox & Company LLC.

Crooked Lane Books and its logo are trademarks of The Quick Brown Fox & Company LLC.

Library of Congress Catalog-in-Publication data available upon request.

ISBN (hardcover): 978-1-63910-701-8
ISBN (ebook): 978-1-63910-702-5

Cover design by Nebojsa Zoric

Printed in the United States.

www.crookedlanebooks.com

Crooked Lane Books
34 West 27th St., 10th Floor
New York, NY 10001

First Edition: March 2024

10 9 8 7 6 5 4 3 2 1

For Diana again, forever and always

CHAPTER

1

Saturday

E VEN AT 7:20 in the morning, JFK was a hive of activity. Anxious early birds rushed through the terminal toward their gates, glancing briefly at the departure screens for the words "On Time" next to their flight number. Impatient travelers stared at their cell phones while they waited for spouses or family members outside the restroom, or waited in line for a much-needed dose of caffeine. Pilots and flight crew, dressed in their crisply pressed suits and tailored uniforms, strolled briskly as they towed their carry-ons with one hand and sipped coffee with the other. A squad of excited cheerleaders dressed in blue and gold practiced a victory routine at the edge of the busy concourse while an electric cart, carrying an elderly couple with a small Pomeranian, beeped through the ever-shifting multitude.

At the opposite end of the energy scale, brain-dead passengers trudged through the jetway doors, backpacks slung over hunched shoulders and inflated pillows tucked under sagging arms. They slogged forward like mindless zombies, their jet-lagged synapses not yet firing as they lumbered around compulsive texters, slow walkers, and arm swingers.

Joining this pack of weary nomads, I lugged my rollaboard behind me as I navigated the madding crowd. I'd managed about three hours of sleep since lifting off from LAX just before midnight, and my bones ached. I really wanted a cup of dark roast but wanted to get out of the airport even more. My neck hurt from leaning against the window, my folded sport coat serving as a makeshift cushion. I flexed my tight shoulders and felt something crunch in my spine as I zigzagged around a couple of parents herding a passel of kids, then dodged an airport attendant pushing an empty wheelchair. I made a quick but necessary detour into the men's room, stepping around a janitor slinging a mop around the tile floor.

When I came back out into the terminal, I turned in the direction of the exit, and that's when I felt a sharp nudge as someone in a great hurry pressed by me. Instinctively I reached for my wallet—*still there*—and glowered at the guy who'd bumped me. Salt-and-pepper hair that certainly was a toupee and matching goatee, which appeared to be real. Late forties, maybe fifty, dark Cartier sunglasses covering his eyes—even though he was still indoors—studying his phone with one hand, carrying a briefcase in the other.

Without looking up, he mumbled, "Business coming through," and kept going, weaving in and about the people streaming toward him, like a fish moving to his desired spawning ground.

"Money on the move," I instinctively replied. I wasn't sure he could hear me, but he glanced back at me with what seemed to be a look of annoyance. Or was it alarm that I had responded the way I did, with those precise words?

In the next instant, I was hit by the blunt force of an old memory coming at me like a freight train. This noxious jerk, with the expensive rug and designer shades, was the son of a bitch who had killed my wife.

I'd only caught his profile as he hurried past, and it had been over a year since I'd last seen his corrupt and venal face, but there was enough of a resemblance—even in this age of cosmetic surgery and aesthetic enhancements—to force me to do a serious mental double take as I numbly watched him hustle toward the terminal exit, picking up speed as he passed the security guard stationed under a sign that read "No Reentry Beyond This Point."

But there was more to it than just his physical appearance. It was his voice—stressed and cracked—and my automatic response that sent a red alert to my red-eyed brain: "Business coming through. Money on the move."

Maxwell Harding's absolute favorite aphorism, which I'd heard him utter numerous times at Alison's work functions and holiday parties, where spouses were invited to attend. She'd explained that it was a line from a bad off-Broadway play he'd invested in that barely made it through previews before closing. That one line was the only thing of value he'd salvaged from it, she had joked.

"Hey, you—stop," I yelled, instantly realizing how ridiculous that sounded. Just like a horror-movie ingenue calling *"Who's there?"* into a darkened basement.

But Harding—if that's really who he was—was not about to stop. I sensed a nervous acceleration in the man's pace, but that could just have been my own imagination playing tricks on me. In fact, the bastard clearly had no intention of doing anything except disappearing through the tempered glass door that separated the friendly skies from the rest of the world. And when he did, he would be lost for good.

That was the jump of absurdist logic my mind was trying to deal with, because Maxwell Harding could not possibly be at JFK. Not today or any other day. The son of a bitch had died in the same fiery crash that had taken my amazing and brilliant Alison, a horrific event that had suddenly carved a dark void in my world and left my daughter without a mother. As the TV news reports kept reminding me for days afterward, the Lamborghini Aventador—Italian V-12, seven hundred super-charged horses, seven-speed automatic—had all but melted from the intense heat, although much of the lightweight carbon fiber body had held up against the raging inferno.

"Extreme multiple injuries" was how the official certificate had listed the cause of death, and the grisly implication of those three words had fueled my vivid imagination for months afterward. I'd spent the early years of my career as a photographer for the Associated Press, back when news outlets actually paid people with cameras to chronicle the world's events, rather than shell out a few bucks for an amateur snapshot taken with a cell phone. I had covered many of the world's hotspots, captured hundreds of pained faces and grim atrocities that remained indelibly imprinted in my memory: a deadly earthquake in Haiti, the start of the Arab Spring in Tunisia, even the devastating wildfires in Colorado. Even though I had not been on that stretch of I-80 in rural New Jersey that night, the blazing moment of impact was burned into my mental receptors like any prize-winning photograph.

Besides, there had been no doubt my wife had died in that crash. Her dental records had confirmed it—same with Harding.

End of story.

Yet here the bastard was.

Except there wasn't a chance in hell. Not possible, no way. That sort of thing fell into the deep category of D-E-N-I-A-L, a good dose of which I'd put myself through during the days after the crash. I had told myself there was no way she'd been strapped into the passenger seat next to Harding. Alison would not have gotten into a car with him, not after everything he had done and all the federal charges he was facing. Even though the camera on the second level of the parking garage on Sixth Avenue showed her sitting beside him, Harding easily could have dropped her off just two blocks later and picked up someone else. And the simple gold band and charred engagement ring found fused to her wedding finger could have belonged to anyone.

Whatever pitiful tricks my brain played on me after the accident, none of them were rational. Eventually I accepted the inevitable conclusion that my wife was not coming home, and there was nothing I could do to turn back time. Alison was dead. She was gone, and after the memorial service, I had flown down to Charleston to scatter her ashes on her favorite beach in the world. Sabrina—our daughter—had come with me, joined by Alison's parents and a dozen family friends. If the tears that had fallen and the prayers offered that day weren't proof enough, the empty space in our bed when we arrived home confirmed the bleak and dismal truth.

Alison was not coming back.

On top of all that, why would Harding be here at JFK on a Saturday morning in April? In his former life, he'd kept a leased Learjet out at Teterboro Airport in New Jersey, and a chartered Bell 407GX chopper could be waiting for him at the East 34th Street Heliport on ten minutes' notice. Yet here he was—or so the reactive side of my brain told me—hurrying down a public concourse at JFK, part of the plebian masses for which he always seemed to hold so much disdain.

"Stop!" I yelled again.

A jolt of raw adrenaline plunged into my bloodstream, and my heart began to race. An instant later I was dodging men, women, and luggage as I wove my way through the terminal, like a running back trying to break through the defensive line.

I practically crashed through the reinforced exit door, the lone security guard advising me, "Sir, slow down," as I charged by.

But I had no intention of slowing down—or giving up. Neither did the man in the rug. I figured him for an inch over six feet and maybe one-ninety, roughly the same height and build as my wife's former boss.

I lost him for a few seconds, then picked him up again as he pressed past a line of limo drivers patiently holding name signs, waiting for their passengers. He seemed to slow down just a second to glance at them, or maybe it was just my imagination dealing another card from the deck of delusion.

Veering around them, I followed his path down the escalator to the ground transportation level. As he navigated the moving stairs, he briefly glanced over his shoulder at me—*or did he?*—then quickly slipped around a woman wrestling with a suitcase, and picked up his pace as if he saw me coming after him.

Making his getaway.

I took the moving stairs two at a time but got trapped momentarily behind a man with an oversized carry-on. I managed to squeeze around the guy just as my target stepped through the sliding doors, joining the buzz of people trying to snag a car or bus into the city. He dodged a black town car as he looked back at me once more while I pushed my way through the same tempered glass doors.

"Harding, stop!" I called again.

The man continued to ignore me, and I didn't blame him. Who was this fool chasing him through the airport, calling him by some strange name? New York was full of crazies, and I knew how I sounded.

He rushed up to a yellow cab that was waiting for a dispatcher to direct the driver to move forward. Several passengers were waiting in line and yelled at him, things like "Wait your turn" and "Who the fuck do you think you are?" He ignored them and yanked the door open, the cabbie probably concerned about being slapped with a fine or being assessed points for picking up a fare out of turn. But the man with the hairpiece and goatee clearly wasn't taking no for an answer as he slid inside and wrenched the door shut.

I raced across multiple lanes of traffic, causing several cars behind me to jam on their brakes. Horns blared in true New York fashion, and more harsh words followed. I anticipated the rending of steel on steel as I closed the distance between the man I knew couldn't possibly be Harding and myself.

A second later the taxi swerved into the stream of traffic. I bolted after him, past the queue of passengers waiting their turn for a ride. I could make out murmurs of "Asshole!" as I ran past, but I didn't care. The cab was gaining speed as it veered around a hotel shuttle bus, and I was beginning to feel a burning in my lungs. Even though I walked my daughter to school every morning, I was out of breath. I slowed, coughing from the kicked-up dust and diesel fumes, then stopped and propped my hands on my knees as I gasped for air.

Damn, I swore to myself. Defeated and desperate, I tried to suck oxygen into my lungs. I closed my eyes a moment, then opened them just as the cab swerved around a black town car and disappeared, giving me just enough time to pick up three letters and a number from the New York license plate.

CHAPTER

2

I CLOSED MY EYES and committed the digits to memory, along with the name of the cab company: ESL6, Empire State Livery. No medallion or fleet number. Unfortunately, the taxi was long gone, and Harding—if that's really who he was—was in the wind.

Which meant I was shit out of luck.

As I wheezed my way back to the curb, I took my phone out of my pocket and entered the cab company's name into the browser. Several seconds later a website gave me a phone number highlighted as an active link. I touched it and waited for the call to connect.

"Empire," a thin voice said in a heavy Brooklyn accent. Male, undetermined age, bored. Maybe Staten Island, if there's such a distinction.

"My name is Kane, and I'm calling from JFK—"

"If you need a car, you can go to our courtesy kiosk," the voice instructed me.

"No—I'm not calling about that," I explained, conjuring up a story as I went. "I just got out of one of your cabs at Terminal Eight and accidentally left my briefcase in it."

"I'm sorry for your loss," he said, a distinct lack of empathy in his voice. "Give me your name and number, and if it turns up at the end of shift, we'll notify you."

"I can't do that," I replied. "I'm getting on a plane to Chicago, and my presentation is in that case. I need it."

"I'm sorry, but there's not much I can do," the dispatcher said again, oozing total disinterest. "Did you get the vehicle number?"

"No, but I have a partial plate. It starts with E-S-L, and the first number is six."

"All our cabs have those letters in their license plates," he explained.

"The driver just picked up a fare when I got out, not five minutes ago. He could have called in where he was going."

"Eventually he will, but that will come into a different dispatcher. Sorry, but there's nothing I can do."

"Maybe you can make a general call to all of your taxis that just left JFK," I pressed. "Terminal Eight."

"It doesn't work that way," she said. "Now, do you want to give me your name?"

No, I did not. I ended the call and stood there a moment, figuring out my next course of action. The practical side of my mind told me I was grasping at strands of a delusional reality, but the lobe that catered to intuition and impulse kept pushing me to trust my instinct, no matter how much it defied logic and rationale. Seconds slipped away, one mental tick after another, until I realized I was wasting time thinking rather than doing.

I took another deep breath, then lugged my carry-on back into the terminal. The escalator took me up to the main level, where passengers were emerging from the same doorway through which I'd run just a couple minutes ago. While

I'd been chasing the man I was convinced was Harding, I'd all but ignored the limo drivers who had been waiting at the exit with their signs. Now I counted eight of them, each one listing the name of the company they worked for, plus the last name of the person they were supposed to meet: Higgins. Wheeler. Zaccaro. Burke. Herrera. Ruan. Shapiro. Matheson. I hung back a bit and recalled that I'd thought Harding had glanced at them as he'd rushed by, not daring to stop with me so close on his heels. I had sensed an almost imperceptible hesitation as he might have slowed, for just a fragment of a second, then continued on his way toward the escalator.

In the end it was a simple process of elimination. Each driver was there for a specific customer, and when that person came through the security checkpoint, he or she approached the chauffeur who held the placard with their name on it. Greetings and handshakes followed, and as each driver departed, a new one arrived. After a few minutes only one of the original drivers remained, and he seemed to be growing increasingly annoyed. He shifted from one foot to the other, occasionally glancing at his watch. Finally, he took a cell phone out of his pocket and placed a call. There was a brief exchange with whoever was on the other end, before he stuffed the phone back into his jacket and appeared resigned to a long wait.

I gave him a few seconds, then walked up to him and said, "Seems Mr. Zaccaro is a no-show."

"Excuse me?" he replied.

"I'm waiting for him too," I explained, nodding at his name sign that indicated he worked for Elite Services LLC. "I'm a courier and have something to give him, but he doesn't seem to have made his flight."

"My office confirms he did," the driver said. He was Black, mid-thirties, rough skin, with a thin line running under one eye. He spoke in an accent that I suspected had originated on the African continent. "He should have cleared Customs by now."

That meant an international flight. "What airline do you have him coming in on?" I asked, taking out my own phone as if to verify my information.

"LATAM, flight 8414 from Rio."

"That's what I have," I grumbled with a feigned scowl as I pretended to glance at my phone. "The plane's either late or he missed his flight."

"The airline app says the plane pulled up to the gate forty minutes ago," the driver said.

"Have you tried calling him?"

"I wasn't given his personal number" was the predictable answer.

Damn. I thought on that a second, then said, "I'd better check in with my boss and see what to do."

The driver shrugged as I walked off and pretended to enter a number into my cell phone. I kept walking but this time followed the signs toward the AirTrain station rather than Ground Transportation.

I hadn't owned a car in over ten years, nor did I care to. The insurance was too expensive, and monthly garage fees in lower Manhattan cost more than a one-bedroom apartment in many American cities. If I ever need to drive outside the city limits, I can rent one and turn it in when I'm done. Dirty and smelly as it was, the subway could take me within several blocks of anywhere I wanted to go in the city, and in much less time than it would take to navigate traffic and find a place to park. That was true now as I boarded the light rail train that would deliver me to Jamaica Station, where I would transfer to the E line that eventually would let me off a few blocks from where my daughter and I lived in the Village.

I remained on my feet for most of the trip into Manhattan. I'd been crammed into an airplane seat all night, and my back and neck remained stiff. I leaned against a floor-to-ceiling pole as I stared out the window at the rooftops of Richmond Hill rolling by. The events of the past few minutes were still bouncing around inside my head, as if I'd popped too many pills and my brain couldn't slow down: Maxwell Harding, or a man who bore a strong resemblance to him in mannerisms and speech, who seemed in a hurry to avoid me. The yellow cab from Empire State Livery, and the surly dispatcher who played by company rules and was no help at all. Flight 8414 from Rio de Janeiro, and a Mr. Zaccaro, who had been a no-show.

Most of all I thought about Sabrina, my seven-year-old daughter. I had dropped her off at the house of a friend on Thursday, explaining that I had to go out of town for a quick trip but would be back Saturday morning. After that I'd headed straight to the airport for my brief roundtrip to California. The purpose for my journey had been a job interview at the world-renowned Bradley Museum, which had a once-in-a-career opening for a senior deputy curator of photography. For some reason, a vice president in human resources had contacted me two weeks ago about the opportunity, which not only came as a complete shock but had caused me to speculate how, or why, they thought I was even remotely qualified to fill the role.

Yesterday's mid-morning appointment had evolved into lunch and ended with cocktails at the Beverly Wilshire

Hotel, where I'd been presented with a formal offer. The salary was well above what I was making now, and the sale of our Greenwich Village condo would afford my daughter and me a larger home with a pool. Maybe even a view of the ocean, or at least the city lights at night. Like many Easterners, I've always had a bit of disdain for the shallow glitz of Hollywood, but the move would allow us to make a fresh start and leave unpleasant memories behind.

I promised to give it serious consideration over the weekend and get back to them on Monday, Tuesday at the latest.

Even though my marital status now is widower—I still find it painful to check that box on applications and tax forms—my own needs take a back seat to those of my daughter. I've managed to shift my hours so I can escort Sabrina to school in the morning and still have time to pick her up before her afternoon day care closes. We cook dinner together almost every night and ritually play Uno and Jenga as part of a school-night routine that's left over from when Alison was alive. I run Sabrina a bath, tuck her into bed, and read a chapter or two from one of her favorite books until her eyes drift shut. Despite the comfortable routine and all this fatherly attention, there's no question that Sabrina misses her mother horribly, and I feel miserable for all my failings. To that end, I make a point of never letting her see me depressed, or even sense that at times I'm just barely treading water.

On the taxi ride back to LAX last night, I'd sorted through the various options on the table, weighed the pros and cons. If Sabrina and I moved to Los Angeles, we would be able to start a new life that was free of any ghosts or haunting memories. No snow, no frigid winds ripping down Tenth Avenue, no ice or slush on the sidewalks. New beginnings abounded: new job, new school, new adventures in a land of

sunshine and beaches and promise. A do-over, with unlim-
ited opportunities for both father and daughter.

On the downside: giving up friends and familiarity.
Sabrina had turned seven just two months ago and had a
solid circle of BFFs. She enjoyed playdates on weekends and
seemed to be achieving well above her age. She'd learned to
read in kindergarten and had graduated from nursery rhymes
and primers to short chapter books. Sabrina could add and
subtract and had taken a special interest in the lives of plants
and animals, especially squirrels, since a growing family of
them lived in the trees bordering our small backyard patio.

Except for the constant emptiness in my life, I'd managed
to convince myself that I was moving on. I viewed every new
morning as the next rung on a rickety ladder that allowed me
to climb out of a vast pit of nothing, and it was time to either
finish the makeover or give up and find a new home.

The light rail dead-ended at Jamaica Station, where I
changed to the E train. When it rolled away from the plat-
form, I slumped against the door—even though a sign said
not to—and let out a tired sigh. So much to think about; so
many decisions in the coming days. So many possibilities; so
many consequences for my daughter and me.

When my phone rang, I dug it out of my pocket, knowing who it was before I even glanced at the screen: Marika
Landry. The ringtone was a riff from Lady Gaga's "Do What
U Want" that she'd downloaded into my cell several weeks
ago. Marika thought it would be a cute way to instantly let
me know she was calling, and I'd gone along with the suggestion. As a new walk-on in my current melodrama—Marika
had literally stumbled into my world three weeks ago—I'd
deliberately left her off the "pro" and "con" lists in my mental
debate about moving to LA. Even though we were in the early

stages of whatever we might or might not become, she figured into my life in a way that could make things complicated.

I should have been thrilled to hear from her, but I'd already misled her about my last-minute trip to LA, explaining that I'd been called out to California to negotiate a particularly tricky licensing deal. I had intended to call her as soon as I landed at JFK, but chasing after the man I knew couldn't possibly be Maxwell Harding had distracted me. And now the past, present, and future were crashing into one another like a rip current after a summer storm.

I waited until the riff played through—I actually liked the song—then slid the phone back into my pocket as the melody faded to silence.

3

"DADDY—WE'RE HOME!" SABRINA shrieked with glee as she raced through the vestibule toward the front door of our condo.

We lived in a renovated prewar row townhouse that had been carved into six condo units, two each on three floors, all of them accessed through a ground-floor entryway with a central staircase and a small elevator. Ours was one of the ground-level residences.

Sabrina shrugged off her *Frozen* backpack and dropped it on the tile floor in front of our door.

"That's right, sugar," I said as I fished through a pocket in my carry-on for my keys.

The sickeningly sweet nickname had been my idea, much to her mother's dismay. *Sugar Kane.* After scouring every baby book in existence, we named her Sabrina at Alison's suggestion—insistence, really—because she was an obsessed Audrey Hepburn fan and absolutely adored her in the movie of the same name, playing opposite William Holden. I'd gone along with the idea, even though my first choice had been Candace, solely because I knew it would be shortened to

Candy. With Kane as her last name—well, at least I thought it was clever. Alison clearly was the wiser parent-to-be.

"I like Hannah's house—she has a canopy bed and a huge TV—but I *love* my room," my daughter gushed. Then her lip curled up, and she added, almost a whisper, "I just wish Mommy was here. I miss her."

Me too, I thought. As I inserted the key in the lock, the door across the vestibule opened, and my neighbor Valerie Hall poked her head out. She and her husband owned a veterinary practice a few blocks away. I'd only once been inside their condo, which was a menagerie of Mammalia that included four cats, a spaniel of some sort, and a ferret that had been abandoned on the doorstep of their animal hospital.

"There you are, Mr. Kane," she said. "Did you get your gas line fixed?"

"My what?" I asked.

"Your gas line. A repairman from National Grid was here yesterday, said he was responding to a call about a possible leak."

"I never called anyone," I said. "Who let him in?"

"I figured it was you or the management company. He seemed to know what he was doing, said he'd only be a few minutes."

Even though there were only a half dozen condos in the building, we had a service contract with a company located uptown that handled repair and maintenance issues. A raw shiver bit at my skin as I turned the key in the deadbolt. It wouldn't be the first instance where there had been a problem with the gas line, but usually someone called ahead and I let them in. This time I'd received no calls, no texts about a service visit from the utility company.

"As far as I know, everything is fine," I said. "I'll be sure to let you know if there's an issue."

"Thanks, Mr. Kane," she replied with a smile. "Hello, Sabrina." Then her head was gone, and I heard a lock firmly click into place.

I pushed the door open and followed Sabrina inside. A single board creaked as I stepped into the foyer, and the first thing I noticed was that the place was cold. Colder than it should have been for a Saturday in late April, so I turned the knob on the thermostat until I heard pipes rattle in the basement. *Maybe the gas inspector did something to the furnace,* I thought as I tossed my keys into a wicker basket on an antique library table while Sabrina began dragging her backpack toward her bedroom.

"Do you need any help unpacking?" I asked.

She shot me an indignant look full of childhood independence and said, "I'm seven years old now, Daddy. I can do it myself."

"I know you can," I replied. "Just let me know if you have any questions about where anything goes."

"I won't," she assured me. "Can we go out and get some pizza? I'm starving."

"After you unpack."

"Hawaiian?"

To my traditionally oriented mind, ham and pineapple did not belong anywhere near a pizza, but Sabrina had gobbled it up at a sleepover last winter, and she'd been obsessed with it ever since. "As you wish," I said, succumbing to a lingering twinge of guilt for abandoning her during my last-minute jaunt to the coast.

As she lugged her bag down the hall, I recalled how little she'd been when we'd moved in not quite four years ago. Sabrina had charged through every corner of the place like the Tasmanian devil in the old Looney Toons cartoons, squealing

with delight when she discovered her own room. Alison fell
in love the moment the realtor had shown us through: bright
and airy, with white walls that would suit whatever color
palette we selected. The place had been recently renovated,
and had hand-hewn hickory floors, and we decorated in what
Alison liked to call eclectic modernism—a hodgepodge of
styles culled from furniture stores and antique shops scattered throughout the neighborhood.

In the end we kept most of the walls white, which made
the space look bigger and sunnier. A half-dozen framed
prints of Alison's favorite photos I'd taken over the years
hung on the walls—mostly portraits of people I'd encoun-
tered on various shoots around the globe. I worried that people might consider the display a self-indulgence that spoke
to vanity, but my wife had insisted on hanging them where
they were sure to be seen. Now that she was gone, I could
have taken them down, but I'd convinced myself that to do
so would defy her best intentions. Plus, I'd grown to like
them.

The kitchen was open to the living room, which in turn
opened out to the enclosed patio where the three of us would
eat dinner on warm summer evenings. After the accident I
tried to respect our routine by getting Sabrina out there several nights a week, but two just didn't feel the same as three.
The food didn't taste as good, the weather seemed chillier,
and the empty chair at the table served as a grim reminder of
better days long gone.

The master bedroom opened off one side of the living
room, and a short hallway led to my study and Sabrina's
bedroom beyond, with a bathroom in between. A foldout
couch in the study was designed to accommodate whatever

guests might drop in for a Manhattan weekend, but no one had visited since Alison's parents had come to town a month after the memorial service. Even then, they had opted to stay uptown at the Sheraton rather than intrude on our space.

Every day of every month since the crash, I'd grown a little more accustomed to living life without Alison. I'd drifted into a world of solitude, and from time to time— usually without much warning—a stray memory would wash over me like an angry sea. Then, just when I thought I might not be able to manage the growing storm, the swells would ease, and the wave of pain would pass. Over time, as weeks turned into months, those moments came less frequently. They usually hit when something triggered a distant memory: hearing a song Alison liked, passing a favorite restaurant, watching Sabrina's mouth turn up in a grin that is so much like her mother's. So many experiences that once had been a big part of our lives and that she would never get to share again.

*　*　*

We did go out for pizza, which we ate at a small table on the sidewalk while pigeons strutted around the pavement. Afterward we walked up to Gansevoort Street and climbed the stairs to the High Line, a New York incongruity that's best described as the narrowest park in the city. A little more than a mile in length and an average of thirty feet wide, it's a pedestrian parkway that runs atop the elevated trestle of the former New York Central Railroad and cuts up the west side of the city.

Occasionally slicing right through the bowels of buildings as it winds along at third-story eye level, the meandering route offers linear views out to the Hudson River and occasional voyeuristic glances into apartments and converted warehouses. On any given day it's the go-to place for grownups, children, and seniors; mimes and clowns; face painters and magicians squirting balloons into the shapes of dogs and flowers. It's still mostly locals, although more and more tourists are discovering its relaxed ambiance and unique character.

When we got to the Chelsea Market area, we stopped at one of the vending booths, where we bought ice-cream cones. Ice cream has always been a High Line requirement for Sabrina and me, and it was the incentive that drove her short legs. While I paid the vendor, my mind jumped back— as it never failed to do—to an earlier time when the three of us would stop here during a weekend stroll. Chocolate for Sabrina, pistachio for me. Alison, however, never ordered the same thing, instead jumping around from banana nut to rocky road to raspberry ice. She was like that: unpredictable, random, impulsive. No set patterns. The flavor of the day, whatever the day happened to bring.

By the time we returned home, my daughter practically dragged herself up the front steps, one at a time. I'm a sucker for expensive cars and had stopped to ogle a black and gold Rolls Royce parked at the curb a few doors up the street. It was the new electric Spectre model, its rear windows darkened with heavy tint, and black trim instead of chrome. Not the sort of vehicle we typically saw in our neighborhood, although I'd spotted at least a dozen of them during my twenty-four hours in LA.

"Daddy, I have to pee," Sabrina said, snatching me from my moment of automotive appreciation.

"Sorry, sugar," I apologized as I let her into the vestibule. Tired as she was, she dragged herself through the condo and made it to the bathroom with barely a second to spare.

By the time she joined me out in the kitchen, I'd totally forgotten about the expensive car and had moved on to figuring out what we were going to have for dinner.

* * *

Sabrina was a typical child, whose diet comprised all four food groups: macaroni and cheese, hot dogs, beefy-Os, and pizza. Since she'd already had pizza for lunch, I fixed a dinner of mac and cheese, and peeled a carrot for a bit of nutrition. After dinner we sat on the living room floor and played a board game. I occasionally glanced at my watch, knowing Marika would be wondering where I was and why I wasn't getting back to her. I realized I should give her a call, but my thoughts were bouncing all over the place.

At one point I looked at Sabrina, seeing for the millionth time how much she resembled Alison. Especially her eyes and that brilliant smile. And for the millionth time, I felt tears well up as I realized Alison would never get to see her little girl grow up and morph into the beautiful young woman she was destined to be.

After we finished our Saturday evening playtime, Sabrina volunteered to put our dishes in the sink, a move I knew was her way of showing me she was mature enough to stay up a few minutes late. When she was done, she shuffled back out into the living room and asked, "Can I watch *Beauty and the Beast*?"

I again glanced at my watch and calculated that the movie would end only fifteen minutes past her bedtime.

Since she always woke up way before I did, I figured the extra quarter hour—just this once—wouldn't harm her.

"We'll make an exception because this is a special weekend," I told her. "As long as you brush every one of your teeth, right now."

"What about dessert?" she asked, those eyes of hers open as wide as they could go. Contrived innocence, something I would have to remember when she became a teenager.

"You know the rules," I reminded her as I walked with her into the kitchen. "On pizza days, dessert is fruit."

"Do we have any of that fruit salad in those plastic cups?" she asked.

"I'll see what I can find," I said. Processed fruit had about as much nutrition as the label wrapped around it, but it was the principle of the thing. "Meanwhile, go ahead and put the movie in the player."

Ten minutes later Sabrina was watching Beauty entangle herself in an inexplicable love for a long-haired Beast that somehow spoke English, even though the story seemed to take place in France. I'd already excused myself with a quick kiss on her forehead and quietly slipped into my study. My desk was positioned at an angle so I could keep an eye on her while I tackled work in the evening, but that was the last thing on my mind tonight.

Two file drawers were built into a side pedestal of my desk, and I pulled out the bottom one that held legal and financial papers. I removed a hanging folder way in the back, labeled "Accident." It contained every report and article I'd been able to find about that night on the dark stretch of highway in western New Jersey. I took the file out of the drawer and opened it with the same trepidation that always hit when I retreated into this section of our past. I didn't do this very often, but sometimes I just needed a "fix" to help get me through the day. Like a jolt of caffeine or, depending on the hour, something much more potent.

The first item was a *New York Times* story that was always on the top of the stack. I gave another quick glance toward my daughter, then picked up the sheet and read it again, as if for the first time:

Indicted Crypto Swindler Maxwell Harding
Killed in Car Crash

NEW YORK, April 28: Maxwell Harding, the Wall Street billionaire who was indicted earlier this year on multiple counts of securities fraud, died Friday night in an automobile accident in western New Jersey.

The Lamborghini sportscar Mr. Harding was driving apparently plunged off Interstate 80 near Hope and hit a tree. The collision killed Mr. Harding and a passenger, Alison Kane, who was an executive vice president at Harding's company in Manhattan.

Highway patrol and state police investigators have begun examining the wreckage of the automobile, which, authorities say, was engulfed in flames when first responders arrived on the scene. The fire prevented authorities from immediately removing the victims from the wreckage. Identification was made using dental records.

Mr. Harding was the former chairman of Harding Financial Services, as well as Bit-XC, the cryptocurrency exchange that filed for Chapter 11 protection last year. Harding was arrested in February on a number of federal charges that included fraud, theft, money laundering, and racketeering. A resident of New York City, he was a Wall Street firebrand whose success with several hedge funds provided him the capital to build a multibillion-dollar financial empire. Investigators from the IRS Criminal Investigative unit say Harding was the mastermind behind a scheme in which billions of dollars were laundered through questionable e-currency transactions, allegedly defrauding thousands of individual and corporate customers worldwide.

They also have linked Mr. Harding to the failure of Tsuka-X, a Japan-based cryptocurrency exchange that dissolved several years ago after it was mysteriously hacked and its assets depleted. Government investigators believe Harding received over $3 billion from that incident and laundered the proceeds through Bit-XC, a charge Harding vehemently denied.

Earlier this year U.S. Attorney Charles Griffith said Bit-XC was a magnet for market fraud, noting, "As online banking technologies continue to emerge, we are seeing a remarkable evolution in the way criminals are subverting new financial systems to perpetuate their nefarious goals."

A federal grand jury indicted Harding on February 14 on multiple counts of financial fraud. Prosecutors asked U.S. District Court Judge William Reese to deny bail, but the judge released Harding on a $10 million personal bond and demanded that he relinquish his passport. Harding's release also required that he be fitted with a GPS tracking device, and he was ordered not to leave the borough of Manhattan without a judge's consent.

Fortune magazine once described Harding as "brilliant, brash, impetuous, impulsive, and reckless." He began his career in the financial world as an analyst at Deutsche Bank, and within four years he had built Harding Financial Services, an investment firm with assets totaling over $5 billion. Working off that success and fascinated by early developments in the digital currency field, Harding subsequently created Bit-XC, a digital exchange that the U.S. government says was nothing more than an elaborate Ponzi scheme.

Prior to Harding's financial collapse, *Forbes* estimated his personal net worth at $4.4 billion, placing him at number 527 on the magazine's annual list of the world's richest people. He is survived by his wife, Nicole, and a son, Cyrus.

Alison Kane joined Harding Financial Services 6 years ago as an executive in the company's strategic development department. When Harding founded Bit-XC, Kane was promoted to her most recent position, overseeing risk management and security algorithms. A former NYU mathematics professor with a PhD from Yale University, Kane was a world-renowned expert on prime numbers and advanced approximation theory. She is survived by her husband, Cameron, an award-winning photojournalist, and a daughter, Sabrina.

The same old questions flooded my brain as I stared at the newspaper clipping with renewed interest. In my typical fashion, I addressed my thoughts to my wife directly, as if she and I were having a mental conversation. First up: *What were you doing with Maxwell Harding that night, Alison? You were cooperating with agents from at least three federal agencies—Justice, Homeland, and Treasury—to unravel his cryptocurrency schemes, so why were you alone with him in the car?* Next: *What were you doing with him in western New Jersey, when a judge had ordered the son of a bitch to wear an ankle bracelet and remain in Manhattan? What caused the car to veer off the highway and careen down an embankment into the trees?*

In the living room I heard animated plates and dishes singing a musical number on the TV, the absurdity of which caused me to realize how delusional all this nonsense was. The official evidence of Alison's death had been solid, and the case was officially closed. It was preposterous to consider an alternate truth, especially one based on seven innocuous words: *"Business coming through. Money on the move,"* spoken in a voice I was sure I recognized. Of course, I'd been preoccupied with new thoughts about the future: new job, new home, new school, new life. *New girlfriend?* My brain had been spinning like a swirling eddy in a stream, and the tentacles of denial had taken advantage of my weakness. Lack of sleep must have pushed me into a fugue state as I'd trudged through the terminal at JFK, and I'd momentarily lost all sense of reason.

The rational side of my brain kept telling me there had to be a reasonable explanation for what I'd experienced. Now that the initial adrenaline rush was over and I was home, I realized I'd probably just bumped into someone who had a similar facial structure and had been one of the few theatergoers in New York to see the same off-Broadway play as the late Maxwell Harding. Wishful thinking was the most likely culprit, and not because I wanted the son of a bitch to still be alive. The bastard was responsible for Alison's death, and he could burn in hell for all I cared. Probably had. The harsh reality was that the man with the toupee and goatee could not possibly have been Maxwell Harding, which meant Alison was dead and gone. Just as she had been yesterday and would be tomorrow.

The simplest, most rational explanation was always the best one.

Occam's razor at work: "When you hear hoofbeats, it's probably horses, not zebras."

Still . . .

Halfway through the movie I got up from the desk and wandered into the living room. Sabrina was stretched out on a quilt on the floor, her head resting on a sofa pillow, eyes closed. I wasn't surprised; I had yet to see her last even a few minutes past her bedtime, movie or not.

I gathered her in my arms and gently carried her into her bedroom. I tucked her into bed and gave her a kiss on the forehead. She squirmed a bit in her sleep and made a soft snuffling sound as I pulled the covers and shimmery lavender comforter up to her chin. I checked to make sure her plastic cup was filled with water, then backed out of the room and clicked off the lamp. Sabrina liked to sleep with the door cracked open a few inches, to allow in just enough light so she could see her things in the dark. And so her mommy could see her too, *wherever she might be.*

I tiptoed into the kitchen and uncorked a bottle of bourbon stashed in the cabinet above the refrigerator. I poured two generous fingers and brought the glass back into the study, where I sat back down and let a slow, contemplative sip flow over my tongue.

It all began around seven thirty that night almost a year ago. It was a Friday, and Alison had called to say she would be working late. *Again.* She'd been tied up all week in a conference room with federal investigators and a battalion of pin-striped attorneys. Everyone was systematically poring through boxes of potential evidence, trying to untangle untold layers of cryptocurrency, money transfers, and blockchain ledgers. I knew a little about Bitcoin but hadn't even heard of blockchain until Harding's indictment, and when Alison attempted to explain the details, all she managed to do was confound me with geek speak. I was more puzzled than ever, so I looked it up on Wikipedia and learned it was a digital technology through which cryptocurrency transactions were recorded in chronological order, with full transparency, so no one could challenge the legitimacy of a Bitcoin purchase or transfer.

Harding had been brought in that final night to explain an issue with his blockchain accounting. Despite his pleas of innocence, he'd been cooperating with the feds, up to a point. Somehow—and no one was ever able to explain this to me sufficiently—Alison ended up in his car, and they drove off together. Less than an hour later, they were both dead, and the subsequent questions far outnumbered the answers.

Had I been suspicious? Perhaps jealous? Of course I was, even though I refused to admit it at the time. "Working late" was one of those age-old euphemisms that loosely translated to "intimate entanglement," and even before those last few weeks when she'd been working side by side with the lawyers, she often didn't come home until almost midnight. Harding always had some sort of critical project that caused her to work sixty—sometimes eighty—hours a week, but since Alison earned a lot more than I did, who was I to complain? Besides, she'd never given me any reason to believe there was anything romantic going on between them, although I admit to a conflicting sense of relief when the feds showed up at his penthouse waving a pair of cuffs and a search warrant.

When Alison slipped into our condo on those late evenings, she would tiptoe into the bedroom, trying not to make a sound. Sometimes I would be asleep, and if I woke, I'd groggily encourage her to look in on Sabrina before coming to bed. She always smelled like the skin conditioner or baby powder she bought at a boutique on Bleecker Street, and never a hint of another man.

I took another sip of bourbon and focused on what had brought me to this point in my life. I was forty-three, a widower, and a single dad. Six months before Sabrina was born, I'd made a major job change, giving up my globe-trotting career to sit behind a desk in midtown Manhattan. Gone were long flights to remote corners of the world and the adrenaline jolts that came with sneaking into war zones, rebel strongholds, and refugee camps. Now I was simply licensing someone else's digital images to online publishers and news agencies.

In the beginning I'd missed the energy rush, but my new desk job had allowed me to adjust my hours so I could be home whenever Alison had to work late. Anyone raising a child in Manhattan is acutely aware of the cost of all things, especially a solid roof, quality schools, and the mounting expense of future college tuition. The two-parent working family is a necessity, not a preference, so after Alison went on Harding's payroll, it fell on me to pick up Sabrina from her day care in the afternoon and have dinner ready when Alison came home—whatever hour that might be.

That's how it had been the night of the crash, and I had actually anticipated the call before the phone started ringing.

"I'm sorry, hon—looks like it's going to be another late one" was how it began.

"You've been having a lot of those lately." We'd already had this discussion a number of times, and I couldn't help but point it out. Looking back on how that evening had ended, I now felt like a total dick. But as they say, hindsight is always twenty–twenty.

"You know my job has always kept me busy," she'd reminded me. "That's why I make the big bucks."

Hard to argue with that. Alison was always on the go, but her salary more than made up for the long hours. Solid six figures, with bonuses and benefits that made it all worthwhile. I never could understand how a math geek with an IQ of 170 could play such a vital role in a cryptocurrency firm, but the job paid many times more than a tenure-track professorship at NYU. In any event, that last night she'd sounded more defensive than usual . . . or maybe I was reflecting backward, knowing now what I didn't know at the time.

"I thought your schedule might ease up when Harding got hauled off to jail," I'd said.

"I don't have control over my hours," she'd explained, sounding exasperated. "The feds are looking at everything, and when they say 'jump,' I have to do what they tell me. You know how they are."

No, I didn't know how they were, because Alison repeatedly insisted she couldn't talk about things like that: investigations and no-knock warrants and sealed indictments.

"Anyway, the FBI and SEC and IRS keep coming with demands for more stuff," Alison continued. "And Homeland has gotten particularly fastidious."

"Yeah, okay," I had said, sounding resolute. "Just so you know, there's some leftover Chinese from King Wok in the fridge."

"Thanks, but we'll probably order out before we wrap up here," Alison said to me.

"Well, try not to be too late," I told her. "Morning rolls around fast enough as it is."

"I'll be home as soon as I can," she'd said, then asked me to hand the phone to Sabrina so she could say good night. The two of them chatted for a minute or two, and they both made kissy noises before Alison asked to speak with me again. Sabrina gave one last smooch to the phone, then handed the phone back to me.

"I promise, this is going to all be over soon," my wife assured me.

"I can't wait," I replied, probably with less enthusiasm than she was hoping for.

"And hon?" she continued. "I want you to know . . . I love you, more than anything. I don't think I tell you that as much as I should, and I just want you to know."

"I love you too," I'd replied. "Double."

That was how the conversation ended, the last words either of us ever spoke to each other. As I set the phone down, I'd wondered if our marriage was in trouble. By all measures it was not, but appearances can be deceiving. Alison kissed me on the cheek and the back of the neck a little less than during our first years together, and we said "I love you" a little less too. But that was the natural progression of things after nine years of marriage, right?

Then again, had it been a signal that something deeper and more troubling had been in the works? Marriage is one of those learn-as-you-go things, and I didn't know what I was learning or where our marriage had been going. I still loved Alison as much as I had that first night we'd made love, and the next night and the next. But I also knew it was a different kind of love. The first blush of wild passion that fueled every new romance naturally softened over the years. I understood the evolving nature of intimacy, and I'm pretty sure Alison did too. I still wondered if she missed the thrill ride of falling head over heels and whether she had rekindled some of that thrill by working around an eccentric billionaire like Harding.

Alison had not come home that night, of course, and was still gone when I walked Sabrina to a prearranged playdate the next morning. I'd repeatedly called her office and her cell, but there was no answer on either number. I phoned a few of our friends, but I didn't want to come right out and ask if they'd heard from her. What does it say about your marriage if your spouse doesn't come home after spending a late night at work in the company of another man, and you don't know where she is? I also called the NYPD, but the woman I spoke with didn't have anything to tell me, and I didn't even consider turning on the news. Looking back, I don't think I wanted to acknowledge what that might imply. Not until I'd had a chance to sit down with her, face-to-face.

Even though it was a weekend, I'd taken the subway uptown to my office. I busied myself sorting through the latest batch of photos that had been downloaded overnight, but I couldn't focus. Instead, I kept seeing images of Alison with her boss, and the more I allowed myself to think about the two of them together, the more my imagination fed upon itself. My wife was a good lover, attentive and inventive in most aspects of the bedroom. And now I couldn't stop picturing her with him, doing all those things that

until this moment now were the sole province of our marriage. My calm, practical side told me to slow down, not to
rush to judgment—or persecution. There simply had to be
a reasonable explanation for where she was. But the jealous,
reactive side . . . well, that side wanted to go out and find
that crypto bastard and ram his blockchain right down his
throat.

The call came in just before noon, and within seconds
both sides of my brain caved in from the weight of the truth.
At that moment I felt my world implode, and I simply placed
my cell on my desk as stray words kept playing over and over
in my head.

"Mr. Kane . . . this is Captain Estes from the Warren
County Sheriff's Office in New Jersey. I tried calling you at
home, but there was no answer . . ." Somewhere around that
point I stopped listening, tuning him out until I heard the
words, ". . . all indications are she did not suffer."

In the end I learned that she most likely *did* suffer. It
was hard not to imagine the intense horror and pain when
your car leaves the road at a high rate of speed, flies over an
embankment, and slams headfirst into an oak tree. Or when
the gas tank explodes in a massive fireball, the flames engulf-
ing the wreckage so thoroughly that even the license plates
melt. As I later discovered, there was only one Lamborghini
Aventador in the state of New York whose tags contained the
four digits that remained partially visible after the inferno,
and that car was registered to Maxwell Harding.

The process of deduction had been quick and precise.
Harding's wife confirmed to the police that her husband had
not returned home that night either. Surveillance cameras in
the parking garage where he kept the car showed Alison had
been in the passenger seat at eight forty-five—just an hour

and a quarter after she'd called about staying late. Another camera showed the vehicle leaving the garage two minutes later, turning from Sixth Avenue onto 47th Street, and EZ Pass records confirmed it traveled through the Lincoln Tunnel and, later, onto the Garden State Parkway.

The next thing I remembered was the police telling me they were going to need dental records to make a positive identification.

I shook off the imagery and lifted the autopsy summary from the manila file. I'd first tried to read it just a week after the crash, but that had been a mistake. Despite its cold and academic description of what had happened that night, it still was far too graphic for me to deal with back then, and after thirty seconds, I put it down. That's why the medical examiner had refused to give me a copy in the first place, but I'd convinced myself I *needed* to know. *Had the right to know.* I had to see everything connected with Alison's death, so I'd found another way to get a copy.

The report I now held was stamped in red ink at the top with the words "Official Document: Not For Public Distribution."

From the County of Warren, Department of Coroner, it consisted of three letter-sized pages. The name of the deceased listed at the top of the first page was Alison Leigh Kane, along with the case file number.

The report was painfully straightforward, beginning with a three-paragraph summary of the official investigation the night of the crash. At 22:17 hours, Officer Morgan Wright of the New Jersey Highway Patrol received a dispatch call to check out a possible automobile accident off Interstate 80 just west of the town of Hope. Upon arrival, he found the burning wreckage of a vehicle approximately one hundred

feet from the pavement, with flames so hot he was unable
to go near it. Officer Wright radioed for assistance, and two
more units arrived on the scene within minutes. Ten minutes later a fire company pumper truck arrived, and with
the help of several extension hoses coupled together, the
crew was able to smother the flames. By the time the inferno
was fully extinguished, the Lamborghini had burned for
approximately thirty minutes, totally immolating everything
inside—including what appeared to be two humans strapped
into the twin bucket seats.

As Natalie Cook, the Warren County medical examiner, had written in her report, "Both the automobile and the
occupants were so badly burned that not only was it difficult
to identify the make of the vehicle but also the sex of both the
driver and passenger. Initial identification was ascertained
from the vehicle's front license plate, which, despite the high
degree of heat, yielded partial digits that confirmed owner-
ship of the vehicle. Positive identification of both victims,
however, was not possible until dental records were supplied
by relatives of the deceased."

The final section of the autopsy report covered "body
examination," and it had been the cause of nightmares for
weeks after the accident:

> Decedent 2 was identified from charts provided
> by Dr. David Nguyen, DDS, which confirmed she
> was a female Caucasian named Alison Kane. Severe
> burns covered 100 percent of her body, which was
> in a pugilistic position when physically separated
> from the charred seat in which she died. Most of her
> flesh had been burned from her body, and much of
> her skeletal frame, including her skull, was visible

during autopsy. Her teeth were still affixed to her upper jaw and mandible, making identification from dental X-rays possible . . .

My eyes had just gotten to the bottom of the paragraph when my attention was interrupted by the Lady Gaga riff on my phone. I glanced at the screen, which confirmed what I already knew: Marika. I let it play a few more seconds before I finally touched the "Talk" button and said, "You are the goddess of good timing." I'm sure my voice sounded hushed because I didn't want to wake up Sabrina in the other room.

"Mr. K," she said in that bright, cheery voice that just yesterday would have made any dark day seem brighter. She had called me Mr. K from the moment I introduced myself at Deutsche Bank Center three weeks ago, and it had stuck. "I was beginning to think that after two days out on the coast I was one of those out-of-sight, out-of-mind type of things."

"Nothing could be further from the truth," I replied. "I didn't get much sleep on the plane, and it's been a busy day. I just put Sabrina to bed and was catching up on emails before I called you."

"You didn't get my messages?" she asked in a tone that was playful but accusatory at the same time.

"I did, but I decided to wait until I had a good opportunity to call you back."

She could have said, *"You might have tried texting,"* but didn't. Instead she said, "I get that. I just missed you, is all, and wanted to hear your voice."

"And I wanted to hear yours," I told her. And I really did.

"Well, here I am." Upbeat and buoyant as usual. "So—how did it go out in California?"

"It's cold and it's damp, just like the song says. But we have a deal in the works, and it's good to be home." Not exactly a lie, really, if you accept the ambiguity of words.

"So, when do I get to see my man?" she asked.

"When do you have in mind?"

"Is right this very second too early?"

"Patience is a virtue," I said.

"And I think I've made my virtues very well known to you," she said with a giggle. "And I've been as patient as any woman could possibly be."

A little backstory here: I'd started seeing Marika three weeks ago in a deliberate attempt to put my past behind me. Everyone kept telling me I needed to move on; Alison was gone, and she wasn't coming back. Time to look out for my own needs, keep an eye on the future, and truck all those yesterdays to the landfill of the past.

That's when Marika wandered into my life, on the "up" escalator at the Deutsche Bank Center at Columbus Circle. Her Hermes scarf got snagged by the moving stairs, and I'd managed to pull it free without shredding it. She'd given it a cursory inspection, then asked me if she could pay me back by buying me a cup of coffee. I'd said yes, which led me to then invite Marika to dinner several nights later, followed by a jazz brunch the following Sunday. I explained my life up to that point over eggs Benedict and French toast: widower, single dad, great job with flextime that allowed me to work around Sabrina's school hours. Marika seemed to understand my circumspection, but I could see she was eager to get more intimate. So was I, but now I wasn't sure how that would sit with a job offer to move to LA. Something I would need to mention to her when the time was right. Full disclosure, and all that.

I thought for a moment, then said, "Sabrina and I have a full day planned tomorrow with my brother. Father–daughter time."

"Maybe we all could grab dinner when you get home?" Marika pressed.

"Nice thought, but it's a school night," I said.

"And you're going to tell me it's the same thing all week, right?"

"Unfortunately."

"Are you trying to avoid me, Mr. K?" she asked me then, just enough weight in her question to take the edge off her usual playfulness.

"Not even a remote possibility," I replied, maybe a little too quickly. But there was a guilty ring of truth in what she was saying, so I added, "Maybe we can try for lunch on Tuesday."

"It's a long time between now and then."

"Good things come to those who wait."

"And the best things come to those who make them happen."

"Then let's make this happen. Tuesday, noon."

"I'm not sure I can hold out that long, but it sounds like I'm going to have to," she said.

I told her I couldn't wait either, then hit "End" and set the phone down. I sat there and thought about what I'd just done, arranging a date with the wonderful woman who had recently entered my life. Nothing wrong with it except my brain was dealing with equal parts conflict and guilt.

* * *

Sometime later I was awakened by a sudden riff of drums that indicated a text had arrived in my phone. I didn't recognize the number at all, but it began with a 201 area code: New Jersey. *Probably another goddamn marketing pitch,* I thought, and almost didn't check the message. But curiosity got the better of me and I touched the SMS icon, which opened up a text that contained just four words:

My dearest huckleberry friend . . .

That was all. Nothing more. But that's all it took for a brain freeze to grip my head.

Huckleberry friend.

The secret nickname Alison had given me one night after we'd watched *Breakfast at Tiffany's* for the twentieth time, a line right out of Johnny Mercer's haunting theme song, "Moon River."

Who the fuck could possibly know what that term meant to me, and why would he—or she—be messing with my mind?

Without thinking, I texted back: *Alison? Is that you?*

It was a simple question that should have taken no more than a second to reply, but I got no response in return. I waited a full minute, then five. Not giving up, I typed another text, this one demanding, *Who is this?* As if that were going to get a more immediate response.

It didn't, of course.

Undaunted, I dialed the New Jersey number from which the message had been sent, listened patiently as the call clicked from satellite to satellite, cell to cell. Tower to tower.

Nothing. Zilch.

I dialed again and again, somehow expecting a different response each time. The truest definition of insanity.

I checked again to see if I might have missed another incoming text, and that's when I watched the impossible happen: the four-word message simply vanished, as if it had never arrived on my phone in the first place. Along with the phone number in Jersey.

Here one second, gone the next.

Just like my late wife.

5

Sunday

O N WEEKEND MORNINGS Sabrina usually stayed in her room until I was up, playing with her dollhouse or coloring in one of her books. TV was off-limits unless I gave her permission, but she wasn't much of a watcher anyway. She was more of a doer, and this morning she was engrossed in creating her own storyboard with a set of vinyl Colorforms that her grandparents had sent for her birthday. I remembered playing with the same toy when I was a child—Scooby-Doo and Batman were my favorites—and I'd had no idea that they were still a thing.

Sundays were waffle mornings, and I dragged myself into the kitchen and started mixing batter. I'd managed no more than five hours of sleep, felt anxious and conflicted. I busied myself by cutting a grapefruit, then showing Sabrina how to cook up some veggie sausage links. Now that I was awake, she was impatient, hurrying through the breakfast routine as she kept an eye on the second hand of the kitchen wall clock.

"How long now?" Sabrina asked when she finished her waffle and had mopped up the syrup on her plate.

"Maybe you can figure it out," I told her as I took a long sip of much-needed coffee. "The show starts at one o'clock, and it's nine o'clock now."

She frowned at my question—everything she asked me seemed to turn into a learning experience—but I could see her brain working on the puzzle. Eventually she brightened and said, "Four clocks?"

"Four *hours*, but yes, you're right," I said.

"That's a long time."

"It will go by real fast if you don't keep thinking about it."

That brought another frown as she ate her last bite of sausage. "Can we go to the park this morning?" Sabrina asked. "To look at the dogs?"

"Sounds like a plan," I replied as I warmed my hands on the coffee mug. In my mind, as long as we watched the dogs, we didn't actually have to get one.

* * *

The show that was at one o'clock—and which had Sabrina in a complete dither—was the annual Disney on Ice extravaganza at Madison Square Garden. It seemed to me that mid-spring was a bit late in the year to go to a skating spectacular, but my brother, Elliot, had given her the tickets for her birthday. He had a daughter named Julia who was a year older than Sabrina, and the two girls had grown particularly close over the last year. The one o'clock matinee had been conceived as a father–daughter thing, which meant Elliot's wife had the afternoon free.

I hadn't been to an ice show since Elliot and I were kids. Our parents had driven us down from Connecticut for the experience, a three-hour road trip that began with an argument in the car less than ten minutes after we'd hit the road. Mom had found something in Dad's briefcase, and the fight escalated when he demanded to know why she was going through his things in the first place. The deep freeze that engulfed the car that morning made the event chillier than advertised, and the drive home ushered in the next Ice Age. Memories of all those dancing sorcerers and magical princesses gliding around on skates were long gone by the time we pulled into our driveway that night.

One of the reasons I'd been looking forward to the performance today was because Sabrina and I could spend some quality time with my brother and Julia. But that was before yesterday's events at JFK, and the ludicrous hypothesis that was knocking around in my head. As preposterous as my wafer-thin thesis was, I wanted to get Elliot's take on whether I was out of my mind for even remotely thinking Maxwell Harding could still be alive. Let alone my wife.

They lived on the Upper East Side, a half dozen blocks from the Guggenheim, and we had agreed to meet up at the subway stop inside Penn Station, near the Garden. The place was packed with parents and kids, many of them dressed up as their favorite Disney characters. Sabrina and I arrived first and got involved in playing a variation on I Spy, me saying I'd just spotted Pluto or Olaf the Snowman, and Sabrina frantically glancing around to locate him or her. My daughter was dressed in a yellow Belle dress from *Beauty and the Beast*, her favorite of favorites, although she'd pouted for a good five minutes when I had given her a firm no to a request for some of the real makeup that was still in the drawer where her mother had kept it.

Squeals of delight erupted when Julia and her father appeared at the top of the escalator, and Elliot and I exchanged hearty man hugs. Julia was wearing a blue dress that Sabrina correctly surmised was Elsa's in *Frozen*, and within seconds they began debating whether pandas or koalas were cuter. They were off in their own world, and once I was certain they were paying no attention to my brother and me, I guardedly spelled out for him what I'd experienced at the airport yesterday. The man bumping me, the words "business coming through," and his reaction when I responded with "money on the move."

"That's fucking nuts, bro, and you know it," Elliot told me when I finished, checking to make sure the girls were out of earshot. No mincing of words, no sugarcoating. No indulgence of any kind. "Crazyland Express."

"That's what my left brain keeps telling me," I acknowledged as we dodged a family of seven that were all dressed like the dwarves from Snow White. I wondered if the parents had any idea how much embarrassment they were putting their children through, trauma that likely would result in expensive therapy as they grew older.

"Then listen to it," he said. "The left side, I mean."

"I know, I know. The best explanation is the rational one. But then my right brain clicks in and my mind just starts racing."

"Well, you need to hit the brakes on that," Elliot replied. "Before your brain spins out of control."

"It's already doing that," I confessed. "Besides, there's just too much that happened to simply be a coincidence."

"Like what? Seven words from a rotten play? Thousands of people could have seen it."

"More like a couple dozen," I replied. "It never even made it out of previews."

"Listen, Cam," he said. "I suspect I know where you're going with this, but you just have to accept the fact that

Harding wasn't the only asshole in New York who might have seen that play. What was the name of it?"

"*Dead Cat Bounce*," I replied. "It was all about Wall Street greed."

"Sounds like a lot of people in this town," my brother said. "Still, it's just a random line. Proves nothing."

"Not by itself, no. But he was the same height, and his facial structure was similar."

"But not identical, right?"

"Not exactly," I conceded. "He easily could have had reconstructive surgery."

"Sounds totally convincing to me," he said, sarcasm battling cynicism in his voice.

"You weren't there, Elliot. I was. I know what I saw . . . and heard."

But Elliot wasn't buying it. He gripped my arm firmly, and said, "Tell that to your logical, rational side. And pay real close attention to the answer."

I smiled politely, but the right side of my brain was fully engaged now, and I couldn't let this one go. "So maybe you can explain why he ran away when I yelled for him to stop," I challenged him.

"Seriously?" my brother replied, looking me square in the eye. "The easiest explanation is the guy was in a hurry. Or he could have been worried that some nutjob was chasing after him in the airport. Or maybe it was just your brain playing tricks on you, telling you he was trying to get away."

"He *was* trying to get away," I insisted. "He walked right past the driver who was waiting with all the others and had a sign with a name on it."

"And you know this how?" Elliot asked.

Just for a second, I tuned in on the girls' conversation, noted that they had drifted from koalas and pandas to kangaroos and platypuses. This indicated at least one of them had some understanding of Australia.

"Because I went back and talked to the chauffeur," I explained. "After Harding jumped in the cab and sped off."

"Maybe this guy—Harding, or not Harding—just didn't see his driver with the sign. That happened to me once in Miami." My brother was the managing editor of a weekly checkout line celebrity magazine, and he did a lot of traveling. That would have explained the presence of a car and driver waiting for him in Florida.

"I don't think that's what happened here," I told him. "I think he saw his name on the sign but kept going for a reason."

"The name on the sign was Harding?"

I shook my head in irritation, annoyed at Elliot's negativity. Although I really hadn't expected anything different; my brother had always been the pragmatic one, weighing all sides of every issue before committing to anything. The voice of reason. On the other hand, I'd always been impulsive and impetuous, such as the time I'd jumped on a plane to Kenya, two months after graduating from college, because I'd landed a stringer assignment to take photos of the violence following the US embassy bombing. The entire Kane family had been horrified that I dove right into a lion's den, but it landed me a full-time gig with the Associated Press that had continued until Sabrina was on the way.

"No," I replied. "The name on the sign was 'Zaccaro,' and when I spoke with the driver, he seemed perplexed that his customer didn't show. The designated flight from Rio de Janeiro landed on time, but they never connected."

"Did you get the name of the limo company?"

"In fact, I did," I told him. "Elite Services."

"Have you called them to check on this Mr. Zaccaro?"

I had to admit I had not; why, I didn't know. "I'll do that tonight," I said. "Although I don't know what good it will do."

"It might put an end to this ludicrous flight of fancy," he suggested.

Given my brother's totally rational rejoinders to what I knew sounded like a delusional rant, I was hesitant to mention the text I'd received in the middle of the night. His response would be predictable, and I'd just be opening myself up to more of his brotherly ridicule. But there was no cogent explanation for what I'd experienced, so I filled him in on what had occurred from the moment my phone pinged.

"When did this happen?" he asked when I was finished.

"Around two o'clock, maybe a little later," I said.

"Out of the blue." More of a statement than a question.

"One hundred percent."

He studied me, and I got the feeling he was trying to see if I was trying to pull some elaborate joke or had truly slipped into the realm of the deranged.

"And this message just disappeared on its own?" he finally asked.

"I know how it sounds, but they have that kind of technology now."

"Whoever *they* are."

"Look, Elliot—I accept that you don't believe me, but I know what I saw."

He nodded, and for a second I thought he might finally be getting the picture. Then he said, "Sometimes a banana is just a banana."

"Meaning what?"

We were nearing the entrance to the Garden, and we herded our respective daughters into the security queue. "Meaning there could be any number of reasons why the guy said what he said, looked how he looked, bypassed his ride, and took a cab," Elliot replied. "Like I said."

I stared at my brother for a few long seconds, but Elliot's words—as maddening as they were to my right brain—made total sense to the left side. What I was proposing was ludicrous, and I knew how it sounded. Dental records and autopsies and police reports all confirmed the same thing: Alison was dead. To think otherwise was to risk falling into a delusional labyrinth based on conjecture and wishful thinking, and was, quite possibly, evidence of a psychotic break.

6

THE ICE SHOW was a welcome diversion, and Elliot and I spoiled our girls with all sorts of vendor food that was sure to make them sick. The Garden was packed, the fresh ice made it unseasonably cold, and I had forgotten to bring a sweatshirt for either of us. By the time the encore had finished, both Sabrina and Julia were shivering, but they still pleaded for us to take them to get ice cream. I knew my daughter was going to complain of a stomachache later, and when she brought up the idea of pizza for dinner again, I put my foot down.

"You've had enough junk food for one day," I explained as I unlocked our front door. "I think I'll make fish sticks and a big salad with cucumbers and carrots."

She groaned, then asked if we could have dinner while watching a Disney movie. But another rule in the Kane house was that Sunday night dinners were free of external stimulation—no TV, no toys, no games at the table. The only exception was the glass of wine I poured while rinsing lettuce and slicing tomatoes. I had no idea how Sabrina could possibly want to see or hear more of the same Fantasyland schtick we'd just witnessed on skates at the Garden, but then

I remembered going to my first rock concert when I was in high school. My buddies and I stood on our feet for over three hours of Bruce Springsteen and the E Street Band, and on the drive home from the Civic Center in Hartford, Joey Kearns popped a CD into the dashboard and we sang along with the Boss all the way home.

It was close to eight when Sabrina finally climbed under the covers, just a few minutes past her regular bedtime. I read her a chapter from *Stuart Little*, which was quickly replacing *Charlotte's Web* as her new favorite story. She had a full shelf of newer, more contemporary books that had been gifts from relatives, but the older ones were considered classics for a reason. Eventually she ran out of excuses for me to keep the light on, so I clicked it off and kissed her forehead. I started to get up from the edge of her bed when she said, "I think Mommy would have liked today."

I sensed a sharp tug at my heart, the way it always feels when my daughter and I are thinking the same thing. "She would have loved it," I assured her, giving her one last hug. "Every single moment."

"Can we see it again?"

"Next year, sugar," I said.

"Maybe Marika can come with us," Sabrina mused. "I think she'd like it too."

I had introduced the two of them just last weekend, an afternoon outing to the Alice in Wonderland statue in Central Park. They had gotten along famously, and both had been genuine in saying they couldn't wait to do it again.

"I'm sure she would," I told her, my mind flashing on Los Angeles and my meeting just forty-eight hours ago, and all the changes our lives might go through over the next twelve months. Marika possibly being one of those changes.

After making sure Sabrina's door was closed just the right amount, I wandered out to the living room and ran a search for the phone number for Elite Services LLC. My brain was in the neutral zone between right and left, but the website said they were open 24/7, so I punched in the ten digits and prepared myself for the same sort of runaround I received when I called Empire Livery.

"I'm sorry, sir, but that's confidential client information," a woman on the other end said when I'd explained what I wanted.

"So Mr. Zaccaro is a client?" I asked.

"Everyone who arranges a car with us is considered a client," she said. "I can't tell you anything more than that."

"Can you at least tell me where your chauffeur was supposed to drive this client?"

"No, sir. I cannot."

I knew the answer to my next question before I asked it, but I was already all in on this. "What about a phone number?"

"I'm sorry, sir, but if you're not going to make a reservation, I'm going to have to end this call right now."

I think we both took the same action at the same instant, and after I put down my phone, I walked over to the door that opened out onto our little back patio and stared out at the darkness. I replayed Elliot's voice of reason from earlier in the day, but once again my right brain had started careening down a track of random memories, gathering speed as one spark of consciousness followed another, in no particular order or time frame. Alison's eyes, her smile, her laugh. Her brilliant mind, her capacity to find order in confusion, her gentle touch and acceptance of my personal quirks. Her selflessness, her dedication to our daughter, and her commitment to make our small but expensive condo a home.

My mental wandering took me back in time twelve years, to the night I first laid eyes on her. Jake's on the Creek, a waterfront restaurant set on a marsh just outside Charleston, where Alison was born and raised. I hadn't known any of that at the time, of course; all I was aware of was how she was leaning against the deck rail, glass of chardonnay in her hand, staring out at the dolphins and fishing boats. I couldn't take my eyes off her, and I had been gripped with an eerie sense of certainty that the woman who would define the rest of my life was standing just a few feet away, gazing at the orange hues of the Carolina sunset. I wondered who she was, why she was there at that very moment, who might be with her. Only later did I learn that she had just defended her doctoral dissertation at Yale and had flown down to visit her folks while she waited to learn whether she'd earned her degree.

I was in town to take photographs of a visit from the vice president, who had flown down from Washington for some sort of military commemoration. One of my colleagues had insisted on getting she-crab soup and shrimp and grits, and Jake's had come highly recommended for all of the above. I remembered the long oak bar set off to the right, the dining room with floor-to-ceiling windows, music playing on the overhead sound system. Glass doors opened onto the outdoor dining deck at the edge of the creek, the very same deck where I'd walked up to the future Alison Kane and asked— quite seriously—"Would you like to dance?"

She'd looked at me over the rim of her wineglass, then set it down and, without a word, tugged me onto the outside dance floor. We eased into the Carolina beach tempo almost seamlessly: triple step, triple step, rock step. I still remember the song that was playing: "Be Young, Be Foolish, Be

Happy," by the Tams. She was a better dancer than I was, but after I got my groove on, we'd moved around the floor to every song the band played.

Neither of us wanted the night to end, nor the next, nor the one after that. I kept delaying my flight back to New York, opting instead to take long walks on the beach and dance the night away with this woman who was becoming a smooth segue between my past and my future. A few weeks later she flew up to New York to spend a long weekend with me, which included attending her doctoral ceremony in New Haven, where she had been named the university's latest PhD in quantum mathematics and number theory.

Three years after that, she had taken my hand and said, "I do," and two years later she'd given me a little girl, who now was sleeping right down the hall.

* * *

I must have fallen asleep in my chair, because my eyes abruptly blinked open from the sound of a clanking pipe down in the basement. After I determined the origin of the sound, I looked in on Sabrina, who was sound asleep with her knees drawn up in the fetal position. She had started sleeping like that just days after her mother died, which made me wonder if her life would ever return to normal. Whatever "normal" might be for a little girl whose mom would never be there to see her graduate from high school and college, or walk down the aisle in a flowing white dress. I didn't even know what "normal" was for a man in his early forties who had lost the love of his life and wasn't sure that he'd ever find someone who could bridge the pain that had cracked his heart. Someone who could press away the grief and anger, a void that all the best sex in the world couldn't possibly touch.

Sabrina made a noise, but it was part of a dream that I dared not disturb. Night terrors were one thing, and there had been plenty of those in the early days. But now her dreams seemed to be of the regular variety that were an ordinary part of a seven-year-old girl's life. I watched her for a moment, just to assure myself that she was okay, then quietly pulled her door closed a few inches, leaving it as I had found it.

By now it was well past my own bedtime, but as I gathered up my phone and headed down the hall to my room, a random thought hit me, and I made a U-turn back to my study. My computer was still powered up, so I sat down in front of it and clicked on the link for my wireless carrier. Seemed there always was some sort of problem with my bill, and I'd bookmarked the web address so I wouldn't have to google it each time.

I logged into the site, scrolled down through my options, selected "See Current Activity." I knew from past searches that this would show me a running tab of all calls and texts during the most recent thirty-day period, incoming and outgoing. Not the specific conversations or messages themselves, just the ten-digit number for each and whether it was incoming or outgoing. I figured that whoever had deleted the Huckleberry text last night might not have been able to achieve the same result with the incoming call log.

I figured right. There it was, a text that had arrived at 2:11 that very morning. From a 201 number, just as I'd thought. Maybe I wasn't going nuts after all—at least not about that.

I was just about to log off when my brain caught something my eyes didn't. I had to search the log line by line to find it, and finally located it near the top of the activity log. Another entry from the same number, three weeks and two days ago. This time a phone call that lasted all of two seconds, probably just enough time to connect, but not ring before the user on the other end hung up.

Had Alison tried to contact me back then as well? If so, why had she ended the call so quickly? Whose phone was she using? Or was some marketing spoofer over in Jersey just trying to sell me an extended warranty on a car I didn't own?

Acting on impulse, I dialed the number, expecting it to ring and ring. Highly doubtful that a real live person would pick up. Instead, I just got the constant *beep beep beep* of a circuit-busy signal, indicating the system was down, or the phone was turned off or, in the case of a prepaid, out of minutes. I tried again, getting the same result.

The number was definitely real, not just the remnant of a fading dream I'd had the night before. Probably a discarded burner that was sleeping with the fishes, or lying at the bottom of a dumpster somewhere, smashed into a dozen pieces.

7

Monday

MORNING CAME EARLY, as it usually did at the Kane house.

Sabrina was the first to rise, and as I swung my legs over the side of the bed, I heard her racing from room to room. She finally came to my door and knocked, then called out, "Have you seen my socks?"

"Which ones?" I asked.

She popped her head inside the room and said, "The yellow ones with the wiener dogs."

"Those are dachshunds," I corrected for what had to be the tenth time. Alison had made a tradition of giving our daughter specialty socks for every birthday and holiday since she was three, and I'd kept up the ritual. Santa had left the dachshunds in her stocking last Christmas, and Sabrina had all but worn them out.

"Have you seen them?"

"We packed them for your sleepover," I reminded her. "Check your backpack."

Her face brightened and she said, "Oh, right," then raced back to her own room.

I managed to get half a banana and a frozen waffle into her, then made sure her shoes were tied and teeth were brushed, again. When she was finished I walked her the ten blocks to school, kissing her goodbye at the front gate, as I always did. There were too many child abductions these days to give her anything less than door-to-door service, and I wasn't taking any chances.

The Jameson Preparatory Learning Academy was located on 13th Street in a prewar brownstone that looked as if it came right out of an old sepia photograph. A set of granite steps that had been highly polished by the soles of time led up to the main entrance, which opened onto a lobby where the administrative offices were located. Stairs and a small elevator accessed the classrooms on the second, third, and fourth floors, and a rear ground-level door opened out onto a grassy play area out back.

Alison loved it the moment we set foot inside, and decided to enroll Sabrina on the spot. But that's not how the process worked; the application for matriculating firstgraders seemed longer than anything I remembered filling out for college, and the wait until we heard about our daughter's educational future was excruciating. The pressure almost justified the tuition once we received the letter informing us that Sabrina Kane had been accepted into the next first-grade class.

Something Alison had not lived to experience.

I watched my daughter bound up the steps of the brick building, and once she disappeared inside, I felt a profound sense of accomplishment. Sometimes the morning delays could last for hours, but this Monday morning—miracle of all miracles—Sabrina managed, just barely, to get to school on time. Even if her dachshund socks were inside out.

* * *

Confusion also had kicked into high gear where I worked at the headquarters of Meridian Image and Light, Inc., on the eighth floor of a postmodern building on Avenue of the Americas. Within ninety seconds of my arrival, I learned that, in the short time I'd been gone, the North American video editor had texted her immediate resignation from the company. As a result, William Trent—the CEO—was storming around the open workspace in a fit of rage. Plus, one of the assistant photo editors had allegedly made an unwanted advance on an intern from NYU, and the young woman he'd hit on was talking inappropriate sexual contact and lawsuit. The young employee who allegedly made the improper suggestion was sulking in his cubicle, insisting to anyone within earshot that his intentions had been misunderstood.

I managed to make it through a full slate of morning meetings without too many distractions. I was brought up to date on where the company's contract photographers were positioned in the newest hotspots around the globe and which news organizations might be interested in licensing their work. I started to doze off during a gratuitous and tedious teleconference with a marketing group that was interested in signing a multiyear contract, but I caught my head as it began to bob and mentally slapped myself awake.

A half hour before lunch, William Trent stopped by my office and plopped himself down on a leather chair in front of my desk. He was casually dressed in tan khakis and a plaid button-down dress shirt, no tie. I had been studying a particularly graphic photograph of a Sudanese child cradling his dead baby sister, taken less than twenty-four hours before. Both were covered in dried mucus and black flies, and the little boy appeared not to have eaten in days. I looked away from the desktop monitor and leaned back in my chair as Trent made himself comfortable.

"Thanks again for letting me take those days off last week," I said as he settled in.

"Not a problem," Trent replied. He was a tall and wiry man who, like me, had put in his years out in the field before succumbing to life in a corner office in midtown Manhattan. Running with the bulls was a hell of a lot more fun than pushing a mouse around, and he'd picked up a few scars and two Pulitzer nominations over the years. He'd also acquired a family and had made the tough decision to put the peripatetic adventures of his career behind him. "A few days away from here, toes kicking up the sand, is good for the soul."

"Great way to recharge the batteries, that's for sure," I agreed. I had not told Trent that I'd actually made a quick trip out to LA in pursuit of a total midlife makeover and had come back with a job offer tucked neatly in my pocket. A job offer that required an answer, preferably today and no later than close of business tomorrow. I wondered why Trent was here in my office, since the man was not known for engaging in casual banter with his employees.

"For some reason I never forget a date," he said in a way that suggested he had something to share but wasn't going to get directly to the point."

"What are you telling me?"

"I know this coming Saturday is the one-year anniversary."

And there it was. I hadn't forgotten either, of course, but I hadn't expected Trent to think of it. Or anyone else, for that matter.

"Most people wouldn't remember."

"How could I not?"

"That's the curse of having an eidetic memory," I replied.

"Actually, I remembered because I've walked in your shoes."

His words caught me by surprise, and I found myself leaning forward, folding my hands together on my desk. "What do you mean?"

Trent lowered his head in confirmation, a resolute look in his tired eyes. "I don't share this with many people, but I was married once before," he said. "Many years ago, before I ever did my first overseas gig. Her name was Beverly. We met at Fordham, and she was beautiful in just about every way a scrawny young goofball in his early twenties could imagine beautiful to be. She was smart and sophisticated and witty."

I wondered why he was telling me all this, since he rarely spoke of his personal life with anyone. All morning he'd been jumping from one debacle to the next, and now he was kicking back in my office, sharing his life's secrets. I didn't want to break the flow, however, so I just let him continue.

"She laughed at my dumb jokes and shrugged off my moods," he carried on. "We never fought; at least, the bright side of my memory doesn't remember us ever getting mad at each other. Her parents thought we were too young to get married, but when we did, they accepted it for what it was. Accepted me too, even though I didn't have an MBA or any conceivable way to earn the sort of living they thought their daughter deserved. We had a small ceremony and a beautiful honeymoon in Key West, and settled down to start a life together. Three months later she was gone."

Wham! I wasn't sure if my eyes actually bugged out, but after a second, I forced a blink. "I had no idea about any of this. Do you mind if I ask how—"

Trent waved me off as if the statute of limitations on tiptoeing around such things had expired long ago. "We were living in DC at the time," he said. "Right across the river, actually, in Alexandria. I'd flown to Texas for a quick photo shoot, and we were supposed to go to her sister's wedding in Maine that weekend. If I'd been home, we would have driven up together, but since I had to fly up from Waco, we decided she'd pick me up in Portland. The best anyone could figure, she was tired and fell asleep at the wheel, drifted into the wrong lane and collided with a tanker truck hauling milk."

"Damn . . . I am so sorry."

Trent shook his head and said, "Thank you. But as I said, that was a long time ago, and since then my life has gone on in many wonderful and miraculous directions. I guess that's why I'm telling you all this."

"To reassure me?"

"To soften the impact of this coming weekend." Trent rose from his chair and gazed out the window a moment, as if studying the brick building across the street. "I know from experience that when you hit that first anniversary, your mind can play funny tricks on you. For instance, don't drive. I know you don't have a car, but your mind will be drifting, and you'll run a great risk of not paying attention. A few days before the first anniversary of Bev's death, I could swear I saw her come out of a restaurant we liked in Georgetown. And one night I was sure I smelled her perfume on the sheets as I got into bed."

"What did you do?" I asked as I felt my skin go clammy. "Did you try to find her?"

"I poured a double Scotch on the rocks and told myself it was time to break from a past I couldn't change. You need to do the same thing."

"I don't really care for Scotch," I replied.

"That's not the point. What I'm trying to tell you is you need to get on with your life."

Trent was right, and he wasn't the only person telling me that I needed to stop living in the past and get on with the future. For my sake and Sabrina's. And for the memory of Alison.

Plus, I did like Scotch, especially when he was pouring from his private stash.

"Message understood," I said.

*   *   *

My afternoon was filled with the tasks that had piled up while I was in California, even though I'd only been gone two days. I tackled them from the top of the heap down, but the stack never seemed to get smaller. I knew I needed to call Claire Beckett, the woman from the Bradley Museum, and give her my answer. She'd made the job seem like a dream opportunity that would transform my career path forever, but I wasn't sure I was ready to climb out of the comfort zone I'd created for Sabrina and me.

A little after three I closed my door and made a half dozen personal calls. I could have waited until I was on my way to collect Sabrina from her after-school day-care program, but I wanted to strike while the impulse—*obsession*—was hot. I compiled a list of people I wanted to speak with and began to dial, so I could set some things in motion before Manhattan's workforce crowded the subway tunnels and bus lines, in an effort to get home.

By the time I was finished, I had just under an hour before I had to pick up Sabrina, so I quietly slipped out of the office. I stepped out onto the sidewalk and thrust my hand in the air to hail a cab. Three minutes later I was barreling down 51st Street in a stream of yellow cars, delivery trucks, and suicidal bike messengers. At the end of the block, the driver turned left onto Ninth Avenue, heading downtown in lurching stop-and-go traffic.

8

A FEW MINUTES LATER I was sitting in the corner of a Starbucks on Sixth Avenue. I knew I was perilously late, but this was a stop I felt I needed to make. Sitting across from me was Lillian Sloane, a longtime friend and former colleague with whom I'd shared numerous work exploits when our careers had crossed paths in the field. She was staring at me with such concentration that it told me she was genuinely worried about me. Worried for everything I had just laid out on the table for her.

"You do realize how insane this sounds," she said, her hands clasped in front of her. She furtively glanced around as if to see if anyone in her friendly neighborhood coffee lounge had been eavesdropping on our conversation. "Please don't tell a living soul what you just told me."

"I haven't—not yet," I assured her, not mentioning my conversation with my brother on Sunday.

"It's a classic case of not being able to let go of reality," she went on, as if I didn't already know that. Lillian had always been blunt, and she'd wasted no time getting right to it. "You told me you'd moved beyond that."

"And I did," I told her. "I've read all the right books and done all the right things. I've even started seeing someone. And I don't mean a shrink."

"Well, that's all good news." She picked up the remains of a cranberry scone and nibbled at the edge. "As a friend, I must say I'm happy for you. And you know how much respect I have for you as a career man and father. But what you're telling me . . . well, you really don't want to hear what I have to say."

"Try me."

When I'd first met Lillian, she'd been a hard-edged reporter for the AP when I was a photographer, and now she was an adjunct professor of journalism at City College. I'd thought she was beautiful, in an athletic, outdoorsy way that fit her career, and little had changed since then, except the setting. She was wearing a gray knit dress, cinched with a thin black belt tied at the side. She never paid much attention to makeup or accessories—she didn't need to—and this afternoon she was wearing square glasses with lenses that looked like little television screens, and large silver hoops hung from her ears.

"For starters, Cam, if you start telling people you think Harding is alive simply because of a short line from a lousy play, they'll ship you off to Bellevue in a nanosecond."

"I'm not bonkers, Lillian. And I'm not asking you to buy my story. All I want you to do is contact your friend. The ex-cop. You once told me he's the best there is at cracking cases that can't be cracked. Tell him I want to talk to him. I just want to see what he can find out, and I have the money."

"Think about what you're saying," she replied as she let out a sad sigh. "If by some small miracle Harding is alive, think what that implies. If he didn't die when that car went off the road, someone else did. Same thing goes for your wife."

"I've already gone through all this in my mind," I said. "Police reports, autopsy results, dental records. I know how preposterous it sounds, but just humor me."

"Do I look like I'm laughing?" She studied me intently, but I couldn't tell what she was thinking. "Just listen to me here. If even a thread of what you're saying is true, can you imagine what sort of macabre coordination it would take to pull off? You sound like those *truthers* who believe the twin towers conspiracy."

"Thanks for your support," I told her.

"I'm serious, Cam. Do you realize what you're suggesting?"

"I know what I know."

"You believe what you believe," she corrected me. "Don't confuse the two."

"I am not confused—"

Lillian raised her hand, palm outward: *"Stop right there."* "Nice try, but that's not at all what I said. Have you given any thought to the whole question of why? *Why* kill two innocent people just to . . . to do *what*? Make two other people disappear?"

"Harding was anything but innocent," I reminded her.

"I didn't say he was. But even if he didn't die in the crash, what makes you think Alison is still alive? Have you thought about that?"

"I know, you're right," I said as I glanced at my watch. "If *P* doesn't necessarily mean *Q*."

"Harding couldn't have concocted this on his own," Lillian pointed out. "He would have needed major help."

"That son of a bitch raked in billions of dollars through cryptocurrency fraud. I'm sure he had associates who knew their way around the dark web."

"And there's a reason it's called that," she reminded him. "If what you're proposing is even a sliver of the truth, it still leads back to the fact that two innocent people are dead."

I let out a deep sigh of exasperation and said, "You don't think I've already gone over all this in my head a hundred times?"

"Of course you have," Lillian replied. "I know how your brain works. And ultimately, I know you're a highly rational man. That's why I've always liked you. And I really admire how you've dealt with your wife's death, especially where Sabrina was concerned. Which is why it's very important that you keep a level head."

"That's why I needed to meet with you," I told her. "I want you to imagine, just for a second, what it would mean if there were some vast, crazy conspiracy that caused Harding—and maybe my wife—to disappear. What if they put two totally random people in that car and caused it to fly off the highway? Think about that. Consider what it would mean if Harding got away with murder—and who knows what else. Right now, at this very moment, he and his dark web cohorts could be up to something very crooked and sinister, and they're getting away with it. And my wife might be caught in the middle of it."

She must have detected the sincerity in my voice, as a faint smile eased onto her face. "Now, that's the Cameron Kane I met all those years ago," she said, letting out a long breath. "The young crusader, off to the action with a backpack, a camera, and an AP badge. Slogging through forests and deserts and refugee camps in search of the truth."

"I had a good instinct for finding it too," I reminded her. "So did you. And as absurd as this might sound, I think there's a greater truth here that needs to be found. Please, Lillian—will you just call your cop friend?"

She took another nibble of her scone but remained silent. I imagined the cogs in her brain turning methodically as she tapped a fingernail on the tabletop. Finally, she reached for her iPhone and began flipping through her contacts.

"I just want you to know I'm doing this for the Cameron Kane I know is not full-tilt crazy," she said. "The Cameron Kane who won accolades, married the most beautiful woman in the world, and is the greatest dad on the planet. Just be forewarned: if you're not crazy—if there is some truth in what you're saying—you might just not like what you find out. And whoever is behind it sure as shit won't either."

* * *

I was late. *Expensively late.* If I didn't collect Sabrina from the after-school program before five thirty, my monthly account would be dinged a dollar for every minute I was tardy.

The subway got me downtown in nine minutes, and as the train shot through the tunnel, I replayed my conversation with Lillian. She had every reason to doubt what I said; there was nothing about my story that sounded even remotely plausible. The empirical evidence all pointed to a terrifying and fiery car accident in the New Jersey countryside, a crash that had killed my wife and her arrogant, felonious boss. To even consider an alternate reality—one in which Harding might still be alive—not only was certifiably nuts but predictable for a widower who was nearing the first-year anniversary of a tragic death.

Just as William Trent had said.

As I dashed up the subway stairs to the street, my mind was working on dueling scenarios. Neither made any sense, and they came back to one thing: if Harding had not died in the accident, he had to be living somewhere.

Maybe right here in the City.

Which, in my mind, meant that Alison could still be here too.

And that brought me back around to *why*? I could understand why Harding might stage his own death; he was facing decades of life in prison, and orange jumpsuits were not his taste in threads. But why would Alison assist him? She had loved Sabrina with all her heart, and I thought she loved me just as much. Sure, I'd grown suspicious when she'd started spending long nights at the office, but now I wondered whether those late evenings might have involved something much more nefarious than an affair. Something that resulted in the murder of a man and a woman who had somehow come to be behind the wheel of Harding's Lamborghini that night.

I played out every possibility as I hurried down Eighth Avenue. For the past sixty hours, I'd been chasing windmills based solely on a random nudge after stepping off a crowded, stuffy red-eye from LAX. My brother had a description for the wild ride I'd climbed aboard: Crazyland Express. Which brought me back to the dental records. They were the forensic foundation of identification in both cases, and the autopsy report had made it clear that Alison had perished in the impact and fire. Harding too. I saw neither reason nor motive for someone to have forged it, which meant case closed.

Closed, until the text message landed in my phone.

My dearest Huckleberry friend.

* * *

Sabrina was standing just inside the glass door when I rounded the corner and raced up the steps. I was twelve dollars late, as the lone remaining college intern dutifully reminded me when I pushed my way inside.

"I'm sorry to have to charge you extra, Mr. Kane, but rules are rules," she apologized, although the tight grin on her lips suggested she enjoyed playing day-care cop.

"I understand," I said. "I'll do my best to make sure it doesn't happen again."

Outdoors on the sidewalk, Sabrina handed me her tiny backpack as if I were her private Sherpa, then gushed: "Guess what, Daddy? My teacher loved my story so much she asked me to read it to the whole class."

"That's great, sugar." I leaned down and kissed her on the forehead, wondering what story she was talking about. Had I missed something in all the activity of the last few days? "Which one did she ask you to read?"

"The one about the squirrels," Sabrina said. "It was my best one. Mrs. Erskine said I should pick that one for her to write down."

Mrs. Erskine was the mother of Pattie Erskine, one of Sabrina's classmates, and she helped out in the classroom several days a week. She was a writer—who had published several novels for young teens—and had been helping the class with an oral language project. Each student would make up a story and share it with Mrs. Erskine, who then would type it into a computer and print it out. Each young author would illustrate his or her story and bind it into a real picture book.

"Why don't you tell me the story while we walk home?" I suggested as we headed up the sidewalk toward the corner.

"Okay," Sabrina agreed, and in that one word I sensed an enthusiasm I hadn't heard in a long time. Not even when we'd visited the shark exhibit at the aquarium at Coney Island last summer. "See, Suzy Squirrel lived in a big oak tree out in the country. She lived there with her mommy and daddy in a hole in the trunk, and they ate nuts. Lots of nuts. They ate nuts for breakfast, they ate nuts for lunch, and they ate nuts for dinner. And even though it was summer, her daddy was always going out to look for more nuts to save up for the winter. One day, Suzy told her mother, 'I hate nuts. That's all we ever eat.' And her mother said, 'We're squirrels, Suzy. That's what we do.' And Suzy said, 'Well, I'm tired of nuts. I want to try something else.'"

"Like mac and cheese?" I suggested.

"*Dad-dy*," Sabrina said, "squirrels don't eat mac and cheese."

"That's right," I said. "They eat nuts."

Sabrina flashed me one of those "you're-being-like-that-again" looks. "Can I just tell the story?" she said.

"Of course," I said. "I'm sorry."

She furrowed her brow in a look that suggested I *should* be sorry. "Anyway, the next morning Suzy woke up, and her mother was gone. She asked her daddy where she was, and he said, 'She went out to look for something new to eat. I guess she doesn't know that squirrels only eat nuts.' Suzy was really worried, because if something happened to her mother, it would be her own fault. The thing is, her mother didn't come home that night, and she didn't come home the next day. She didn't come home the day after that either."

Sabrina fell silent and stared down at the sidewalk. I waited for her to continue, but when she didn't, I asked her, "When did her mother come home?"

"Well, that's the thing, Daddy. She never *did* come home. Suzy's mother is still out there, somewhere, still looking for something for me—I mean for Suzy—to eat. Besides nuts."

Holy shit, I thought as we turned onto Hudson Street. Could Sabrina somehow believe she had something to do with her mother's death? I'd tried to talk to her about it numerous times over the past year, but I never got anywhere. Sabrina would shake her head and immerse herself in a coloring book or play with her toys. And now, after all this time, it seemed she might still be thinking that her mother was out there somewhere.

Well, stand in line for that one, I thought as I cast a doleful glance at my daughter.

"That's a very sad story," I finally said.

"Not really, Daddy," Sabrina said, a childlike brightness in her voice. "It's not sad at all."

"It's not?" I asked, more than a little bewildered.

"Nope. 'Cause, you see, there's another story, one of those—I forget what you call them, but like a movie that comes after the first one."

"A sequel?"

"Yep. It's going to make everything better. I told my teacher, and she said it would also make a great story."

"Can you tell me that one too?" I asked.

"Nope," she said, making a zipper gesture across her lips. "I'm still working on it."

So am I, sugar, I wanted to say. *So am I.* Problem was, I knew that real life didn't always work out the way it does in movies. Or sequels.

* * *

We ate mac and cheese for dinner. My mention of it on the walk home had given Sabrina a craving, so we had that along with some steamed peas. After, we played three rounds of Chutes and Ladders, and Sabrina won every one of them.

At this point in her life, I thought it was better for her to enjoy the thrill of victory rather than the agony of defeat. She'd already lost enough at such a young age, and life would always be full of tough lessons.

When we finished, I ran her a bath, and she played with a set of plastic mermaids until I managed to convince her she was going to shrivel up like a prune. She got out of the tub and slipped into her nightgown by herself, then brushed her teeth before heading to bed. She started to crawl under the covers, then stopped and glanced over at the window.

"Is that locked?" she asked.

"I think so, but I can open it to let in some fresh air—"

"No!" Her voice wasn't quite a shriek, but it was firm and absolute. "Can you make sure?"

"Of course, sugar." I walked to the window and thumbed the latch to confirm it was. "Is everything okay?"

"It is now," Sabrina said as she pulled the sheet and bed-spread up to her chin.

"Did you hear something outside?"

"No," she replied quickly. "And I'm not scared."

"I know you're not," I said. "But it's a good idea to double-check sometimes."

She nodded as she made herself comfortable, then said, "Will you read me a story?"

"Wouldn't miss it for the world. How 'bout some *Stuart Little*?"

"Yes, please. But there's something I don't get."

"What's that?"

"Well, I don't know how someone's child could be a mouse."

I got through ten pages before her eyelids drooped, and when I heard gentle snuffling, I quietly closed the book and set it on the nightstand. I made sure the water cup was full and kissed her on the forehead. Then I turned off the light and slipped out into the hallway, partially closing the door until just enough light seeped in so if she woke up, she would see she was safe in her own room.

I tiptoed into the living room and tried to watch television, but nothing grabbed my attention, so I turned it off. I picked up a thriller I'd bought at LAX but lasted three minutes before I set it back down on the table. I checked my text messages but found nothing new, so I wandered into my study and found a yellow legal pad. I sharpened a handful of pencils, grabbed a clipboard, and took them into the living room. I put an old Cowboy Junkies CD on the stereo, turned it down low, and settled onto the recliner. I mostly listened to my Roku these days, but tonight seemed like a good time for a real album, especially since it was one of Alison's favorites.

I collected my thoughts, then scribbled a few words at the top of the page. I retraced each letter several times, wearing down the lead, until each word stood out in bold letters: **Things to Check Out re: Alison**.

Below that I jotted down stray thoughts as they came to me, highlighting them with bullets as I wrote:

- *Talk to medical examiner who performed autopsy (Dr. Cook).*
- *Talk to Dr. Nguyen about dental records.*
- *Reread all newspaper stories re: accident.*
- *Track down 201 number.*
- *Talk to Mrs. Harding, if she's willing.*
- *Talk to Jersey cops who responded to 911 call.*
- *Talk to NYPD cops who responded to burglary.*

Damn! How could I have forgotten the break-in on the day of Alison's memorial service?

My mind backpedaled to that Saturday afternoon a year ago, one week after the crash. The spring weather had cooperated, with temperatures in the mid-seventies and a light breeze blowing in from the Hudson. William Trent had pulled some serious strings and reserved a small area of Central Park near the lake for a private gathering of family and friends. Alison had once mused that if she died before I did, she wanted a memorial service somewhere outdoors, surrounded by wind, woods, and water. The three *W*s, she called them. Trent—who, as it turned out, had once walked in my shoes—made it all happen.

For the first time in a very long week, I'd felt a lift in my spirits, buoyed by all the wonderful things Alison's friends and colleagues had said about her. Funny things, loving things, quirky things—all intended to encompass a full spectrum of emotions, although it seemed that the primary objective was to wring out as many tears as possible. Their collective words accomplished that goal, and I'd kept wiping my eyes with a handkerchief someone had given to me. Finally, we headed home, where I knew I was going to have to do my best not to fall apart as soon as I turned the key.

But I didn't have to worry about any of that, because as soon as I opened the front door, I could see that thieves had struck. I'd read about this sort of thing: professional burglars regularly scan the obituaries to find the time and location of funerals and memorial services. Then, while the grieving family is out of the way, they hit the house, quickly making off with anything of value.

"Brazen, insensitive assholes" is what the NYPD officer called them when he walked with me through the house, looking at what the scumbags had done.

The burglars had been highly selective in what they'd taken, skipping over the digital media player and soundbar while helping themselves to the sterling silver flatware and candlesticks that we rarely used because they required too much polishing. In the bedroom they'd found a diamond and sapphire ring that had belonged to Alison's grandmother, an heirloom I'd planned on saving for Sabrina until she got older, but had not yet stashed in our safety deposit box. Alison had never been much into jewelry, and on most days she'd only worn her wedding and engagement rings. And those had been destroyed in the fiery crash.

But now I remembered they'd also taken Alison's old MacBook, the one that seemed to dwell permanently on the coffee table in the living room. She'd bought it not long after she went to work for Harding, and occasionally used it to devise the sudoku puzzles she sold to game publishers as a hobby.

Was something on that laptop? I wondered now as I found myself checking the window locks. *What could have been so important to break into the condo to get it? On that day, of all days?*

At some point I dozed off, because I snorted myself out of a forgettable dream and realized the CD had finished playing. The pad of paper was on my lap, but the pencils had rolled to the floor. I picked them up and decided it was time to go to bed. Another day would be waiting in the morning, no matter how much sleep I got.

What were you involved with, Alison? I asked myself again as I turned out the lights. *Was it something you knew or something you did?* For a fleeting moment I considered whether she might have been embroiled in something sinister, and the only way to get out of it was to fake her death. But just as quickly I put the thought out of my mind, or at least tried to. The Alison I knew could not willingly kill a spider, so there was no way she could be involved with the death of another human being.

But someone very likely was, and the rational side of my brain was beginning to accept the possibility that all was not as it seemed.

CHAPTER

9

Tuesday

THE NEXT MORNING Sabrina was dressed early, bright and cheery and asking for a second helping of cereal. No slow-motion movement around the house today. In fact, she was a chatterbox as she told me that she had figured out what to do with her squirrel story.

"Please tell me," I said as I smeared peanut butter on a piece of toast.

"Nope," she said, fiercely shaking her head. "You'll have to read it when it's on Amazon."

I practically spit out a laugh as I stood there at the kitchen counter. How would a seven-year-old know about that? When I was that age, I'm sure I didn't even know the Amazon was a river. Or a mythical tribe of women warriors. And the online retail giant was still years away from being even a flicker of an idea.

"Well, I can't wait," I told her. "Do you know when that's going to be?"

"I don't know yet." She shrugged. "I have to wait until the next time Mrs. Erskine comes in."

"I'm looking forward to reading it. Or hearing it, if you want to read it to me."

"That's what I'm going to do," she said as she dug her spoon into her second bowl. Then she pointed at my mouth and added, "No talking and chewing at the same time."

"See? Even parents forget the rules sometimes."

"Maybe there shouldn't be so many." She grinned. She finished the rest of her cereal, then got up and carried her bowl to the sink. "Did you sign my form?"

I had to think a moment, then remembered the note Sabrina had brought home from school last week, before I'd flown out to LA. The entire first grade was going on a field trip to the Central Park Zoo at the end of the week, and parents had to sign off on it.

"It's right there on the counter," I assured her. "I wouldn't want you to miss the monkeys and leopards."

"And the pandas," she added.

"And the snakes."

"And the frogs."

"And the leopards."

Thus, it went on for the next ten minutes as we walked to school, both of us adding to the list of animals that lived at the zoo. "Don't forget the mynah birds," I reminded her as we stopped at the front gate.

"And the penguins."

"They have penguins at the zoo?" I asked her.

"Don't you remember *Mr. Popper*?"

"Oh, right."

She hesitated a moment, glancing around at whoever might see her, then gave me a quick kiss. "Love you, Daddy," she said.

"Love you too, sugar."

"Love you three." Sabrina grinned.

I knew from experience how this could go, ever since her teacher taught the class how to count and write to two hundred. "Three is good," I told her.

"But four is better." Sabrina giggled, then raced up the stairs before I could raise the number to five.

* * *

While I was walking Sabrina to school, Natalie Cook, MD, had returned my phone call from yesterday afternoon. She left a voicemail agreeing to spare a few minutes if I could come by her office around ten. That meant I'd have to rearrange my entire morning, but I knew she possessed answers to some of my questions, so I really had no choice. I called my office and left a message for William Trent, informing him that Sabrina had come down with a cold and I was trying to find a sitter for her. Not easy to do at the last minute, and I would try to make it in as soon as I could. I knew I was taking advantage of his good nature, but I really saw no alternative.

I also needed to call Claire Beckett at the Bradley Museum, fully aware that I was delaying the inevitable decision as long as I could. I had no idea what I was going to tell her, and after a few seconds of mental ping-pong, I decided to put it off again.

Natalie Cook was the medical examiner who oversaw Warren, Morris, and Sussex counties in central New Jersey and had personally supervised the autopsies of my wife and Maxwell Harding. Her office was in Morristown, a ninety-minute drive once I picked up a rental car in midtown Manhattan. I could have simply spoken with her on the phone, but I've always preferred face-to-face communication. As a photographer, you learn a lot about a person by watching their eyes and hands, making it easier to interpret a full range of emotions—including honesty, or the lack thereof. Besides, I had something else I wanted to do in New Jersey, and a car was critical.

I pulled the compact Hyundai into a parking lot off West Hanover Avenue in Morristown and followed the building signs to the ME's office. I explained to the receptionist that I was there for an appointment with Dr. Cook, who was expecting me.

"She's running late this morning," the woman said. She had shoulder-length hair, dark and shiny, and beautiful earrings that looked like ancient Mayan art. "Motorcycle crash in Union Sunday night. Passenger wasn't wearing a helmet. She's doing the cut now."

"I'm sorry to hear that," I told her. "About the passenger, I mean. If she's going to be tied up for a while, I can come back."

But the woman shook her head as if this sort of thing happened all the time. "That's not necessary," she said, glancing at her watch. "She keeps to a tight schedule, so I'm sure she'll only be delayed a few minutes longer. Please, have a seat."

I chose a straight-back chair that was set against a stark white wall, and picked up a copy of *Web MD* magazine. As I thumbed through it, I was struck by the irony of reading a health magazine in the waiting room of a doctor whose patients were dead. I'd just begun an article on the early warning signs of irritable bowel syndrome when the phone on the desk buzzed. The receptionist answered in a hushed tone, then hung up and said, "Mr. Kane? Dr. Cook is in her office. Down the hall, third door on the left."

I thanked her and followed her simple directions. Sure enough, the third door had a brass and faux wood nameplate beside it that read: "Natalie Cook, MD, Medical Examiner."

I stood in the corridor a moment to straighten my jacket lapel, then knocked.

I heard a voice inside, low and feminine, and guessed the doctor was on the phone. I knocked again, and she called out in a firm voice, "Don't be bashful. Come in."

I pushed the door open and stepped inside. Dr. Cook was seated behind an industrial steel desk cluttered with manila files, diagnostic books, and mountains of stray papers. The room carried the faint smell of formaldehyde or formalin, or whatever fluids were used during autopsies these days. There was also the hint of an industrial disinfectant that I suspected was used to decontaminate the autopsy room and anyone who came in contact with it.

"Cameron Kane," I said as I extended my hand. My eyes naturally drifted to a shelf that held an assortment of vials and specimen jars with pickled organs and fleshy tumors floating in them. "You said you could see me this morning at ten."

Dr. Cook rose from her chair and leaned over the desk, grasping my hand with a solid grip. She had pewter eyes and short hair the color of deep mahogany. No makeup or fingernail polish, at least none that I could detect.

"Gloria put it on my calendar," she said as she waved me into a chair in front of her desk. It was made of the same industrial steel and was cushioned with just a thin layer of padding, clearly designed to make visitors disinclined to remain seated for long. I arranged myself squarely in front of her, my hands resting on the metal arms.

"Thank you for agreeing to see me on such short notice," I said.

The ME gave the slightest of nods, then said, "On the phone you said you only needed ten minutes of my time, so let's get started."

So much for polite chitchat. I shifted my posture and edged back in my chair, then took a deep breath. "Well, as I mentioned in my message, I want to ask about an old case," I said.

"Your wife was Alison Kane," she replied.

"That would be correct."

She made a clicking sound with her tongue, then lightly bit her lower lip. "You called me a year ago to ask about the autopsy."

"You remember that?"

"For reasons that don't bear repeating," she said.

I suspected the reasons were directly related to the description I'd read in the autopsy report. "My life had just gone off the rails, and hundreds of questions were spinning through my head," I explained. "I figured you'd be able to answer a couple of them."

"But I didn't, did I?"

"No, ma'am. You said it wouldn't be a good idea to speak with me directly."

She nodded slowly, then proceeded to pull a paper-clip chain out of a small porcelain dish on her desk. "What makes you think I would've changed my mind after a year?" she asked as she began to fidget with it.

"I'm hoping it's because I'm sitting across this desk from you," I told her.

She did that clicking thing with her tongue again, then set the paper clips down on her desk. Finally, she said, "You're looking for closure."

"Excuse me?"

"Closure," she repeated. "It's very common, Mr. Kane. Most relatives, when they lose a loved one—particularly in a sudden death situation—they end up seeking closure long after the incident occurred. A year, two years. Often more than that."

"I guess I'm just a common cliché," I said without emotion. "But that's not why I'm here. Please . . . just let me explain."

Dr. Cook glanced at her watch. "In your voicemail you asked for ten minutes. We're down to six."

My eyes again drifted to the array of specimen jars set on the corner of her desk, one in particular that appeared to contain some sort of blob that seemed enlarged or swollen. I tried not to imagine what it was or how it came to be in her office.

"I want to know the process you used to identify my wife," I said.

She fixed me with a dark scowl and tapped a finger on her desk for a good five seconds before she responded. "Dental records, as I recall," she said. "The oral X-rays eliminated any question of identity. I'll spare you the details except to say that we examined the files and positively matched them to the victim's dental structure."

"I understand all that," I replied. "I've studied the reports and newspaper stories until I've almost memorized them. My question is: Can you be absolutely certain—beyond any sort of doubt—that the victim was my wife?"

"Dental records don't lie, Mr. Kane."

"No one is accusing anyone of lying," I quickly assured her. I was here only because of her good graces, and I didn't want to betray whatever trust I may have built. "All I want to know is how you confirmed that the dental records you used for identification were those of my wife?"

She studied me warily for a moment, then eventually said, "We got them from her dentist, Mr. Kane. *Your* dentist. With your direct assistance, if memory serves. The file would have had her name on it."

"Was it sealed?"

"Signed and delivered. Both dentists—yours and the Hardings'—sent them by bonded courier. Standard practice."

"Could someone have tampered with the file while it was in transit?"

"Please . . . you're grasping—"

"You must still have those records in your files," I pressed.

Dr. Cook sighed impatiently and leaned forward in her chair. She fixed me with her dark eyes again, this time a hard glare that wouldn't let go. "Mr. Kane, I believe this conversation is far from constructive. And a good illustration of why I don't meet with relatives of my patients, as you call them."

"Please, ma'am—*Doctor*. I'm just trying to tie up loose ends."

"And I'm telling you, this is tighter than tight."

"Closure, like you said," I conceded, just to buy myself a little extra time.

"What it sounds like is a strong case of denial," she countered. "Again, it's pretty common. A surviving relative can't accept the idea that his spouse or child or parent is dead, and needs to go through the entire investigative process again. Let me assure you—the ID was conclusive. And final."

"Would those records be in your file cabinet?"

She rolled her eyes and let out a long sigh. "It's been a year, Mr. Kane. They'd be in off-site storage."

"Is there any way I can take a look at them?"

"No. And while I appreciate your interest in dental forensics, I'm now going to politely ask you to stop wasting my time."

"Please, Dr. Cook," I said. "It's just one file. I know I'm a pitiful cliché, but just humor me. If only to ease my mind."

She leveled me with an intensive stare, then surprised me and said, "I'll send my assistant over during his lunch break. Give me your email address."

"Thank you." I scribbled it on a slip of paper and handed it to her while I rose to my feet. I turned toward the door and gave one last glance at the array of specimens arranged on the corner of her desk. "Interesting collection," I observed.

"Amazing, the things you can buy on eBay," she said. "Goodbye, Mr. Kane."

CHAPTER

10

WHEN I GOT back to my rental car, I checked my phone and found a voicemail from Officer Morgan Wright. He was one of the state troopers who'd responded to the 911 call about the accident, and he was returning my call from earlier. Wright said he was out on patrol but was five minutes from a fast-food taco joint in Stanhope, and when I told him I was in Morristown, he agreed to wait until I got there. Unless a dispatch call came in, and then all bets were off.

"Don't get a ticket," he warned me. "The fines run pretty steep out here."

It took me close to twenty minutes to get there, and Officer Wright was just walking out of the place with a to-go bag and a large soda when I pulled into the lot. "Thought you might've gotten lost," the state trooper said in a thick Jersey accent.

"Damned GPS got me turned around," I replied by way of apology. "And I totally understand if you have to be somewhere."

"I always have to be somewhere, but I can spare a couple minutes."

Officer Wright appeared younger than I'd expected, late twenties, with a broad nose and dark, focused eyes that some people might describe as beady. His chin was square, and his head looked as if it had just gotten a boot-camp buzz cut. He seemed to lurch when he walked, but I figured the motion was due to all the stiff, squeaking leather strapped to his waist.

"I appreciate you meeting me like this," I told him as we shook hands.

"Part of the job," Wright said, lifting a shoulder in a shrug. "Your message said you had some questions about an accident?"

"That's right. But I may not have been completely precise in my message."

"Yeah, I guessed that," Officer Wright said. "Since you left your name, I did some checking and figured out who you are. How can I help you?"

"The thing is, there are a few things that are still puzzling me about that night."

Wright took a sip from his soda and said, "That was almost a year ago, sir. Long time to still have questions."

"You remember it?"

"Like it was yesterday. I assume it's the one-year thing that has you asking about it."

"People keep telling me I'm looking for closure, and they're probably right."

"It's always better to look to the future, not the past," Officer Wright replied. "What is it you'd like to know?"

"To tell you the truth, I'm not really sure. I guess I'd like to hear your version of that night and what you found when you arrived on the scene."

"You're asking for personal reasons, right? Nothing legal or financial?"

"Just between us." I dug my wallet out of my pocket, showed him my driver's license. "Off the record, no lawsuits or newspaper stories."

Officer Wright was silent for a moment. I wondered if it was because he was trying to kick-start his memory, or maybe he was trying to compartmentalize what he had seen that cold April evening.

"Shortly after ten o'clock that night, I got a call from dispatch that a car had gone off the interstate. It took me maybe eight minutes to get there, even with the blue lights. It wasn't hard to find the site of the accident, even though the car was way down the embankment."

"Because of the fire," I said. It was a statement, not a question.

"You could see the glow a half mile away. I arrived in the westbound lane and pulled off the pavement. It was dark and there'd been some rain. I figured the driver must've lost control and shot over the edge. There's quite a slope there, and the car rode down thirty, forty yards before it came to a rest. That's what I figured when I got there, anyways."

"And the car was in flames when you arrived?" I already knew the answer to this, but I asked the question anyway.

"Totally engulfed. Those people never had a chance." Wright hesitated a moment, then added, "I'm sorry . . . this has to be difficult."

I made a show of trying to shrug it off, but I don't think it worked. Then I said, "Tell me: When you arrived on the scene, did you see skid marks? Any indication the car had swerved or maybe tried to stop?"

Officer Wright took a minute to think this through, then said, "Like I told you, it had rained earlier. But I don't think anyone found tire tracks or other evidence that the driver used his brakes."

"The accident report says you moved down the embankment to get closer to the car."

"Tried to. Got maybe ten, fifteen yards from it, but the fire was too hot."

I didn't like to think about that and had tried not to for months after the accident. The mental image still made me shudder. But now that there was even the slimmest chance that Harding might still be alive, the notion of the blaze wasn't quite as hard to stomach.

"Tell me about the car," I said. "What it looked like."

Officer Wright flashed me a look that said, *"Do you really want to go there?"* Then he said, "It was a Lamborghini, as I'm sure you know. The whole thing had gone up in flames, a blaze so hot it even started burning the carbon fiber. That's why they had such a hard time identifying the driver."

"Any estimate how long it burned?" I asked. Tough question, fetching an even tougher answer, but it was something I felt I needed to know.

Officer Wright took a breath, exhaled slowly. "The first pumper truck got there six minutes after I did. By the time the others showed up and they got the hoses down the embankment—well, I'd say about thirty minutes. By then it had started going out since there wasn't much left to burn."

I nodded at what the cop was saying; it was pretty close to how the papers and the official reports had told it. "How long until anyone was able to get close to the wreckage?"

"Quite a while," Wright told me. "Even after the fire was out, all that metal still put off a lot of heat. Maybe twenty, thirty minutes."

"That's when they found the bodies," I pressed him.

"Yeah. Look, Mr. Kane—I really think you need to let it go."

"And I will," I assured him. "I just want to know the basics."

"Fact is, with all those investigators arriving, I wasn't really needed. I made my way back up to the road, talked to some other officers, and not long after that I got another call and took off."

"Did you see the news the next day?" I wanted to know.

"I don't read the paper, but it was all over the TV," Wright said. "Far as I could tell, they got it pretty much how it was."

He cast an impatient glance out at the road, and I sensed this conversation was coming to a close. "Well, I want to thank you for going over all this shit again," I said. "I'm not sure what I was expecting by talking to you, but I think it eased my mind a bit."

"If you say so," the cop said. He opened the door and settled his frame into a large depression in the cloth seat. He turned the key in the ignition, then looked up at me and said, "You want a piece of advice, Mr. Kane? Listen to your friends and put all this behind you. Like my grandma used to say, 'Ain't no good comes from picking through dying embers.'"

11

Twenty minutes after leaving the taco joint in Stan-hope, I nudged the rental car as far as I could onto the shoulder of I-80 and cut the engine.

The patch of gravel was narrow, and there was barely enough room to open my door without getting clipped by passing cars. I knew I only had a few minutes before another state trooper—maybe even Officer Wright—would come by and either order me to move along or write me up for some sort of violation. But I'd needed to come out here, endure the events of that night one more time. I'd driven out to this spot with my brother a month after the crash, and that had been a colossal mistake. The muddy tracks and scorched earth and blackened tree were clearly visible, and it didn't take much imagination to visualize how it had happened. Harding's Lamborghini careening down the embankment, Alison screaming inside, strapped into her seat, helpless to do anything in those final seconds as she hurtled toward a horrifying death.

But today was different. Call it denial or wishful thinking, but for the first time in a year I had the slightest fragment of optimism that all was not what it seemed. I waited for a black SUV to speed past, then slipped out of the driver's seat and edged around the front fender before another car raced by.

Along this stretch of highway in western New Jersey, the westbound lanes were separated from the eastbound lanes by dense woods that fill the wide median. There were no guard-rails keeping vehicles from swerving off the pavement here, and it would have been easy for Harding—or whoever had been behind the wheel—to lose control and plunge down the embankment.

How did they engineer it? I wondered. *Jam the pedal to the floor with a rock, or maybe a block of ice that would melt and leave no trace?*

I stood on the gravel shoulder and looked down at the massive oak tree where the car had come to rest. The tire tracks had filled in over the passing seasons, and the grass on the side of the road was still draped with the dull brown of mid-spring. Just as it had been a year ago. The trees were beginning to bud, and the oak that had borne the force of the collision had generated a layer of scarred bark over the scorched trunk. If I hadn't known precisely where the accident had occurred, I would have thought I was standing in the wrong place. Except for one other thing that had changed over the past twelve months.

Someone had placed a white cross near the point of impact. Two crosses, in fact.

I started to make my way down the steep bank but only got a few yards before a state trooper pulled up behind my Hyundai and slowed to a stop. No one got out right away, and I figured the officer inside was running the plates through his onboard computer. Eventually the door opened, and a uni-formed cop unfolded from the driver's seat.

"Hey, mister . . . you can't go down there."

I started walking toward him and said, "I just wanted to take a look—"

"Not today. Not here."

I stopped, held my hands out in front of me. Unarmed and harmless. "I just wanted to see where it happened."

"Yeah, we get a lot of lookie-loos out here," the man said, touching a finger to the brim of his hat. "Nothing to see. Not anymore."

"Someone put up crosses," I observed.

"Yeah, one day they were just there, and we decided to leave 'em. Respect for the dead, and all that."

I figured there was no need to bring up my wife, Maxwell Harding, or anything that smacked of ancient history. "Interesting" was all I could bring myself to say.

"Yeah, well, you need to move along. Else I'm going to have to write you up." The cop emphasized his words by holding up his summons pad.

"Like you said, not much to see," I replied. "I'm on my way."

* * *

I'd just returned the rental car two hours later when my phone rang. I hit the "Talk" button and said, "This is Kane."

"Cameron, it's been way too long," a woman replied. "It was so wonderful to hear your voice yesterday, when I got your message."

"Lexi Lawler?" I guessed.

"Yes, it's Lexi. You have no idea how delighted I was to hear from you yesterday, out of the blue. I was just thinking the other day how it's been . . . well, almost a year."

"A long time, and in some ways just an instant," I said. "I appreciate you calling me back."

"Of course I'd call you back. Alison was one of my favorite people in the whole world. Not a day goes by that I don't think about her."

Lexi was short for Alexis. She and Alison had worked together at Harding's financial firm until the feds moved in and took him down. They had handled different things in different departments on different floors, Alison heading up the Risk Management division while Lexi was the assistant to the executive vice president of Procurement. What they procured I did not know, nor was it my place to ask. The two women had become close friends, going shopping, having lunch, and occasionally grabbing a glass of wine at the end of a long day before heading home to their respective families.

"Alison really treasured your friendship," I said, afraid my words came out too measured or impersonal.

"She took the sting out of my job, that's for sure," Lexi said. "But I could tell from your message that's not why you called."

"No, it's not," I admitted. "In fact, there's something I'd like to talk to you about. I was hoping you might have a few minutes to meet."

"Today?"

"Today, tomorrow, whenever," I told her. "No real rush."

There was a short silence on the other end, then Lexi said, "Hey, look at this. I've got an entire half hour totally clear tomorrow afternoon at three o'clock. Does that work?"

I mentally checked my schedule, figured I could juggle some appointments. That would still give me plenty of time to get down to Sabrina's after-school program and pick her up before the late charges began to pile up.

"That'll be great," I told her. "Where are you working these days?"

"A private equity boutique downtown, just a block from the Cortlandt Street station," she replied, and gave me the address. "Not quite the same money, but at least those damn feds aren't crawling all over the place."

"Yeah, that's one of the things I'd like to talk about."

"You're sure you want to go through all that again?"

"Closure," I told her. I was quickly learning that people liked that word.

"A noble reason," Lexi said. "But a year ago, all that poking around ended up with Alison and Maxwell dead. See you tomorrow."

As soon as she hung up, I considered what she said. Had Lexi suspected there was a connection between the federal probe into Harding's finances and his death? I'd heard the rumors that he'd driven his car into the tree on purpose, but I'd never believed them. He was too much of a narcissist to take his own life, especially when he maintained he'd done nothing wrong and insisted the eighteen charges against him were just part of a government witch hunt. Try as I did, I just couldn't see him checking out without a fight.

* * *

When I'd spoken with Marika Saturday night, we'd agreed to meet for lunch on Tuesday. That was today. Prior to my trip to LA and my chance encounter with Harding/not-Harding at JFK, I would have been looking forward to the occasion. Still was, in fact. Up to this point I'd conducted what I considered a methodical, slow-go approach to our relationship, and I'd finally begun letting go of that reluctance to move on past my life with Alison. I couldn't be the grieving widower forever, and I needed the fulfillment that emotional and physical involvement with another woman would bring.

Fact was, I truly cared for Marika. She was warm, tender, giving, considerate. And, it seemed, on a far more accelerated path to intimacy than I allowed myself. Part of my hesitancy, at least at the start, was our age gap: I was forty-three, and she had just turned twenty-seven. A sixteen-year difference that she insisted she wasn't concerned about, but I knew how it might look to her friends. And mine.

We had agreed to meet at Café Protégé, a trendy spot half a block off Amsterdam Avenue that was light and airy, mostly small plates that weren't overly pricey, even by New York standards. Spacious booths and linen tablecloths and great acoustics that made it easy to talk and listen. While I had no intention of mentioning my crazy notion about Max Harding, I had decided to come clean about the real reason for my quick journey out to the coast.

Marika was already seated at a corner table in the rear, sipping on a glass of wine. As I approached, she stood and gently kissed me on the lips, then gave my hand a comforting squeeze. I apologized for being late, an atonement she waved off, and I sat down across from her.

"He lives; he breathes," she said in a playful tone. "And look . . . he even manages a smile now and then."

She was right; I was smiling. "How can I not smile when I'm in the presence of such a beautiful woman?" I asked.

Let me emphasize that I truly had grown very fond of Marika, in my own cautious way. I know *fond* is one of those words, like *friend*, when it turns out that someone you're madly in love with doesn't feel the same way. Under any other circumstances we would have been tearing it up in bed by now, retreating to the Cape for romantic weekends. Scooting out of our respective offices for afternoon quickies. All the wonderful things one does while experiencing the pleasure of falling in love, although it had been years since I had been in the dating scene. Something I'd never thought I would have to revisit once I married Alison.

Marika asked me how Sabrina was doing, what she'd thought of the ice show at the Garden on Sunday. In turn, I inquired about her day and yesterday and the day before that. Easy pleasantries to navigate, and eventually I steered the conversation around to the West Coast.

"Did you see any stars?" she asked.

I shook my head and said, "I thought maybe I recognized that guy who played Bosch, except I'm not very good with faces. But there is something I want to talk to you about."

"What's that?" she asked, studying me over the rim of her wineglass.

"The thing is, I wasn't particularly forthcoming about my reason for going out there," I replied.

"To sign some long-term contract?" she said. "No way. I figured it was a job interview you didn't think you could tell me about."

"I'm that easy to read?"

"Like *The Cat in the Hat*. Did you get the part?"

"Get what?" I was still stuck on how my cover story hadn't fooled her. Not one bit.

"The job, silly. They'd be crazy not to hire you."

"It doesn't bother you?" I replied, not answering her question. "The fact that Sabrina and I might be moving?"

"Why would it? I work in television sales. New York and LA are the two biggest media markets in the country."

Marika was an account representative for a major cable news network with a worldwide audience. She was good at what she did, earning a generous salary with commissions

that paid for a glass apartment on the West Side with an awesome view of the Hudson.

"So, you wouldn't mind if I tell them yes?" I asked.

"I'd mind if you didn't," she replied.

"Then I'll phone first thing after work," I assured her. I
actually reached across the table and held her hand, instantly
feeling like a lout because I knew full well I'd find a way to
delay the call.

12

I GOT SABRINA TO bed right at eight and read her a few pages until her eyes eased shut and her breathing slowed to a steady snuffle. Before I'd turned out the light, she had asked me again about her bedroom window, this time whether it would be safe to leave it open just a bit to catch the breeze. I showed her how it could be locked in an open position about an inch above the sill, not nearly enough room for a squirrel to squeeze through.

"But could one come in if she tried?"

I caught the gender reference and wondered if Sabrina was thinking about the mother squirrel in her story. "They can't get past the screen," I explained.

She seemed to ponder that answer for a moment, then said, "That's okay."

Once I was sure she was asleep, I poured myself a shot of bourbon and sat down at the computer in my study. Something had been nagging me all day, and now that my daughter was in bed and the night was quiet—at least as quiet as it was going to be in the West Village—I went to work on

Google. I wasn't sure what I was looking for, just whatever would fit a steadily emerging sense of curiosity.

I began with the word *missing*, then added *man* and *Caucasian*. They were rather ambiguous key words, and a fraction of a second later Google returned over a half million hits, including several paid ads for detective agencies and investigative services. I glanced at the first few pages and found exactly what I'd asked for: missing white men all around the world. That was way too broad for my purposes, so I added additional terms to narrow my search: *New York* and *April*.

I scrolled through pages and pages of hits, some of them touching on one or two qualifying factors in my hypothesis. Quite a few men had been reported missing close to the time of the accident, but all were either too young or hadn't disappeared until after the crash. I considered refining my search parameters further, but then a listing leaped off the screen at me:

New Canaan Man Still Missing After A Week

I clicked on the link and found a story from the *Stamford Advocate* nearly a year ago:

> Connecticut State Police report Jason Dillon, a forty-eight-year-old professor at the University of Bridgeport, remains missing following an intensive search of his New Canaan neighborhood.
>
> Mr. Dillon was reported to have disappeared last Wednesday evening. His wife, Elise Dillon, said that when she arrived home late from her job in Norwalk, her husband was not there. He did not answer his phone, and subsequent calls

to the university informed her that he did not show up to teach his classes that day. She called the Connecticut State Police, who told her there were no accidents involving Mr. Dillon or his vehicle. Several hours later she called the New Canaan Police and reported him missing.

Mrs. Dillon said she last saw her husband when he was getting ready for his regular morning run through Mead Memorial Park. An entrance to the park is not far from their home, and she said he regularly ran three miles every morning before going to the university. On the day of his disappearance, he was scheduled to have lunch with one of the deans, but he did not show up for that meeting either.

Mrs. Dillon told this reporter that she and her husband were not having personal problems, and insisted their marriage was fine. She also said she was certain he was not involved with another woman.

"This is so not like Jason," she said when questioned at her house on Saturday. "He is so set in his routine, that for him to disappear like this—well, it's just not something he would do."

Police mounted an extensive search of the neighborhood, including the nearby park, but turned up no clues as to his whereabouts. Mr. Dillon's car was in the garage, and his credit and debit cards have not been used. Authorities also checked airline manifests and rental car records, but so far those inquiries have turned up nothing.

"It's very unusual for men in their forties to disappear like this," New Canaan Police Captain David Milliken said. "We are continuing our search for Mr. Dillon and are optimistic that he will turn up safely. I want to make it clear that, at this point of our investigation, there is no reason to believe that he has met with foul play of any kind."

I reread the article two more times, then narrowed my search just to stories about Jason Dillon. It turned out the police hadn't had much luck finding him, and the case slipped into a state of perpetual investigative limbo. Elise Dillon eventually hired a private detective to look into her husband's whereabouts, but those efforts—and, I presumed, a significant amount of cash—went unrewarded. The last story I could find on the subject was a small squib published just a month ago in the *New Canaan News*, reporting that almost a year later the detective had not come any closer to learning what had happened to Jason Dillon.

He had simply vanished.

Most of the articles I found included a photograph of the missing man, and I was struck by the close resemblance between Dillon and Maxwell Harding. I realized that hair and skin tone didn't matter; bone structure was what counted if a forensic specialist was called in to help confirm a burned victim's identity. Both men had the same square chin and high, pronounced cheekbones, strong brows that made his eyes appear dark and intense. Dillon also had a full smile with straight teeth that bore a strong resemblance to Harding's. The accompanying description said he was just a little over six feet tall, which would have come close to Harding's height. And their weight seemed to be within a few pounds of each other's.

I knew it was a crazy long shot, but if the body found in Harding's Lamborghini actually was that of Jason Dillon, it stood to reason that Alison's stand-in would have disappeared around the same time. If she had a stand-in, that is. As logic dictated, even if there was a remote chance that Harding was still alive, it was distinctly possible that Alison was not.

At that moment my phone rang. I glanced at the screen, saw the call was from Lillian Sloane, and answered with a pensive "Hello."

"I spoke with Mick," she said. "Without going into any details, I told him you wanted to meet with him."

"And?"

"He said you can buy him a beer tomorrow at noon. Place on 47th Street called Ryan's, near the corner of Madison."

"What did you tell him about me?" I asked.

"You mean, did I tell him you're probably nuts? No, I decided to let him figure that one out for himself."

CHAPTER

13

Wednesday

THE SUBWAY WAS as sluggish as usual during the morning commute, and the car I boarded downtown at 14th Street grew more crowded the farther north it went.

At one point I noticed a young man in jeans, a black T-shirt, and a black baseball cap with the Led Zeppelin *ZoSo* symbol on it, standing at the far end of the car. He was looking directly at me, but when I returned his stare, he quickly turned away. For the next two stops, we played a cat-and-mouse game of covert glances, and I had a troublesome feeling that he was keeping an eye on me. *How long has he been in the car?* I wondered. *Was he here when I boarded in the Village, or did he follow me?*

Either way, whatever the story, I got off at Rockefeller Center, one stop early, and trudged up the stairs to the street. I couldn't tell if he followed me off the train, and when I emerged into the sunlight, I was stopped by security guards. A TV cop drama was shooting a scene on the sidewalk, and the cameras were rolling. A clog of humanity crowded around me, grumbling about "this fucking city" and "gotta get to the goddamn office." Eventually the action stopped, and the guards allowed the stream of passengers to cross the street, but by now I was certifiably late.

I had back-to-back meetings starting at nine, and I slipped into our corporate conference room with thirty seconds to spare. Meeting one merged into two, then three, and it was close to lunchtime by the time I made it back to my own office. I couldn't complain; Trent hadn't mentioned my absence yesterday except to inquire how Sabrina was feeling, and he'd already extended some latitude to help me make it through a tough week. But this morning I found I was unable to focus on digital rights packages and legal clauses; none of that stuff seemed to matter. I was not a lawyer and never in my life intended to be, and the marathon meetings only reinforced this resolve.

I hadn't called the museum out in LA after work yesterday, of course, and it was too early to do so now. The West Coast was just waking up, I told myself. Instead, I attempted to read a report that had landed on my desk last Friday when I was gone, but I just couldn't focus on the details. I glanced through a folder I'd pulled together after I'd kissed Sabrina good night, information about the accident that could be pertinent to whatever investigation might result from my lunch meeting. As well as a check in the amount Lillian had suggested was her friend's usual retainer.

* * *

I had never been to Ryan's Grill and Bar on 47th Street, but I'd passed it countless times. A holdover from an age before steel and glass took over the Manhattan skyline, it was easy to miss if you weren't looking for it. I almost missed it anyway, as it was buried under six floors of scaffolding that seemed to keep it in a perpetual shadow. Pedestrians were routed around the entrance by a plywood fence that was papered with flyers for obscure off-off-Broadway productions and poetry slams in SoHo, and I retraced my steps twice before I found the front door.

I spotted the ex-cop I assumed was Mickey Donovan the moment I walked in. He had that police officer look about him: solid, no-nonsense, dark eyes that caught my entrance as soon as the door opened. I wondered if he was carrying a concealed weapon. He gave me a slight nod of recognition, and I walked over to the bar, where he'd already found a stool.

I scooted up on the one beside him, and we made small chat until the bartender brought us two beers, whereupon I launched into the story of my life. At least the part that began when I'd met Alison, and everything pertinent leading up to the crash. I became more tentative as I launched into my encounter with Harding/not-Harding at JFK, the mysterious Huckleberry text, and a previous two-second call I'd received from the same number.

"To answer your question, Mr. Kane—no, I don't think you're crazy," the ex-cop Mickey Donovan told me after patiently listening to my story for the past ten minutes. "Grasping, maybe, but not crazy."

We were sitting on stools at the far end of the bar. It was as good a place as any to talk without an audience, and it allowed us to keep an eye on the front door. I studied the former cop in the mirror behind the shelves of bottles: bald head speckled with discolored patches of skin, long face, tight mouth, thin lips. A faint scar ran from his left ear several inches down his jaw—good restorative surgery at some point in his past—and his dark, searching eyes seemed to be aware of everything and everyone in the place.

"You'll look into it, then?" I asked.

"Lucky for you, I'm a little light on work right now," Donovan said with a nod. "I suspect I know what I'm going to find out, and I can't guarantee you the results you think you want. But I have impeccable resources at my disposal, so if there's anything to find, I'll find it."

"All sounds good," I told him. "What else do you need from me?"

Donovan tapped the folder that I'd just handed to him, which now sat on the bar. "You said everything is in here?" he asked.

"Accident report, death certificate, newspaper clippings. Even the autopsy summary. And your retainer."

"Sounds organized," Donovan said. "It'll give me a place to start. But first I'd like you to tell me a little bit about your wife and what she was up to the last months of her life. I know it's been almost a year, but anything you can remember would be helpful."

I picked up a cocktail straw and bent it down the middle, then began twisting it. Purely a mental distraction while I considered what Donovan was asking me. Finally, I said, "I believe I told you how Alison and I met."

"That restaurant on the creek down in Charleston," Donovan said. "She was getting her PhD in mathematics?"

"Numerical linear algebra and advanced approximation theory."

Donovan rolled his eyes and shook his head at the same time. "I don't think I even know what that means," he said.

"Join the club. Filling out expense reports is still the best I can do. But Alison, she was a math prodigy. Ate it, breathed

it, slept it. Wrote her dissertation on a Parisian monk named
Mersenne who discovered some sort of special prime numbers. What's so special about them I couldn't tell you. But
she was the most beautiful mathematician I'd ever met, and
I told her so. I even called her Math."

"Such a romantic," Donovan said, the sarcasm thick in
his voice.

"It was an acronym for 'More Awesome Than Hepburn,'" I explained. "She was a big fan of *Breakfast at Tiffany's* and *Roman Holiday*—anything with Audrey Hepburn
in it. We named our daughter after the character she played
in *Sabrina*."

"When did she start working for Maxwell Harding?"
Donovan asked.

"Six years ago . . . Sabrina wasn't quite one," I said. "Alison had gone to a math conference in Chicago, a big meeting
of brainiacs. She'd been invited to give a presentation on the
factorization of Mersenne prime numbers, or something like
that. She'd actually made a name for herself in that particular
niche and almost discovered one of them herself."

"Discovered what?" Donovan wanted to know.

"One of the prime numbers. They're very rare, and some
are millions of digits long. Only about fifty of them have ever
been discovered."

"Sorry I asked," the ex-cop said with a grin. "Go on."

"After her session, she was mobbed by a bunch of attend-
ees who wanted to talk to her. After they all cleared out,
Maxwell Harding went up and introduced himself."

Donovan creased his brow and said, "What was he doing
there? A Wall Street banker at a math conference?"

I had no idea, and told him so. "His story was that he was
fascinated by her presentation, even if he didn't understand

much of it," I explained. "Said he wanted to ask her a few questions about this Mersenne guy and approximation theory, and did she have any plans for lunch."

"And he hired her?"

"No . . . not on the spot," I told him. "Over the next few weeks he kept coming back to her with more questions. He seemed to really be into these prime numbers, but I never fully grasped what she was talking about when she got into it."

Donovan nodded and took a swig of beer, then used his sleeve to wipe the foam from his mouth. "So how long before she was working for him?" he asked.

"The math conference was in early fall—September, I think. Her first day at Harding's company was the Monday after New Year's. She started out working on all sorts of things relating to probability, permutations, mutually exclusive events. She seemed to love her work, and she was making a great salary. Much better than the teaching job she'd given up at NYU. I really didn't pay much attention to what he had her doing."

"Except when she started working late and on weekends."

I shot him a hard look and said, "What makes you say that?"

Donovan glanced around at the lunch crowd that was filling the joint despite the scaffolding outside, then back at me. "Like I already said, you don't seem to like Mr. Harding very much."

"He was rich, he was a narcissist, and he was what a lot of women would consider good-looking. And he was spending a lot more time with my wife than I was."

Donovan nodded, as if he'd heard this sort of thing before. "Was there ever any indication something might have been going on between them?"

I quickly shook my head and said, "Once or twice I dropped some not-so-subtle hints, but she just laughed and insisted I was silly."

Donovan slowly swiveled on his stool and leveled his eyes at me. "Did you believe her?"

"Of course I did," I replied. "She was my wife. She told me she was working on some complex calculations, and when equations started flowing in her head, she had to work through them until they were solved. Of course, after Harding was indicted and the FBI tore his office apart, it was all about helping the feds nail him to the wall."

"They must have been tough on her, her boss being arrested for financial fraud."

I considered Donovan's words and what he might be implying. "I can assure you, my wife was not involved in any of the legal shit that came down on him," I told him.

"I don't doubt it for a minute. But it must not have sat too well with Harding, his trusted gal Friday turning on him the way she did."

"She was not his gal Friday," I told him.

"Sorry . . . poor choice of words," he said.

"And the feds never once implicated her in any improprieties. Bastard deserved everything he had coming."

"And he might have thought the same thing about her," the former NYPD detective said. "Retribution can be a bitch."

"Suggesting what?"

"You have to look at all sides of this, Mr. Kane. If what you're saying turns out to contain even a grain of truth, there's a thin chance Harding is alive and well. But you also need to accept that your wife still might have been the passenger in his car that night."

"I get that," I assured him. "But one way or the other I need to know."

The retired cop took a deep breath as the bartender came up and asked if we wanted another round. Yes for Donovan, but one was enough for me. When he wandered off, Donovan said, "Tell me about Harding."

"There's a whole bio on him in that file there."

"And I'll read it." Just then, two men in dark suits entered the bar and stood in the doorway, soaking up the light. Donovan seemed to size them up for a moment, then picked up his beer and took another healthy swig. "But I want you to tell me your own impression of him. Whether you felt he was honest or devious or opportunistic. That sort of thing."

"He was a crook and a scumbag," I said. "His arrest was all over the news."

"Yeah, I know. Comparisons to Bernie Madoff and that guy from FTX a year or two ago. But I'm not interested in what was in the news. I want your take on the man."

I was studying the bottles lined up on the glass shelves on the other side of the bar. A person can tell a lot about a pub's clientele from what kind of booze it stocks. This one seemed to have an abundance of Irish whiskey, which, with a name like Ryan's, made perfect sense.

"The first time I met Harding was at the company's Christmas party," I told him. "He rented out the entire Museum of Natural History for the night. Alison hadn't started working for him yet, but he insisted that she attend—and bring me along."

"And your first impression?"

"He was everything Alison said he was. Cordial, engaging, friendly, and more than a bit extreme."

"Extreme?" Donovan repeated.

"He was always on. And always up, almost as if he were on something."

"And what did she say?"

"She just laughed and said he couldn't possibly be, since no one ever remembered seeing him anything but hyper," I told him.

At that moment a man and a woman wandered down the length of the bar and sat down next to me, on my right. I turned to face Donovan and lowered my voice a notch. "I remember that something distracted Harding at the party that night, and he became really agitated until it got resolved. I forget what it was that set him off, but he went from zero to sixty in a flash. Then he went right back to being cordial and pleasant, like the snap of a finger."

"How did he come across to you?" Donovan asked.

"You mean, did he seem like the founder of a huge crypto empire that no one knew was swindling investors out of billions of dollars?"

"Something like that, yeah."

"I learned a long time ago that rich people shit and sleep like everyone else," I observed.

"When Harding was indicted, did you notice a change in your wife?"

"Those last few weeks, yeah," I admitted. "She seemed on edge and tense, but so was I, since the big paychecks had stopped coming. Plus, there was a legal shitstorm raining down on her boss. Anything more than that . . . well, it's hard to remember now because so much has happened since then."

Donovan dipped his head in an empathetic nod and said, "I understand. I lost my Charlotte several years ago. Two-year battle with breast cancer."

"I'm sorry . . . I had no idea—"

The hardened ex-NYPD detective raised his hand to stop me. "Everything I remember about her is absolutely wonderful. I suspect there were some not-so-good times too, but I can't for the life of me figure out what they might have been."

"I know exactly what you mean," I said, then considered what he'd just asked me. "The thing is, even back then I had this odd sense about whatever she'd been working on, she seemed to be holding back. Or at least not being completely upfront when she talked about work."

"There was a lot going on in that company that had nothing to do with honesty," Donovan pointed out. "Do you think your wife could have been helping Harding with his scheme?"

I could have been angry at the suggestion, but it was a question Donovan had to ask directly. One, I admit, I had contemplated myself. "Not possible," I said. "Alison just wasn't wired for high crimes or misdemeanors."

"Still, you thought she was keeping something from you."

"That's just it—I don't know." I sighed, then picked up another cocktail straw and began to twist it, just like I had with the previous five. "I really don't think she was involved with Harding's scams, or even knew anything about them. In fact, she tried to get her parents to invest their retirement accounts in Harding's latest venture, Bit-XC. She wouldn't have done that if she'd known it was a fraud."

"Bit-XC . . . that's the thing that went down the toilet, right?"

"One of several, yeah. In a nutshell, it was a digital firm that traded in crypto, but the feds believed it was used largely for banks and the super-rich to launder gobs of money. Mostly dollars and rubles."

"Rubles?" Donovan asked. "The Russians were part of this?"

"Whenever there's crooked money involved, they're like pigs to the trough."

"Do you recall what Harding was charged with when it all came tumbling down?"

"The US District Court here in New York handed down eighteen counts," I told him. "Everything from operating an unlicensed currency transmittal business to money laundering, to ransomware hacking. The feds also got him for stealing from other exchanges, identity theft, and even facilitating the trafficking of narcotics. Son of a bitch was looking at decades behind bars."

"What about your wife?"

"I already told you, she wasn't involved in anything illegal. You have to believe me."

"I do," he replied. "What matters here is what the feds believed."

"Well, I guess they had to be suspicious since Alison wrote the company's blockchain program. But she had no idea that Harding was using it for any sort of illegal activity."

"Wait . . . back up a bit. What do you mean by blockchain?"

"I asked Alison that once, and she got all nerdy about it. I had to look it up myself. Essentially, it's a sort of open digital ledger that tracks financial transactions between a person or a company and another person or company, making a permanent record of it. By definition, cryptocurrency doesn't exist in any tangible form, so there has to be a way to keep track of all the purchases and sales, splits and permutations. Harding wanted his own proprietary system."

"I'm sorry I asked," Donovan said, rolling his eyes. "Is that why he hired your wife? To write one of these blockchain things?"

"He wanted an exclusive programming language, if you get down to it. He was impressed by her knowledge of numerical linear algebra."

"You're losing me again," the ex-cop said, shaking his head.

"Been there myself," I assured him. "To make a complicated story short, Harding seemed obsessed with the whole thing, and he wanted Alison to create a new language function that somehow made his blockchain impenetrable and error-proof."

"And that's what she was helping the feds with?"

"Unraveling the transactions to see where the fraud occurred," I confirmed.

"At least, that's what she told you."

"I've told you, my wife did nothing wrong."

"Relax, Mr. Kane. I've been a detective for twenty-six years. It's in my nature to question everything and trust no one. That includes Harding, your wife—even you. You've come to me with a highly fanciful story that strains all belief, and I've put my trust in you. If you want me to help you on this thing, you need to trust me as well."

"Fair enough," I said.

"So . . . what do you remember about the night of the accident?" Donovan asked, abruptly changing the subject.

"Everything."

"Understandable. But what I'm getting at is, western New Jersey is a long way from Manhattan. Any idea what they were doing out there?"

I tossed my twisted straw on the counter with all the others. "As I recall, Harding owned a house in the Poconos,"

I explained. "If you can call thirty thousand square feet with an indoor swimming pool, private movie theater, ballroom, and bowling alley a house."

Donovan let out a low whistle. "Damn . . . that's almost three-quarters of an acre."

"The thing is, I'm pretty sure the feds had already seized it by then. Look, Mr. Donovan—"

"Please, call me Mickey."

"Okay. Mickey. That's the part I just don't get. The feds had Harding on a short leash. He'd given up his passport and bonded out for ten million, and they took everything he owned. They even locked a GPS monitor on his leg."

"So why was he going to Pennsylvania that night?"

"A question I keep asking myself," I said with a shrug. "Thing is, aside from the ten bedrooms, fourteen bathrooms, and private ballroom that he no longer owned, the place also had a helipad. He could have been planning on fleeing the country and taking Alison with him."

"Maybe," Donovan conceded. "But that theory falls apart if the car crash was staged. Tell me again everything that happened when you got off that plane at JFK last Saturday."

I led him through my story one more time: chasing Harding to the front of the taxi queue, where he made a hasty escape in a cab. The partial license plate number, and my chat with the limo driver who was waiting for a client that never showed. LATAM, flight 8414 from Rio de Janeiro.

"You say this guy's name was Zaccaro?" Mickey Donovan asked when I had finished.

"That's what it said on the sign," I said, spelling it for him. "No first name."

The detective hadn't taken one note during our entire conversation, and he didn't bother to start now. Instead, he poured the last of his Sam Adams down his throat, then abruptly slid off his stool. Just like that, our meeting was over.

"I know a guy, a real righteous dude who has access to things no one else even knows exists," Donovan said as he turned the collar of his lightweight jacket up around his neck. "I'll see what he can dig up."

"Do you trust him to keep this to himself?"

"I'm not sure what *this* is, but believe me—he's not the type to breathe a word to anyone." He extended his hand and we shook; then he said, "I'll give you a call when I have something."

I nodded, figuring the meter started now. "Remember, any expenses, put 'em on my tab," I said.

"Count on it," Donovan said, and then he was gone.

14

THE LOBBY OF my office building was a cavernous space with high ceilings, rich wood paneling, and a dark marble floor. A formal security desk was set off to one side, and two guards were running ID checks on prospective visitors. I was just pushing through the double glass doors from the sidewalk when my phone rang. Lady Gaga.

"Miss me already?" I said when I answered.

"Always, sweetie. What're you up to?"

"Heading from one meeting to another," I replied. "Hope it ends before I have to go pick up Sabrina."

"Actually, that's why I was calling," she said, her voice brightening. "Sabrina, I mean."

"What about her?" I asked, almost too abruptly.

"Well, my sales manager scheduled some sort of lame training exercise for this afternoon, but it just got canceled. I don't have anything set up for the rest of the day, and I was thinking maybe I could play hooky for a few hours and pick up Sabrina from school. We could go and do some girl things."

Marika had made no secret that she wanted to get to know my daughter better. No woman can ever replace a little girl's mother, and she was okay with that. There was no way she was going to try to be a surrogate mother for Alison. But she had made it clear to me that if she was going to be part of my life, short-term or longer, she wanted it to include Sabrina. I'd felt a sudden warmth at her sincerity and told her that, by all means, if she ever wanted to spend time with my daughter, she could. As long as it was okay with Sabrina.

But now things had changed . . . sort of.

"I think that's a great idea," I told her, ignoring the big "what if" that had taken up residence in my brain. "I'll have to call the school and put you on the official pickup list."

"That would be wonderful," Marika said, sounding relieved. "Do you mind if I take her to do a little clothes shopping?"

"You don't like the outfits I buy her?"

"You have excellent taste in clothing, sweetie," she said diplomatically. "For a man. But sometimes a girl needs the special touch of a woman."

"I think I've just been insulted, but I'm going to ignore it." I laughed.

"Actually, Sabrina isn't the only one who needs the special touch," Marika continued, a sexy playfulness in her voice. "Did I mention that I have the whole night free too?"

"Tonight's a school night," I found myself saying on impulse. "Sabrina has to be up early."

"Which means she has to go to bed early too," Marika pointed out. "If you know what I mean."

Oh yeah, I knew exactly what she meant. And there was a strong side of me that would have liked to tell her to stay for dinner and plan on a late dessert. But the other side of my brain—the side that had been distracted by the events of the last few days—was making a loud, screeching sound, like emergency brakes trying to stop a locomotive on hot steel tracks.

"Tell you what," I said. "Why don't you pick up Sabrina and do your girls' thing, then bring her home when you're done? I should be back by then, and you can stay and have dinner. We'll figure out the rest as we go."

"What do you mean, 'figure out the rest'?" She sounded guarded, as if she was getting ready for the proverbial "other shoe" to drop.

I read the caution in her voice and didn't want to tip her to the conflict I was dealing with. So I quickly answered, "All I'm saying is we need to be discreet when Sabrina's around."

There was a pause on the other end as Marika apparently thought this through. Then she said, "You're starting to sound like my mother."

"She's my daughter, Marika. I'm trying to raise her the best way I know how."

A fact that was hard to argue with, and she wasn't about to try. Instead, she said, "Okay, sweetie. You're her father. But I'd still like to pick her up, take her out to buy her a new dress, maybe some shoes. If you think that's all right."

"I think that would be fabulous," I assured her as I got on the elevator. I pushed the button for my floor, then added, "And you'll stay for dinner too?"

"I'll do you one better. I'll pick some things up on the way, whip up one of my specialties. And as you said, we'll figure out the rest as we go."

I detected a lingering note of dismay in her voice, but I decided to let it pass. After all, Marika was the odd one out in this little trio, and she had feelings too. "Sounds like a plan," I agreed.

"See you at your place, then," she said.

"See you tonight."

*   *   *

"Cameron Kane!" Lexi Lawler practically leaped from behind her desk and threw her arms around me. She planted a kiss on my cheek, then stepped back and looked me in the eyes, the way a distant aunt looks at her nephew after not seeing him since forever. "It's so good to see you—you haven't changed at all."

"You're a horrible liar," I told her, self-consciously running a hand through hair that I knew was much thinner than it had been a year ago. "It's you who looks as fabulous as ever."

They were polite platitudes, standard chitchat for two people who hadn't seen each other for almost a year. Lexi took my hands in hers and gave an appreciative squeeze, then motioned for me to follow her to an unused meeting room. It was located on the perimeter of a cube farm where worker bees were buzzing over a network of computers, two or three monitors per desk.

"The Dow and S&P are both up today," she explained. "Lots of trading going on."

"So I see," I said as I followed her into the glass conference room. "What goes down must go up."

"That's the general promise of economics, but it doesn't always work that way," she pointed out. Her ginger hair seemed to be shorter than the last time I'd seen her, but the same freckles dotted her cheeks, and her blue eyes seemed just as bright and cheery. She wore a light gray skirt and matching jacket, and a white blouse that was buttoned at the neck. She gently closed the door, then indicated for me to sit in one of a dozen chairs positioned around a polished table. A phone that resembled an intergalactic landing craft was set in the center of it, next to a black box that looked like some sort of digital hookup. "And I doubt you're here for wealth management advice."

I peered out the floor-to-ceiling glass wall to Zuccotti Park and the Canyon of Heroes ten floors below. "Do I need a reason to visit one of Alison's best friends?" I asked.

"Of course not," she said as she eased into a chair across from me. "But I know you better than you think I do. I hear nothing from you for months, and then just a couple days before . . . well, before the one-year mark, you give me a call out of the blue?"

"Busted," I admitted. The last time I'd seen Lexi was at the memorial service in Central Park, but we'd only managed to share a few words that day before the tears took over. Hers and mine. "Thank you for making time for me on what has to be a crazy day."

"Each day is crazier than the last." She shrugged. "On the phone you said you had something you wanted to discuss, and given the timing I assume it has to do with Alison. So . . . what gives?"

When I'd first called Lexi on Monday, my brain was spinning with unsorted ideas and notions, and I'd had plenty of time since then to process them. Or at least feed them through a filter of reason and rationale. I'd actually come close to canceling this meeting, but the impulsive side of my brain had pushed me to go ahead and take the subway all the way downtown rather than listen to my own voice of doubt.

"You're right—my timing is not a coincidence." Little pads of notepaper and pencils had been placed at every seat in the conference room, and I absently picked up one of the pencils and started rolling it between my fingers. It was a good replacement for cocktail straws. "I guess the date kind of crept up on me."

"Totally expected," Lexi said. "I've found myself thinking a lot about Alison lately too. So what's this all about?"

I shifted in my chair and set the pencil down. "Well, I know this may sound idiotic, but I was hoping you might remember some things about Alison from those last few weeks."

"I remember lots of things, and none of them would be idiotic," Lexi told me. She touched her hand to an eye and wiped away a bead of moisture. "I remember how she always had a smile on her face, even though she was under a lot of pressure. She always seemed to be working on a sudoku puzzle, even in executive staff meetings—creating them, not solving them. She was the most logical person I knew, to the point where a lot of people around the office started calling her Spock. She always had a bounce in her step, like she was doing the jitterbug. She insisted on being called Alison, spelled with one *l*, and never Ali. And I remember how she always was going on about prime numbers and algorithms and theorems, the way other women talk about George Clooney and Brad Pitt."

I grinned at that and said, "Yes, she did have a passion for numbers. But what about other things?"

"What other things?"

This was where it was going to get a little difficult, if not embarrassing. "Well, like her relationship with Maxwell Harding."

"What relationship?" Lexi asked.

"You tell me."

She stared at me as if she didn't quite understand what I was getting at. Then her brow tightened in a noticeable crease. "You can't possibly be suggesting—"

"I don't know what I'm suggesting, Lexi."

"You'd have to be out of your mind if you think Alison and Harding were . . . Oh my God, you do, don't you?"

"No. Yes. I really don't know."

Lexi started giggling, shaking her head at the same time. "Men can be so dumb," she said, stifling an all-out laugh. "And totally blind. But let me spell it out for you, just so there's no ambiguity. Alison loved you. No . . . she *adored* you. And she adored Sabrina. She lived for you and your family, everything you guys had. She even developed a mathematical equation to describe how much she loved you."

"She did?"

"She never showed it to you?" With that, Lexi picked up a pencil and scribbled on one of the notepads, then turned it around so I could see it:

$$L = CK^n.$$

I stared at the chicken scratch a second, then asked, "What does it mean? Luck?"

"You idiot. It means Love equals Cameron Kane to the nth power."

I sensed my face growing red and suddenly felt like the fool I was. "I guess a racing mind can fly off the track sometimes," I conceded.

"It's been known to happen," Lexi replied.

"What about Harding?"

She seemed to consider my question for a moment, then said, "That's a tough one. He was a scoundrel, and I'm pretty sure he found her attractive. But I won't pretend to know how a man thinks." The twinkle in her eye said, *"Not that they ever do."*

"Did Alison ever mention whether he ever tried anything?"

"No, and I doubt he did," Lexi said quickly, brushing aside my suspicion. "Harding was a dirtball, but I think he knew Alison would have kicked him right in his primes."

I laughed at that and let out a breath I realized I'd been holding deep in my lungs. "Thank you," I eventually said. "It's good to hear all this, especially after a year. And I have to admit, it's a bit embarrassing to even ask the question."

"Forget it," Lexi said. "I'm sure you've wondered what Alison was doing with Harding that night, out in western Jersey."

"The media made it sound as if they were on their way to his place in Pennsylvania. You can see how I might've been suspicious."

"Easily," she replied.

"So why would they have been driving out there that night?" I asked, almost more to myself than to Lexi.

"Good question. It never made a lick of sense, because all of his real property had been seized. And after he died, the feds were compelled to drop the criminal charges against him."

"What about the investigation into Bit-XC and all his financial fraud?" I asked her. "Did they drop that too?"

"Last I heard, they were still at it," she answered, raising a single brow. "Word on the street is they still haven't been able to track the billions of dollars he squirreled away before the indictments came down."

Even though my wife had been sworn to secrecy, I'd heard some rumblings at the time. Online, and on the news. She'd also been offered police protection, which she'd rejected out of hand.

"That's what Alison was doing before she died," I said, again more for my benefit than for hers. "Trying to chase down the money trail."

"She was under the strictest orders not to say a word, not to you or anyone else," Lexi replied. "But I can tell you one thing: Harding was pissed at her—beyond pissed; he was furious."

"Furious enough to kill her?" I wanted to know.

"I'm sure it crossed his mind," she replied.

"He must have felt like a cornered rat, with all the indictments and lawyers ripping his world apart. And what he must have perceived as Alison's ultimate betrayal."

"No question," Lexi agreed. "But you're forgetting, he was in that car too. Rat that he was, I never thought him to be the sort of man who would take his own life. I still don't."

CHAPTER

15

D<small>R.</small> D<small>AVID</small> N<small>GUYEN</small>'s office was located in a town house on a tree-lined block of 11th Street, six blocks from our condo. At one time the stonework might have been brown, but over the years the building had been painted over and over, and now it was the color of an old New England barn. Nguyen—pronounced *Win*—shared the address with an orthodontist and a periodontist as well as an architect who didn't seem to fit the overall scope of practice.

"Good afternoon, Mr. Kane," the receptionist said when I stepped into the waiting area. Her name was Annika, and she couldn't hide the accent that said she'd originated from Russia. "Are you scheduled for a cleaning today?"

"No . . . not until August," I told her as I waited for the outer office door to close. "I just stopped by to speak with Dr. Nguyen when he's between patients. It'll only take a minute."

Annika glanced over her shoulder toward the short hallway that led to the exam rooms. "Doctor is finishing up a crown right now," she said. "If you can wait a minute, I'm sure he'll be happy to see you."

That was how I came to read all about marine iguanas in the Galapagos Islands. Despite my former globe-trotting ways, it was one of the places on the planet I had not yet visited, although Alison and I had talked about escaping there someday. Maybe when Sabrina was old enough to appreciate the exotic wildlife, Charles Darwin, and the origins of all species. I was just starting an article about gold mining in Colorado when Dr. Nguyen opened the door and poked his head into the waiting room.

"Mr. Kane . . . what a surprise to see you," the doctor greeted me in his Vietnamese accent. He pulled a nitrile glove off his right hand and extended it for a quick shake.

"I apologize for just dropping in," I said.

"Not at all," Dr. Nguyen told me. "Are you experiencing a toothache or nerve pain?"

I quickly shook my head and said, "No . . . nothing like that. In fact, it's sort of personal. Do you have a place where we might speak in private?"

The dentist reflexively shot me a curious look. "My office," he suggested, nodding toward the back.

I followed Dr. Nguyen to the end of the hall. He ushered me into a cramped room furnished with a small desk, a couple of chrome and plastic chairs, and a shelf full of books that seemed designed more for show than actual reference work. Framed posters depicting the anatomy of the human tooth were fixed to the walls, and a single window was cloaked with thick draperies.

Dr. Nguyen was a thin and wiry man, narrow face, dark eyes that always seemed inquisitive and searching. He waved me into one of the chairs, then sat down behind his desk. "So—what can I do for you?"

There was no easy way to broach this subject, so I simply said, "As you may recall, my wife, Alison, passed away just about a year ago."

"Right, right," the doctor said, dipping his head in a respectful nod. "I wondered if this might be about her. Very tragic, what happened."

"Yes . . . and I never thanked you for sending Alison's file to the ME," I replied.

Dr. Nguyen made a motion with his hand as if to brush away the thought. "So, what might I help you with?"

I shifted in my chair and folded my hands in my lap, trying to appear relaxed and dispassionate. "The thing is, Dr. Nguyen . . . well, I'm curious how dental records are used to identify someone," I said.

He gave the slightest of nods, letting me know he understood where I was coming from. "Identifying a person through his or her dental records is really the best last resort, short of DNA testing," he explained. "Fact is, teeth often are all that's left intact when a body has been burned or decomposed. Tooth structure is extremely resilient and durable, much more so than bone. Even if a person is badly burned, his or her teeth often are free from damage—unless the victim was exposed to an extremely high-temperature fire. Which most of the time is not the case."

"Harding's car all but melted," I pointed out.

"Yes, but as I recall, it was made mostly of carbon fiber, so much of the heat was dispersed. The interior of the car burned, but not at the temperature that would render dental charts useless."

"How do investigators use dental records to identify a burn victim?" I asked him. "Can you walk me through that?"

"Up to a point," Dr. Nguyen replied. "I'm a family dentist, not a forensic one. However, I have assisted in a few victim IDs, so I can share with you what I know."

I eyed a row of tooth-and-gum molds that were sitting on a shelf, and they reminded me of the preserved organs I'd seen yesterday in Dr. Cook's office. Not quite the same common mementos as autographed baseballs or family photos or artwork crayoned by a five-year-old child, but hey—different strokes for different folks.

"Whatever you can do to help educate me," I said. "Keeping in mind I've never cracked a book about dentistry."

"Okay, Mr. Kane. I'll try to keep it to the bullet points." He hesitated, as if mentally outlining how to proceed. "You see, dental structures—what we commonly refer to as teeth—are the hardest parts of the human body. Like I said, they're highly resistant to decomp and fire. So, when a medical examiner uses dental records, it's because there's really no other way to ID the victim. No two oral cavities are alike, and every person's teeth are unique. Now, during an autopsy, the dental evidence that's recovered from the scene of death is compared with the antemortem records for identification."

"Like my wife's," I said.

"Exactly," Dr. Nguyen replied. "As you may know, the enamel is the outermost layer of the tooth. It's harder than any other substance in the human body and can endure temperatures of over two thousand degrees." He stood up and pointed to the layer of enamel depicted on one of the wall posters. "Of course, dental work, such as a gold crown or a filling, might be disfigured by the heat, but it still can aid in the ID process."

"They do it a lot on crime shows," I said.

"Well, TV doesn't always get everything right, but that's the general idea. Anyway, the medical examiner who requested your wife's records—"

"Dr. Cook," I filled in for him.

"Right, right. Since the police were able to narrow down the victims of that horrible crash to just a couple of possibilities, she was able to use your wife's X-rays to get a positive match."

"That's what I heard," I said. "But I hope you don't mind me asking—and please don't take this the wrong way—are you absolutely certain the records you sent to her were Alison's?"

I'd expected the doctor to bristle at the question and anything that might be inferred from it, so I was not surprised by Dr. Nguyen's response. "Mr. Kane . . . I run one of the most respected dental practices in the Village."

"Yes, I know you do," I said quickly. "And I'm not suggesting anything to the contrary. All I'm asking is if there could be any way the file that went to the ME could have belonged to someone else."

Dr. Nguyen stiffened and said, "That wouldn't be possible. I personally copied her chart and double-checked the name on the file. I even sealed the envelope that went to the pathologist."

"Do you still have the originals?"

"Most likely, but it's been almost a year, so they'd be in our storage facility in Brooklyn."

"Did you look at the records before you copied them, to make sure they were Alison's?" I pressed him.

"I am a dentist, Mr. Kane, not a computer. I couldn't possibly memorize the mouths of all my patients. That's why we have records."

"Yes, I know, Dr. Nguyen. I just want to make sure you were absolutely certain those were my wife's records you sent to the medical examiner."

"Believe me . . . they were."

I offered a slight nod and gazed absently at the poster depicting the human tooth. Then said, "How did you send it?"

"It would have been a bonded courier," Dr. Nguyen replied. "I have to say, I really don't like what you're implying."

"I'm sorry," I told him, figuring I might be forced to find a new dentist before my next scheduled exam. "Is there any chance someone could have intercepted that courier or maybe switched the folders?"

The man stared at me long and hard, and I could see the irritation building in his eyes. Or maybe it was exasperation. Finally, he said, "Look, Mr. Kane, the records I gave to the courier are the same records the ME over in New Jersey signed for."

"Do you remember what courier you used?" I pushed him.

"I'm sure it's in our files," the dentist said. "But I really don't see what difference it would make."

"I'd just like to speak with them. It's important to me in order to get complete closure."

Dr. Nguyen let out a sigh of annoyance, then gave a quick nod. "Look . . . it might take a few days to check our system, but I'll see what I can do."

"Thank you," I said, shaking his hand in gratitude. "Please accept my apologies if I've offended you, and I appreciate whatever you can do."

* * *

Earlier that afternoon, after leaving Lexi Lawyer's office, I'd googled Elise Dillon's phone number, and now, as I walked up the street to Sabrina's day care, I dialed it. I hadn't mentally rehearsed how I was going to do this, so I was forced to wing it.

She answered on the third ring with a tentative "Hello."

The hesitation in her voice caused me to think it would be cruel to put the woman through this, especially today. Her husband had disappeared on the Wednesday of the same week of Alison's death, which meant the one-year anniversary was tomorrow. I considered hanging up, and actually had my finger poised over the red "End" icon before I forced all shame from my mind and said, "Mrs. Dillon?"

There was a hitch of indecision; then the voice said, "Who's calling?"

"My name is Cameron Kane, Mrs. Dillon. You don't know me, but I believe we may share a common interest."

"A common interest," Elise Dillon repeated. "Are you with that damned collection agency? I told you people, I'll have the check in the mail by the first."

"No, Mrs. Dillon." Nothing I could say would make this any easier or make me feel any less guilt. "I promise, this isn't one of those calls. Like I said, my name is Cameron Kane, and I've been reading about your husband. I know this might not be a good time, but I thought it might be a good idea to give you a call."

"My husband? You're calling about Jason?"

"Yes, ma'am."

In an instant her tone flipped from wary to fevered. "Have you found him? Do you know where he is?"

"No . . . nothing like that," I said quickly, not wanting to get her hopes up. "But I've read about what you've gone through to find him and . . . like I said, I think we need to talk."

"So you don't know where he is?"

"No, ma'am."

"How do you know him?"

"I don't—"

"Have you ever met him?"

"All I know is what I've read in the papers."

"Yet you think you have something you need to share with me?"

"Yes, Mrs. Dillon," I told her. "For all I know, it may be nothing. But then again, it could actually be something."

"Go ahead and tell me."

"Not on the phone. I know you live in New Canaan, and I'm in Manhattan. I was thinking tomorrow I could come up and we can meet."

"Tomorrow isn't a good day for me," she said. "If you've read all those stories, you know why."

"Yes, ma'am. There's no rush, so I guess it can wait."

"No!" she snapped, changing her mind. "If it has to do with Jason, I need to know. I'll come into the city, and we can get a cup of coffee. I need to get away from this house anyway. Name a place and a time, and I'll be there."

I thought for a second, then said, "The coffee shop in the concourse under Rockefeller Center, near the ice rink." I knew it was a popular place on the Manhattan tourist trail, but it was easy to find and not too far from Grand Central, where her train would be pulling in. "Ten o'clock?"

"Make it ten thirty, just in case Metro-North is running late," she said. "Oh, and, Mr. Kane?"

"Yes?"

"Please tell me one thing—"

"Mrs. Dillon, I don't think this is a good time. Not over the phone."

But Mrs. Dillon continued as if she didn't hear me. Or chose not to. "You're going to tell me my husband is dead, aren't you?" she asked.

"No, ma'am," I assured her. "Like I said, I just have a few questions. I'll see you in the morning."

CHAPTER

16

MARIKA HAD ALREADY let herself and Sabrina into the condo by the time I arrived home a little after six.

On the subway ride downtown, I'd had plenty of time to think about our conversation that afternoon and found I actually was looking forward to seeing her despite my underlying misgivings. I opened the front door and walked into the kitchen, where Marika was sitting at the breakfast bar, her legs crossed, her navy blue business skirt hiked up to midthigh. She looked up at me and ran a tongue over her lips invitingly but made no effort to get up to greet me. Instead, she motioned with her finger for me to come over to where she was sitting. I set down the bottle of pinot grigio I'd picked up on the way home, then gave a quick—*guilty?*—glance over to the hallway that led to Sabrina's bedroom.

Marika turned her face upward as I leaned over to kiss her. *Sorry, Alison.* She grabbed my lower lip with her teeth, lightly, then tasted me with her tongue. I began to respond, but then we both heard Sabrina's footsteps out in the hallway.

I pulled back just as my daughter burst into the room. "Daddy! Daddy! Look what Mika bought me!"

My daughter spun into the middle of the kitchen and struck a runway pose. She held one hand down at her side, curved inward toward her thigh, the other raised up near her face, turned slightly in the opposite direction. Not too different from how a high-fashion model might look as red-carpet cameras clicked. *Where the hell did she pick that one up?* I wondered. She was wearing a brand-new green dress with a white lace collar and looked elegantly beautiful. I realized I was catching my first glimpse of Sabrina as a young lady— seven going on seventeen—and I felt my heart begin to melt.

"You look absolutely lovely," I told her as a huge smile filled my face. I held out my arms, and she came over so I could wrap her up in a big hug.

"Careful, Daddy. This is called taffeta!"

I grinned and released my grip on her. Then I turned and looked over at Marika, who was beaming from Sabrina's elation. And my reaction.

"Tell your father how many places we went to," she said.

"Six," Sabrina told me, holding up five fingers and a thumb.

"We had to find just the right outfits," Marika explained. Then she said to Sabrina, "Go try the other one on."

"The other one?" I asked, shooting Marika an accusatory glance. "What have you done?"

"I've spoiled your daughter," she said with a teasing glimmer in her eye. "And I'm going to keep doing it until she's spoiled rotten."

"I'll be right back," Sabrina said. "You're going to love it." Then she spun out of the kitchen, scampering down the hall to her bedroom.

When she was gone, Marika stood up and placed her hands on my shoulders. She stared at me with those intense eyes and said, her voice barely above a whisper, "Please don't be mad."

"Mad? How could I be mad? She obviously loves that dress." I gave her a quick kiss on the forehead, then said, "I love it too."

"We went to Lord & Taylor, the Children's Place, Macy's, Talbots, April Cornell, even the Disney Store," Marika recounted, ticking them off on her fingers. "She enjoyed every minute of it. When was the last time you took her shopping?"

"It shows?"

"Not in her clothes," she said. "In fact, they're fine. But the look on her face as we were going from store to store—it was absolutely priceless."

"I have a low level of patience for that sort of thing," I conceded.

"Well, your daughter is a young woman, and she loves it," Marika pointed out. "You'd better get used to it."

"It must be a strictly X chromosome thing," I said with a sigh, grinning but shaking my head at the same time.

Sabrina's return to the kitchen was accompanied by the sound of more footsteps racing down the hall. She flew into the kitchen, then braked to an immediate halt and struck the same pose as before. This time she was wearing a blue dress with long, shimmery sleeves that I could only think of as "fluffy."

I felt my heart skip a beat as I wished Alison could be here right now to see our daughter in all her fashion glory. Marika's hiked-up skirt and bare thigh could, however, pose a problem.

"Oh my gosh!" I told Sabrina, fighting hard not to reveal what I was feeling. Which was *It's hard to squeeze a growing chick back into the egg.* "You look absolutely lovely . . . just like Elsa in *Frozen.* I have to say, you have exquisite taste."

Sabrina wrinkled her nose, as if she just had experienced a bad smell. "What does 'exquisite' mean?" she asked.

"It means one hundred percent perfect," I assured her. "Come here, sugar; let me give you another hug."

The smile affixed to her young face grew even bigger, and she squeezed me as hard as her arms would allow. When she was finished, she said, "Can Marika take me shopping again sometime?"

"Of course she can," I told her. I felt Marika's hand on my shoulder, giving me an appreciative squeeze of her own. "Anytime she wants."

"Are you staying for dinner?" Sabrina asked her.

"If I'm still invited," Marika said.

"Darn tootin' you're invited," I assured her. "One big party. We could order out. Pizza or Chinese—"

"Oh no you don't," Marika said. "I told you I was going to fix dinner, but instead we stopped and got lasagna from Panino. With garlic bread and salad."

"Yummy," Sabrina said, licking her lips. "But do I have to eat the salad?"

"Not if you eat some carrots and celery," I told her.

"But I'm getting tired of celery and carrots," she complained with her customary pout. "We have them every day."

"Then you're probably getting tired of dessert every day too," I reminded her.

"Daddy," Sabrina said, her voice just shy of a whine. But she knew this was not a debate she was going to win, and it was best to give up when she was ahead. Instead, she asked, "Can I eat the carrots now, so they don't spoil dinner?"

"I don't see why not." I shrugged. "But first I want you to go change out of that lovely dress. Lasagna can be messy."

"Okay," she said, and without a hint of warning, she dashed out of the room.

Once she was clearly out of earshot, I gave Marika another kiss, this one on the cheek. Despite the confluence of events that was steering my brain out of orbit, I still had a very warm place for her in my heart. She'd had absolutely nothing to do with what I'd experienced out at JFK last Saturday morning, and I couldn't fault her just for being herself.

Or for not being Alison.

"This falls into the category of above and beyond," I told her.

"We had a fun afternoon," she said, kissing me back. "Girls' day out."

"Well, Sabrina definitely had a blast. You can see it in her eyes."

I walked over to the refrigerator and took out a bag of fresh baby carrots. I rinsed a handful of them and placed them in a small plastic dish, which I set on the *Little Mermaid* placemat where Sabrina usually sat. Then I held up the bottle of wine I'd bought, and Marika gave me an enthusiastic nod. I pulled out the cork with a strong, steady pull, and poured a healthy measure for both of us.

"To an extraordinary woman," I proclaimed, clinking my glass against hers.

"And to the extremely rare man who recognizes one when he sees her," she replied. She lifted her glass to her lips and took a small sip. "Now, this isn't so bad, is it?"

I wrinkled my brow and said, "What isn't so bad?"

"This. Me here with you. And Sabrina. On a school night."

"Not bad at all," I conceded, and I meant it. Ever since I'd met Marika at the top of that escalator—one of those chance encounters that could have a profound ripple effect for years to come—she'd been a comfortable person to be around. I'd sorely needed that at the time, and I definitely needed it now.

"I'm not trying to rush things, sweetie," she said, as if reading my mind. "I want you to know that. Believe me, I'm as wary as the next woman when it comes to men. Especially in this town. But I like being around you, and I like spending time with your daughter. And I like to think you feel the same way."

"Of course I feel the same way," I said, and again I meant it. But I also sensed she was crafting her words very carefully. "I just want you to realize that we're both coming at this from different directions, and our timing may not always be in sync."

"I get that." Marika gently swirled the wine in her glass but did not drink. "I really don't mean to push. I just thought that since we seem to have so few evenings to share, you'd have been thrilled that my night suddenly became free."

"I'm always thrilled to see you," I assured her. "And I'm glad your night became free. But that's what I mean about timing. Sometimes people's lives go like this"—I illustrated my point by interlocking my fingers on both hands—"and sometimes they go like this." Making *that* point by having my fingers get all jammed up.

"Do you really think that's us?" Marika asked, nodding at how my fingers were out of sync. "I actually think we're pretty good together."

I sipped my wine, thought I heard Sabrina chugging back down the hallway. She'd be back in the kitchen at any moment. "What I'm saying is that you spent a nice afternoon with my daughter and bought her two absolutely beautiful dresses. You also brought what I know will be a delicious lasagna. We're all going to have a wonderful dinner, you and I will drink some wine, and we'll probably play a few games of Uno with Sabrina afterward. And after I put her to bed and read her a story—well, after that we'll just see how things unfold. That's how I see the evening going."

"Works for me," Marika said. "Except for one thing."

"What's that?" I asked.

"I get to read her a bedtime story."

"Your wish is my command," I said.

"That's what I'm counting on, Mr. K," she said, a twinkle in her eye.

It appeared the storm had passed, at least for now, but I sensed an emotional thunderhead building on the horizon.

CHAPTER

17

Thursday

"DADDY! WAKE UP. Wake up, Daddy!"
I blinked my eyes open at the sound of Sabrina's voice. I rubbed away the remnants of sleep and tried to figure out where I was. In my bed; that was a good sign. Alone—also good, depending on one's perspective.

Then last night came back to me, and I felt a wave of relief wash over me. After putting Sabrina to bed, Marika and I had retreated to the living room, where we had shared some cognac and kisses. We listened to music, talked a bit, and then didn't talk at all. She did her best to convince me that the walls were thicker than my skull, that I was being hard-headed for no reason. I was sorely tempted but declined for reasons I couldn't get into with her. Not yet.

I looked over at the clock. It was five minutes before eight, and Sabrina had to be at school in twenty minutes.

"Did you and Mika stay up late?" she asked as I rolled out of bed, my feet missing the slippers that were always there on the floor, waiting for them.

"She actually left pretty early," I said. I noticed that she'd already slipped on a pair of black jeans and a red knit top with colorful balloons embroidered on the front. "You're already dressed."

"And you're not."

"Give me three minutes," I begged as I darted into the bathroom.

The walk-in closet was off to the left, and I quickly pulled on a pair of khakis and a Jets sweatshirt Alison had given me after she'd thrown out my old Bowdoin hoodie, the one with all the college-era holes and food stains. I brushed my teeth, decided I could shave later, then ran a comb through my hair. I studied my face in the mirror, figured it was the best I could do on such short notice. When I returned to the bedroom, Sabrina was sitting at the foot of my bed, very intent about something.

"One hundred six," she said.

"I didn't know you could count that high," I told her, coming over and kissing the top of her head.

"Ms. Burton taught us," she said. "Is that more than three minutes?"

"Depends on how fast you were counting," I replied. I fished a pair of socks out of a drawer and grabbed a belt. "Let's go get you some breakfast."

"I already ate," she said.

"You got your cereal by yourself?" I asked her.

"No one else was up." She planted her hands on her hips and shot me a classic seven-year-old look of disapproval.

"I'm sorry I slept in, sugar," I apologized. "Your hair smells fresh this morning."

"Mika put something special in it last night," Sabrina told him. "She said it would make it look more."

"More what?"

"Just more," Sabrina said.

"Well, whatever it is, it smells nice," I said. "Did you brush your teeth?"

"Yes, Daddy."

"After you ate your cereal or before?"

She gave me a guilty grin. "Oops," she said, and ran off to her bathroom.

"Count to twenty," I called after her.

* * *

We walked fast, no dawdling, and got to school with seconds to spare. I gave her my usual kiss goodbye, and she turned to run up the steps to the front door, then stopped.

"Is Mika coming over tonight?" she said to me.

"I don't think so," I told her. "She has to work today."

"So do you."

"I know, but Mika's job keeps her pretty busy."

"When will we see her again?" she asked.

"Maybe over the weekend," I said. "We'll see."

"Hope so." Sabrina smiled. "I like her."

"I like her too."

"I know that," she said. "But she's not very good at Uno."

I rushed back home and had just finished shaving when my cell phone chimed, signaling that an email had just arrived. I got a lot of those because of the nature of my work, but this one came from Gloria Ruiz in the Tri-County Medical Examiner's office in Morristown.

The email was short and curt, explaining that the attached PDF contained the dental chart and X-rays that had been used to positively identify my wife. As the ME had assured me in her office, it had been supplied by our dentist and had been delivered by secure and bonded courier. Meaning there was no way it could have been tampered with on its door-to-door journey.

I clicked on the PDF, which opened on the small screen of my phone. Too small for me to actually read, so I hurried into my study and woke my computer up. I clicked on the file attached to the email again and waited for it to open. When it did, I enlarged the first page, which carried an ink stamp from the dental practice of David Nguyen, DDM. Everything was official, just as I'd been assured.

A quick glance at the diagrams of upper and lower teeth, and notations written off to the side, instantly convinced me there wasn't a chance in hell I was looking at a chart of my wife's mouth.

When Alison had been pregnant with Sabrina, she had mentioned that she had never had a filling in her life—something to do with the application of some sort of dental sealant when she was a child. That changed after our daughter was born, but even then, she'd only had a single small cavity that had been filled. Nothing beyond that, and certainly not what I was looking at now.

The X-rays looked like X-rays always look: fuzzy white images on a fuzzy gray background, with stray cracks and lines that only dentists—and medical examiners—are trained to decipher. But my mouth is riddled with metal—as Dr. Nguyen had shown me with my own pictures—and it was clear from what I was seeing that these images had nothing to do with Alison's teeth. A half-dozen fillings, four on the right side and two on the left, were clearly visible in the images. Plus, there was a distinct gray area, at the top of one of the molars, that I suspected was a crown, which Alison certainly did not have.

I was already late for work, and again I was going to have to slip out mid-morning for my ten thirty meeting at Rockefeller Center. As I hurried up the street to the subway station, I quickly called Dr. Cook, whose number was still in my phone log from the other day. She was not in her office, but Gloria Ruiz picked up after several rings. I thanked her profusely for sending me the dental records so quickly, then asked to be patched into the ME's voicemail. I hoped I didn't huff and puff too much as I did the Olympic speed-walk down the sidewalk while leaving her a message, pleading with Dr. Cook to call me back as soon as she had a spare moment.

* * *

I knew what Elise Dillon looked like from a picture I'd downloaded from the Web. I brought it up on my phone, then scanned the underground esplanade that connects the buildings throughout Rockefeller Center. Unless she had changed her appearance since the photo was taken, I was looking for a woman in her early forties. Short dark hair, caramel eyes, and what romance writers might call a heart-shaped face. The photograph showed an infectious smile on her lips, but I doubted she'd done much smiling over the past year.

I was standing at the bottom of an escalator, near the glass that looked out on the open-air restaurant where ice skaters glided around in circles during the winter months. My watch read 10:40, and for a moment I wondered if the train from New Canaan had been late pulling into Grand Central. Or maybe Mrs. Dillon simply had changed her mind.

I finally spotted her, slowly walking past a cluster of tables near the coffee shop. She was glancing around, looking for a man who was looking for her, only she didn't have the advantage of knowing what I looked like. But her hair and eyes matched her appearance in the photo, so I started moving toward her. She seemed to sense my approach and swiveled her head, eyeing me tentatively until I spoke.

"Mrs. Dillon?"

"Yes," she said, same hesitant hitch she'd had in her voice last night. "You must be Mr. Kane."

"Please . . . call me Cameron," I told her.

"Then you must call me Elise."

I extended my hand, which she shook lightly. Then I said, "May I get you a cup of coffee, maybe some tea?"

"No, thank you," she said quickly. "But I think I might need something pretty strong after I hear what I think you're going to tell me."

I neither confirmed nor denied her suspicion. "Let's sit over there," I suggested, indicating a small table with two chairs near the glass wall.

She stood there a moment, as if questioning whether she wanted to go through with this. Then she let out an audible sigh and followed me over.

"How was the train ride in?" I asked once we were comfortably seated across from each other.

"Fine. Crowded. Loud. And please, I'm really not up for small talk. I was awake all night, thinking about your call. Going over what you said on the phone and what I figure you're going to tell me now. So please pardon my abruptness, and let's just get on with this."

"Fair enough," I said. "This isn't easy for either of us."

Mrs. Dillon looked at me but said nothing, her silence urging me to continue.

"One year ago this week my wife was killed in a car crash," I told her, hoping my story might level the playing field. "Out in New Jersey. As you might imagine, it was a difficult time for me."

She nodded, then closed her eyes and lowered her head into her hands. "I am so sorry, Mr. Kane. I had no idea."

It was clear she had not googled me after we'd talked on the phone and thus had no real comprehension of why she was here. She'd come all this way into Manhattan on some vague speculation I'd made on the phone, and I sensed she was still on delicate footing. So was I, but the onus here was on me. I truly empathized with everything she was going through, and the last thing I wanted was to upset her any more than she already was.

"No, you couldn't possibly have known," I said. "And I can't imagine what this past year has been like for you, not hearing anything about your husband."

"So what do you know about him?" she asked.

"I may not know anything at all," I explained. "But I have reason to believe that your husband's disappearance may be connected to what happened to my wife."

She shook her head rapidly at that: automatic denial. Then she said, "I'm afraid I'm not following you."

There was no easy way to go about this, and for a moment I wished I'd never called Mrs. Dillon. What purpose would it serve in the long run? She clearly was still haunted by her husband's vanishing, and nothing I was about to tell her would make a damned thing any better. I hesitated a second, thinking maybe I should just tell her this was all a big mistake, and I was sorry she'd come all the way into Manhattan for nothing.

But it was too late to back out, so I launched into my story. Just the broad framework, leaving out the macabre details. I downplayed just how horrible the crash had been, totally left out the part that the car had practically melted from the heat. She didn't need to hear that sort of thing. Then I jumped ahead a year and gave her a brief thumbnail account of what I'd experienced in Terminal 8 at JFK. I gave her just enough information to imply there was a possibility that a body double might have been sitting behind the wheel in Harding's Lamborghini when it had left the highway that cold April night twelve months ago.

When I was finished, she just stared at me and slowly shook her head.

"That's totally absurd," she told me. "Absolutely insane."

"Exactly what I thought . . . at the start," I replied. "But I know what I saw at the airport. I believe Harding could be alive, and that means everything I was told about the accident could be wrong. Starting with who really was in the car that night."

"Wait a minute. You think someone kidnapped my husband, squeezed him into some goddamn Italian sports car, and crashed him into a tree?"

"As you said, it sounds absolutely crazy."

"Insane is what I said," she snapped. "How did they identify the victims? I mean, if they were so badly burned and all?"

"Dental records," I told her.

"Well . . . there you have it. X-rays and dental charts don't lie."

"So I've been told. But I just received an email that suggests they may have been switched."

"An email? You're basing all this insanity on an email?"

I explained that I didn't believe the dental records used to identify Alison's body actually were hers. No, I was not a forensic dentist, and I had no training in this sort of thing. Yes, my dentist insisted he'd sent the medical examiner the correct file. And yes, I was convinced the fillings that appeared in the X-rays could not have belonged to my wife.

When I finished, she slowly rose from her chair and wandered over to the glass that overlooked the skating rink. The ice was long gone, replaced by tents stretching over tables that were set up for dining. It was too early for lunch, but restaurant staff were laying down place settings and fresh-cut flowers. She stared at them, as if trying to rid herself of a bad dream, then returned to where I was sitting.

She did not sit back down. "This is just too . . . too loony tunes," she said, her words trailing off.

I nodded, hoping to reassure her with my own sense of disbelief. "I know it's hard to take this in, and I'm not asking you to believe me. You hardly even know me. But I was hoping you could do me a small favor."

"Do *you* a *favor*? What kind of favor do you expect me to do after you tell me such horseshit?"

On a scale of one to ten, this was turning into a zero. I should have known better, but I'd put my interests above hers. "Please, Mrs. Dillon. I know how this sounds."

But Mrs. Dillon clearly had heard enough. She placed her hands flat on the table, stared me in the eye, and said, "Look, Mr. Kane." She pronounced my name as if it were a dirty word, which I justly deserved. "I knew what you were going to tell me was going to be bad. But this . . . this is crazy talk!"

"Please . . . just hear me out," I said as she spun on her heels to leave. "Maybe you could check with your dentist to see if he still has your husband's original X-rays somewhere . . ."

Elise Dillon wasn't listening, and I couldn't blame her. She stormed off in anger—*or was it disgust?*—as her shoes click-clacked on the tile floor. She marched toward the escalator, not bothering to look back as she stepped onto the bottom stair.

I sat there, muttering to myself, "Well, that went well."

18

I GAVE MRS. DILLON a five-minute head start before I went
back to the office. I'd already missed one licensing meeting by slipping out mid-morning, and didn't want to make
my absence a regular thing. My plan was to work straight
through lunch, but then my phone rang, and my best intentions spiraled down the drain.

"Mr. Kane," a voice said in my ear. Annoyed and frus-
trated. Dr. Cook. "I got your message. Please, you need to
accept reality—"

"Those aren't my wife's X-rays," I interrupted. I could be
brusque and abrupt too.

"What are you talking about?"

"I'm talking about the PDFs your assistant emailed to me
this morning. I looked at them, and I can guarantee you that
they do not belong to my wife."

"Excuse me for being blunt, but I really think you're
beating a dead horse," she replied.

"Which you'd probably identify with the wrong records,"
I blurted before I could stop myself. Then, before she could
hang up on me, I added, "I apologize for that, Dr. Cook.

Totally uncalled for. But I was married to Alison for nine years, and we dated for three years before that. That's a total of twelve years. Over that span of time, do you suppose a husband gets to know most of what there is to know about his wife, including her mouth?"

"I was married for seventeen years myself, and I have no idea how many cavities Brad had."

"Well, I can tell you right now that Alison never had a filling in her life. Not until she gave birth to our daughter, and even then, only a small one. Calcium deficiency from the pregnancy, the dentist determined. The X-rays you sent me showed six fillings at least. Plus something that looks like a crown, which I know my wife did not have."

There was a long silence on the other end. Eventually she said, "Could she have had other dental work somewhere else without you knowing about it?"

"No, Dr. Cook—we shared everything. There was no need to hide anything like a filling. Or a bunch of them. In fact, the last time she went to the dentist, she came home and said he had told her she stood a good chance of taking her teeth—all of them—to her grave."

"And she had no crowns?"

"Nothing like that."

Another silence followed, ending when she said, "Look, Mr. Kane. I'm probably crazy for even suggesting this, but I'm at a regional symposium of medical examiners here in the city."

"I appreciate you taking the time to call me during what I assume is a busy day."

"What I mean is . . ." She seemed to give serious thought to what she was about to say, then continued. "I just sat through a presentation about achieving the highest possible accuracy in every postmortem and taking another look if there's even the remotest doubt about the evidence."

"Meaning?"

"Meaning, I'll have Gloria send me what she sent you. I'm at the Sheraton on Seventh Avenue."

"I'm just one block over on Sixth."

"Good. Meet me in thirty minutes on the second floor, and we can take care of this once and for all."

"See you then," I agreed.

*   *   *

A half hour later I rode the escalator up from the street level, the hubbub of voices coming from the top of the stairs indicating that a meeting had just broken for lunch. A sign confirmed that the conference was one floor up. When I stepped off, I saw Dr. Cook standing near an anemic potted plant, conversing with a group of people. I gave a wave when she glanced over, but waited at a polite distance until she had finished her discussion.

"I apologize for keeping you waiting," she said when she wandered over to where I stood. She was wearing a charcoal-gray pantsuit with a paisley scarf and stylish beige flats that matched the briefcase she was holding. "When I come to these things, I always run into people I haven't seen in ages."

"No problem," I replied. "I know how it goes."

She looked around the mezzanine area, then pointed to an open door. "We can probably grab a couple of chairs in there," she said.

I followed her to a meeting room across from the lavatories and, quite possibly, the last remaining pay phone in all of Manhattan. The space was empty except for about a hundred chairs, lined up in rows, facing a draped table with microphones set on it. A large screen had been erected in a corner, and a video projector on a rolling stand was pointed at it.

She waved me into one of the chairs, then pivoted the one in front of it so she could face me. She reached into her case and pulled out an iPad, which she thumbed to life.

Right down to business, which was fine with me.

She used her finger to scroll through a jumble of pages, saying, "As we discussed, the victim—your late wife—was burned beyond recognition." Not mincing words, going straight for the facts of the exam. And maybe to shock me back to reality. "We weren't able to make a positive identification until we obtained her official records from Dr. Nguyen, your dentist."

"I spoke with him yesterday," I said. "I don't think he appreciated my visit."

The tri-county ME regarded me curiously, then drew her eyes to the tablet screen and turned it so I could see what she was seeing.

"Is this the chart Gloria sent you?"

I studied it carefully. It had the same stamp from Dr. Nguyen's office, as well as the same four cavities on the right side and two on the left. "Looks like," I replied. "These shadows indicate fillings, right?"

"That's correct."

"And that's a crown."

She confirmed it was.

"Then these definitely aren't Alison's teeth."

"Mr. Kane—"

"Like I told you on the phone, she had one small filling and nothing else," I insisted. "I'm absolutely certain of it."

"Then Gloria must have sent you the wrong records," she said.

"Not possible. It says 'Alison Kane' right there. And there and again there."

Dr. Cook massaged her temples as she studied the screen. Then she said, "Well, if those aren't your wife's records, as you say, I don't know why they have her name on them. Or why your dentist would have sent them. What I'm going to do is call him and then give these charts to a forensic anthropologist we sometimes work with. Usually on those rare situations when all we have to go with is a jawbone or a few tooth fragments. She wasn't involved the first time around, but now I think it would be a good idea to bring her in."

"I give you my word, those aren't Alison's teeth."

She ran a hand through her hair, tucked a few stray strands behind her ear. "I run a forensic pathology lab, Mr. Kane. Your word isn't going to cut it. What I want you to do is get me some good photos of your wife. A full view of the face and right and left profiles would be best. That should provide sufficient information for her to determine once and for all whether these are Alison's records."

"I'm telling you, they're not."

"We still need irrefutable, substantive proof," she insisted. "Plus, the anthropologist might be able to tell from the bone structure and the X-rays what the victim looked like prior to death, without any personal bias."

"What about Maxwell Harding?" I asked.

"I'm going to pull the records we have for him and examine them again," Dr. Cook said. "If one set of records is incorrect, I need to know if the other set is too."

"And if you find that to be the case?"

The medical examiner sat there, her eyes fixed on mine. "Aside from the fact that my reputation will be on the line, there'll be a full investigation. State police, probably FBI.

If it turns out your wife and Mr. Harding are not the victims I had on my table—well, let's see where forensic sci-
ence takes us."

"When do you think you'll be able to go through Harding's file?" I asked.

"This conference is over at four," she told me. "I think
I'll duck out early to beat the traffic and get the folks in
Records to pull Harding's folder before they close. I may find
something in there, or I may need to talk to his dentist. That
would require approval from his widow, and she may not
want to become involved with this. Without her consent, the
dentist probably won't cooperate."

"How long do you think all this will take?"

"I'll put a rush on it, but there's no telling, since accuracy
is of paramount importance."

I started to say, *Not like last time,* but bit my tongue just
in time.

She stood up, signaling that our meeting was drawing
to a close. "Look, Mr. Kane. I can only guess at what you've
gone through in the past year. But if this long-shot idea of
yours comes anywhere close to the truth, you need to consider that A plus B doesn't necessarily add up to C."

"I'm aware of that," I conceded.

"Don't you think it's odd that for almost a full year your
wife didn't try to make contact?"

She did, just the other night, I thought. *Huckleberry friend.*

"All I know is what I know," I replied. "You'll call me
with whatever you find out about Harding?"

"When I learn something, I'll fill you in," she stated. "But
again, if it turns out someone switched the dental records and
God knows what else—you don't want to go anywhere near
this."

"Too late," I replied. "I've already stepped in it."

"Just be careful. Like they say, dead men tell no tales."

"Same thing goes for dead medical examiners."

"Yeah," she agreed. "That thought already crossed my mind."

19

AFTER MY MEETING with Dr. Cook, I found a voicemail from Nicole Harding, Maxwell Harding's wife. I'd placed a call to her Monday and hadn't really expected to hear back from her, especially since I'd had so much difficulty tracking her phone number down. Three numbers, in fact, and I'd left polite messages on all of them.

Based on my experience with Elise Dillon, I thought twice about returning her call. After all, Mrs. Harding was probably going through a similar phase of first-anniversary retrospection and anguish. But I hit "Redial" anyway, and a few seconds later she answered.

I'd only spoken with her on rare occasions, always at a company function in a formal setting. Never on the phone. "Mrs. Harding . . . Cameron Kane," I said. "Thank you so much for returning my call. I hope I'm not intruding on anything."

"Not at all," she said, the upbeat tone in her voice surprising me. "In fact, there's something I want to talk to you about."

Not the response I expected, and all I found myself saying was "What about?"

"Not on the phone, but I'll tell you what. I'm heading out to a late lunch, and if you can make it up to 74th Street, there's a wonderful Indian place that has the best biryani in the city."

"Now?" I asked her, doing the mental calculation in my head. That was about thirty blocks away, and it was lunchtime in Manhattan. Not a good combination for hailing a taxi. At least it wasn't raining.

"Can you think of a better time?" she asked. "I'll see you there."

*   *   *

The restaurant was a modest glass storefront on the shady side of the street, tucked in between an establishment that sold estate jewelry and an upscale nail salon. The place was light and cheery, decorated in various shades of red and yellow, lots of gold, all draped with prayer flags and jeweled lanterns. White linen covered the tables, and the walls were festooned with colorful images of elephants, gardens, and a deity that I recognized as Ganesh, lord of all existing beings. Alison had been a yoga devotee and had adored Indian food, especially veggie samosas and eggplant with tamarind. The pungent aroma of the restaurant brought all that back to me in a torrent of memories, and I sensed my heart miss a beat as I remembered those times . . . *before*.

I recognized Mrs. Harding from her husband's soirees. She was already making her way through a lavish buffet, spooning food onto a plate. Our eyes met and I waved, and she nodded toward a table in the back. I edged my way through the busy restaurant, arriving at the table at the same time she did.

"It's always tough finding a cab this time of day," I said.

She waved off my words as she set her plate on the table. "I forget what it's like trying to hail a ride," she said. "Town cars really can spoil you."

"Quite true," I said, instantly reminded of Alison's access to Harding's fleet of black Lincolns. I glanced at her plate, which was piled high with delicacies, and said, "Looks good."

"The best Tandoor cuisine in all of Manhattan," she replied.

Mrs. Harding seemed older than the last time I'd seen her, at the company Christmas party, but I'm sure I did too. She'd been dressed in a red gown then, with green holiday accents and a string of pearls hung around her neck. Now she wore a trim white dress with a black belt and sapphire earrings. "Please, go get your lunch while it's still hot," she suggested.

I did as I was told, helping myself to more food than I thought I'd ever be able to eat. When I returned to the table, Mrs. Harding was already well into what I suspected was the famed biryani, and used her fork to indicate that I should sit down and get to it.

"I really wasn't expecting to see you this quickly," I told her as I unfolded my napkin in my lap. "Fact is, I wasn't sure you'd even want to meet with me at all."

"Like I said on the phone, there's something I wanted to talk to you about," she said.

"Because it's been almost a year?"

"Because I got a call from a private detective yesterday. He asked me lots of questions about the accident: What I remembered about that night and what my late husband was involved with. The FBI and IRS, the US Attorney's

Office—all of that. I asked him why he was poking around after a year, and all he said was 'privileged client relationship.' The timing seemed a little suspect, so I figured maybe you hired him."

I'd started to take a bite from a samosa, but now I just held the pastry in my hand and said, "Guilty as charged. I hope you're not angry."

"Anger doesn't enter into it," Mrs. Harding said as she took a bite of a pakora. "You're looking into an alternative reality to what happened out there on that highway, aren't you?"

Her direct approach surprised me. "What's past is past, and what's done is done," I replied, just a little too lamely.

"I know you don't really believe that." Clearly a statement, not a question.

"What I believe doesn't matter," I replied. "All that matters are the facts."

"Then tell me about those facts," Mrs. Harding pressed me. "The facts that caused you to hire Magnum P.I."

"I was just looking for closure. Time to get on with my life."

"Bullshit," she said, calling me out as she speared a morsel of lamb with her fork. "I may have been married to Maxwell Harding, but that doesn't make me stupid. As a matter of fact, I've got a pretty good head on my shoulders. Maybe not the same as your wife and her bionic brain, but I know a thing or two."

"I'm sure you do," I said. Wondering if what she knew included her late husband's dubious business dealings, all the dark web activities and cryptocurrency fraud he'd been involved with. Allegedly, since he'd supposedly died before anything could be proven.

"Do you mind if I ask what you're looking into?" Mrs. Harding asked. "I mean, why you hired what I assume is a very expensive detective to go poking into the past?"

"How much did Mr. Harding talk to you about his work?" I replied.

"Not one bit. Max's business dealings completely bored me, and he left all that crap at the office," she told me. "Making money from money, just for the sake of making more money. 'Business coming through. Money on the move.' That's what he always said."

"I take it you saw the play?"

"That horrid thing?" Mrs. Harding said with a visible shudder. "Me and about ten other people, total. Max forced the director to put that line in, threatened to withhold any more funding if he didn't. Not that it mattered in the long run; it was so awful." She seemed to reflect on something, then continued. "Anyway, I had no interest in his business or how he ran it. Sure, I loved having the retreat in the Poconos and the place in Paris, so who was I to question him? Fortunately, I inherited some money when my father passed away, or I'd be out on the street."

A waitress sauntered up to the table and checked the pot of tea. She was dressed in a brightly colored sari and had a vermillion bindi in the center of her forehead, a spot that Alison had told me was the center of the sixth chakra and the seat of concealed wisdom. When the server seemed satisfied that our needs had been met, she wandered off to another table.

"How long were the two of you married?" I asked once the waitress was out of earshot.

"Twenty-two years," she told me. "We met at UPenn. He was enrolled at Wharton, and I was an undergrad. On our first date he boasted that he was going to make his first billion by the age of thirty. He thought I'd be impressed, but I just remember thinking it was so cute. And typical. All the Wharton men believed the same pile of bull, but he was certain he'd be the one to do it."

"And did he?"

"Yes, he did. Beat his goal by four months. Then he set about making the next billion and the next. By that time, I knew he was more in love with money than he was with me, but it was something I could live with. Now, if you don't mind, can you please tell me why you're really here?"

On the cab ride uptown, I'd run through this moment several different ways from several different directions. I had a mental list of questions I wanted to ask her, some crazier than others. Now that the moment was upon me, however, I just reached into my jacket pocket and pulled out the photo of Jason Dillon I'd printed earlier from the online newspaper story.

I handed it to Mrs. Harding and said, "Have you ever seen this man?"

She shot me a quizzical look, then studied the face in the color photo. Broad smile, big teeth, salt-and-pepper hair. A healthy, athletic appearance. She actually gave it a full ten seconds, then handed it back.

"No, but I've seen this picture," she replied. "Just this morning, in fact. Your private detective emailed it to me."

So Donovan is onto something, I thought as another chill raked my spine. "Did he tell you what the man's name is?" I inquired.

"No, and I didn't ask. In fact, I really wasn't all that interested. Look, Mr. Kane, I'm really not into conspiracies or paranoid musings. I believe Neil Armstrong walked on the moon, and I know it was a bunch of deranged terrorists who flew those planes into the twin towers."

"You and me both." I nodded and nibbled on a samosa, trying to figure out the best way to phrase my next question. Straight and direct, just as Mrs. Harding was. "Tell me, how far do you think your husband would go to get himself out of a jam?"

She paused with a forkful of something covered in a brown sauce in midair, and said, "You mean, so he wouldn't have to go to jail for the rest of his life?"

"Something like that, yes."

The fork finished its arc, and the tidbit disappeared into her mouth. "Like I said, whatever it is that my husband did or didn't do, I'm over it. Totally. Our son will be graduating from Choate in a few weeks, and he's heading to Princeton in the fall. I've gone back to work, assistant to the COO of a handbag manufacturer on Seventh Avenue. My co-op is paid for, and I still fly to Paris twice a year, even though I stay in VRBOs and not our own penthouse. Not quite how I thought things would turn out when I fell in love with Max all those years ago, but nothing in life is guaranteed. Or permanent. Now, I suggest you stop asking questions and try the Kashmiri Mughlai. It really is to die for."

Nicole Harding declined to say anything more about her husband, and when I tried to redirect her to the car crash, she changed the subject.

She insisted on paying, and we left the restaurant together. When we hit First Avenue, we shook hands politely, and then she went one way and I went the other. I lingered as she climbed into a waiting town car, then stood at the crosswalk while a stream of traffic raced through the intersection. Including a black-over-gold Rolls Royce Spectre with dark tinting on the rear windows.

Just like the one I'd seen a block from our home on Saturday afternoon.

CHAPTER

20

I WATCHED THE LUXURY automobile glide around a corner at the next block and disappear into the shadows of a tree-lined street. Then the light changed and I stepped off the curb with the horde of pedestrians hurrying back to their offices or cash registers or service vehicles. The moment had passed, and the illusory coincidence faded.

When I reached the other side, I pulled my phone out of my pocket to check for messages. I'd turned the ringer off when I'd entered the restaurant, and my cell had vibrated repeatedly in my pocket. Two calls came from Sabrina's school and two from Marika. My instinct was to phone the school immediately, but before I could punch in the number, the screen lit up. Lady Gaga was singing to me.

I needed to get back to the office, so I let the call go to voicemail as I stuck out my hand and flagged down a passing taxi. Only when I was comfortably settled in the back seat did I listen to her message.

"Mr. K . . . it's Marika," she began in her cheery voice. "Did you know that Sabrina only had a half day today? No worries. The school called me because I'm now on the approved list. Anyway, I picked her up and brought her back here to my place. I'm making tuna sandwiches, and I can rearrange my schedule this afternoon to look after her, but please give me a call when you get this. Love you . . . bye."

Shit. I'd been so damn absorbed in my fishing expedition that I'd totally forgotten the teacher in-service that was scheduled at Sabrina's school this afternoon. Normally she could have just gone to her after-school program, but that didn't begin until two-thirty, which meant there was a two-hour gap when she had nowhere to go. I had no excuse; the note had come home last week, long before I'd hopped the flight out to LA. So much had happened since then that it had totally slipped my mind.

As did my promise to get back to Claire Beckett at the Bradley Museum, who also had left a message: "Mr. Kane . . . I'd expected to hear from you by now regarding our offer of employment. We do have a stand-by candidate, but you're our first choice and we'd like a firm answer before we move on. Please give me a call as soon as you can."

Fuck, I thought as I stared at the ceiling of the cab. I wanted—*needed*—to talk to her, but I didn't know what to tell her. Last Friday night I'd sat at the gate at LAX, convincing myself that there was no way I could pass up a job at the Bradley or a chance for new scenery and building new memories. I'd been ninety-five percent of the way to saying yes, but when I'd gotten off the plane at JFK, my resolve had imploded. And right now, I didn't have time to call her back, having put any decision on hold while I chased my fantasies.

I dialed Marika's number, waiting for the phone to ring on the other end as the cab hung a left at Fifth Avenue.

"Mr. K . . . there you are," Marika said when she answered. "I figured you were in a meeting or something."

"I've been nonstop all day," I told her. "I silenced my phone this morning. Thank you for picking up Sabrina for me . . . I really owe you for this."

"Nonsense," she said. "We're having a great time. But if you feel a real need to pamper me, I have an idea or two."

"I'll just bet you do," I replied. "And hold that thought. Right now, can you put Sabrina on the phone?"

"Of course," Marika told me. "Hang on a sec."

A second later my daughter said, "Hi, Daddy."

"Sabrina . . . I am so sorry for forgetting your half day, but I've been tied up by work all morning," I told her.

"I knew you didn't just leave me there on purpose."

Alison and I had discussed more than once that parent–child separation was a common theme that ran through all childhood fairytales and almost every old Disney movie. *Hansel and Gretel, Dumbo, Bambi, Cinderella*: they all did their best to scare the crap out of kids by taking them away from—or killing off—a parent. And despite all my daughter's protests, I knew that a real thread of fear was still stitched through her entire being.

"Of course I didn't, sugar," I said. "I just got really busy at work and lost track of the time. I hope you're having fun with Marika."

"We're making sandwiches," she replied. "Mika lives really high up in the sky."

"Close to the clouds," I agreed. Marika had invited me home to her apartment a week after we met, and I'd been overwhelmed not just by the view of lights across the Hudson but also by the altitude.

"I like it here," Sabrina said. "It's real quiet, and the air smells different. Clean. Oh, and Daddy?"

"Yes, sugar?"

"Well . . ." She hesitated a moment, then said, "Since my class is going to the zoo tomorrow, Janelle was wondering if maybe I could spend the night at her house. Her mom is one of the *shap . . . shapper . . .* one of the grown-ups who's going with us. I know it's a school night, but it's not. Not really. 'Cause we're going to the zoo. It's almost like the weekend already. Please, Daddy . . . say yes."

Sabrina knew I had a strict rule that on school nights she was to come right home. No sleepovers except on Fridays and Saturdays or when I took a quick job-hunting trip out to California. But what she was saying was true: going to the Central Park Zoo was not the same as learning how to add and subtract or read chapter books. Plus, I was already softened up by the guilt of forgetting about my daughter's half day.

"I'll need to talk to Janelle's mom first," I told her.

"Does that mean yes?" Sabrina asked, a spark of excitement in her voice.

"Only if it's okay with Janelle's mom. I'll give her a call and sort this all out. Can you please put Mika back on the phone?"

"Yippee!" she squealed.

When I finished talking to Marika, I dialed Janelle's mother, Belinda, at the small but luxurious boutique she owned on Christopher Street. I had the number in my contacts because Janelle was Sabrina's best friend, and they were always conspiring for some sort of sleepover or playdate. Belinda assured me that her daughter had already run the sleepover plan up the flagpole, and it was fine with her if Sabrina spent the night. She would simply bring both girls to school tomorrow morning and, as one of the chaperones, keep an eye on them during the field trip.

I thanked her and let her know I would drop off some overnight things at their house later. "I really appreciate this on the spur of the moment," I said. "Sabrina really seems to have her heart set on it."

"She's such a sweet girl," Janelle's mom said. "Very bright too. Anything special I should be aware of?"

"Just the usual stuff. Make sure she brushes her teeth, and not too many sweets."

"Got it. And please don't worry . . . she's going to be fine."

"I know she will," I replied.

CHAPTER

21

THE US ATTORNEY's Office for the Southern District of
New York is located at One St. Andrews Plaza, not far
from where the Brooklyn Bridge empties into Manhattan,
and a few hundred yards from One World Trade, the former
site of the twin towers.

Charles Harmon was the deputy chief of the Criminal
Division, overseeing the Complex Frauds and Cybercrime
Unit, which investigated and prosecuted financial graft,
tax scams, and online criminal activities. The unit worked
closely with the Money Laundering and Asset Forfeiture
Unit, which was responsible for maximizing the recovery
of proceeds from fraudulent investment schemes, eventually
returning the money to victims.

Harmon's was the one name I remembered from those
long nights Alison had spent with the federal suits after Harding had been indicted. His executive assistant told me that
her boss was in a high-level meeting and understandably was
not available on such short notice. Instead, she handed me off
to an assistant regional director named James Hartoonian,
who in turn punted me down the hall to the Investigative

Division. There, a bureaucrat named Lew Myerson made it clear he was juggling a massive caseload and was not happy to have his day disrupted by a taxpayer who seemed to be tilting at some sort of personal windmill. Still, he grudgingly agreed to give up five minutes of his time in a poorly lighted conference room with no windows, where he made a point of not offering me a cup of coffee or even a bottle of water. The message: we weren't going to be meeting long enough to bother with formalities.

I'd almost blown off my unannounced visit to the US Attorney's Office, but Marika assured me that my daughter was in good hands, and I didn't have to hand her off to Janelle's mom until later. Now, a sense of unease nipped at my brain as I wondered how this would all play out if Harding was indeed still alive. As well as Alison, of course. *What a convoluted mess,* I thought as I settled into a chair while Myerson perched his ass on the edge of a credenza. I sized the guy up, wondering if he was a lawyer like everyone else in the building seemed to be.

He explained that he'd worked in the area of cybercrimes for close to fifteen years and was responsible for prosecuting companies and individuals involved with the commission of all sorts of digital thefts, from Nigerian prince rackets to the illegal manipulation of global cybercurrencies. "There was a time when we spent most of our time and resources chasing down good old-fashioned securities and investment fraud, but the internet has changed all that," he told me. "Greed is still as big as ever, but bad actors are finding new ways to bilk their victims, and cybercrime is a growth business. We see everything from IRS phone call scams to bitcoin theft on a worldwide scale."

"Like Maxwell Harding?"

"Exactly, and for every Harding there's a bunch more lurking just below the surface," Myerson said. "But yeah, that piece of shit is a good example. Is that why you're here?"

I placed my cell phone face down on the table and nodded. I hadn't told him the reason for my visit, and he clearly didn't make a connection to my name. Not yet, at least. "I just have a couple questions about him and then I'll be out of your hair," I replied.

"Maxwell Harding is dead," the investigator replied as he tapped the door closed with the toe of his shoe. "I don't know what I can tell you that hasn't been all over the Web."

"At which point I'll be gone."

The expression on Myerson's face suggested he couldn't wait for that moment to arrive. He squinted at me over the rims of his thick plastic-rimmed glasses and said, "You understand this is still an open inquiry, so there's not a whole lot I can tell you."

"Even with Harding gone?"

"The criminal charges were dropped, but his death didn't change the fact that a boatload of money remains unaccounted for." The wary look continued, and deep creases appeared on his forehead. Then he said, "Wait—what did you say your name was?"

I repeated it for him, then a spark seemed to ignite in Myerson's otherwise dark eyes. "Damn . . . I know who you are. You're Alison Kane's husband."

"That's right," I said. "All I want is answers to a few questions."

Myerson nodded, and I could almost detect a hint of sympathy coming over him. He folded his hands together as if erecting an impenetrable wall of fingers and said, "An investigation was opened before he was killed, so we're working in tandem with the Civil Frauds Unit. I wouldn't be violating any confidences to tell you that Harding either stole or defrauded investors out of several billion dollars, and our job is to get it back. Or as much of it as we can."

"Have you had any luck with that?" I asked.

"Harding put failsafe measures in place that are making that task a little . . . problematic."

"Why is that?" I figured that as long as Myerson kept answering my questions, I'd continue to ask them.

"Because no one has ever seen the software language that was used to create his exclusive blockchain. It's a one-off, and there's a firewall no one can get through or around without knowing how it was constructed. You should know all this, since your wife wrote it."

"Seriously? Alison?"

While I had a good grasp of my wife's responsibilities at Harding's company, whenever she had discussed her day over a glass of wine or a late dinner, I usually got lost about fifteen seconds into it. I admitted as much to Myerson now, explaining how it always seemed so technical, so much number theory and quantum mathematics and prime number factorization.

"What about after Harding was indicted?" he asked.

"I know she was cooperating with you guys at the end. FBI, IRS, Treasury. But she said all that stuff was confidential, and never really went into it with me."

Myerson wandered over to where there would have been a window had this been a high-level conference room. The space was getting warm, and he took his time rolling up his shirtsleeves. Then he slowly turned and said, "I'm not sure how I can help you, Mr. Kane. It's been a year, like I said, and we really haven't made much progress."

"You can start by telling me if Alison was ever under suspicion in the Harding case," I replied. "As her husband, I think I have a right to know at least that much."

Myerson fiddled with one of his cuffs, then made a big show of settling into the black chair directly across from me. He leaned back and rested the heel of one shoe on the corner of the table. "Do you know what your wife's role was at Bit-XC?" he asked.

"She was executive vice president in charge of risk management."

"That's what it said on the corporate website and her business cards," Myerson said, dipping his head in a slight nod. "And as an EVP, she also was a member of the executive team that reported to the board of directors."

"Yeah, that sounds about right," I agreed.

"But do you know what she actually did? I mean, what sort of risk she was trying to manage?"

I gave him a slight shrug and said, "The way she explained it, she was involved with assessing financial liability, managing digital transactions, and eliminating the company's exposure to external pressures."

Myerson folded his hands behind his head and fixed his eyes directly on mine. "Yeah, that's how it's worded in the official job description. I studied every page of every employee file at that firm, so I would know. But you were married to her, so you tell me: What does all that really mean?"

He had me there.

Just then my phone vibrated. I looked at the screen, saw it was William Trent, probably checking to see where the hell I was, since I obviously wasn't at the licensing meeting that had been scheduled for our own conference room. I would have to do some serious damage control when this was all over, but right now it could wait. I sent the call to voicemail and set the phone back down on the table.

"Go ahead . . . tell me," I said.

"As I'm sure you know, your wife was one of the world's foremost experts on prime numbers. A particular kind, in fact—"

"Mersenne. Her undergrad expertise was what got her in the door at Yale, and she wrote her doctoral thesis about them."

"Exactly," Myerson again confirmed. "And from everything we've been able to dig up, Harding had a thing for them."

"That's why he hired her."

"Correct. But it wasn't just so he could discuss the topic at cocktail parties and impress other people with his knowledge. Harding was convinced that primes, as common as they are, also are some of the most transcendent mathematical concepts in the ordered universe. Almost as if they were the molecular mortar that held the cosmos together. He was a nut about them, figured they were mystical in some way. Spiritual, even."

I gave Myerson a quizzical look and said, "Okay, but Harding didn't hire Alison just so he could discuss prime numbers with her."

Myerson removed his shoe from the edge of the table and scooted his chair in. "No, he did not," he said. "Alison was involved with a lot of high-level security issues at the firm, and she adapted a form of advanced approximation theory to write Harding's cryptocurrency security program."

"She mentioned that sort of stuff from time to time," I told him. "But I never came close to knowing what she was talking about."

"Me neither," Myerson admitted with a tight grin. "Your wife was very helpful in our investigation, but after she died . . . well, we had to bring in a bunch of geeks to help us figure out what she'd done."

"How did that go?"

"All I can tell you is that she was focused on creating a predictor program that had to do with approximating algorithmic functions and—pardon me if I don't get this exactly right—quantitatively characterizing any errors introduced through those algorithms."

"This is where she usually lost me," I said with a flustered sigh. "Can you just tell me what this all means?"

The assistant chief of the cybercrime investigative unit eyed me with a look of sympathy, maybe even compassion. "I've already told you more than I should have," he said. "Like I said, it's still an active investigation."

"And all I want to know is whether Alison was cleared of all the stuff her boss was charged with," I countered.

He didn't answer right away, but when he did, it was preceded by a long sigh. "As I've mentioned, we've had trouble cracking the proprietary blockchain," he said.

"The digital ledger that kept track of the company's bitcoin transactions."

"Yes, but there was more to it than that. Before she . . . well, before the accident, she told us that she'd started to grow suspicious that Harding's intentions at Bit-XC were less than honorable. In fact, the word she used was 'nefarious.' He demanded that she create a digital backdoor into the program, which she was worried would allow him to get past the firewall and manipulate the data."

"And siphon money out of the company," I guessed.

"Exactly. She went ahead and did what he asked—her employment at the firm depended on it—but she also devised a worm that would tunnel into any computer that tried to slip through that backdoor. Whereupon it would shut it down."

"Like a ransomware attack?"

Myerson's forehead creased in a deep scowl, and he said, "Same principle. It would launch a program that would erase the entire hard drive, along with any others that might be connected to the corporate network."

"And when Harding went through that backdoor, the firewall shut his computer down."

Myerson gave me a weary nod and said, "That one and then another and then another. The company's entire network crashed. Harding started getting desperate, and for good reason. By our estimation, over four billion dollars in cybercurrency—depending on daily market fluctuations—was sitting out there in the ether, and he had no idea how to get to it."

"What about Alison? She had to know."

"That's what she was helping us with," Myerson said. "The worm she planted in the program was designed to shut the whole thing down, and she used advanced approximation theory to create a sort of countermeasure, should one ever be needed."

"And with her gone . . . " I said, my words trailing off.

"We've tried everything, but we haven't been able to figure out how the damned thing works. And the hackers from Princeton and MIT—even a couple from China and Russia—couldn't do shit. Alison was a math prodigy, and no one has been able to come close to reproducing what she created. Anything more than that, you'll have to talk to Deputy Director Brody at Homeland."

"Who's that?"

"The piece of bureaucratic red tape that's been holding this whole thing together," Myerson explained.

"How can I get in touch with him? Do you have a number?"

"What I have is a piece of advice," he said. "Leave this alone."

"I just want a word with him."

Myerson raised his palm to stop me, indicating that was all. "Listen, Mr. Kane, you're free to track down Deputy Director Brody if you want to. I can't stop you. But I can tell you this: you want nothing to do with that man. Scumbag would eat his own children for breakfast if he ran out of bacon."

CHAPTER

22

B Y THE TIME I hit the lobby downstairs, I was already
dialing the general number for Homeland Security in
Washington.

A live person picked up on the second ring, which I
thought was promising until she slipped me into voicemail
hell. I chose the instructions in English, listened thoroughly
to all the selections because the menu had changed, then
punched in the options that might bring me closer to my
goal. Just as I arrived at the Chambers Street subway station, I actually tagged another live person, who didn't prove
any more useful than when I'd entered the automated phone
labyrinth.

"Is the deputy director expecting your call?" the man on
the other end asked.

"He should be," I lied. Cell reception could be spotty
down in the subway tunnels, so I remained up on the
street, leaning against the concrete barrier that kept drunks
and kids from toppling into the New York underground.
"Please tell him it's regarding the Maxwell Harding case in
New York."

"I'm sorry, but Mr. Brody isn't available to take calls at the moment," the man on the phone said.

"But he is in the office?"

"I really don't know, Mr. . . ."

"Kane. Cameron Kane. If you can just let Mr. Brody know that I'm calling, I'm sure he'd want to speak with me."

"That may be, sir. But I don't have access to the deputy director at this time. We're not even in the same building. I'd be happy to put you through to his voicemail."

Voicemail he'll never return, I knew. But I had no other option here, so I said, "Okay, that would be fine."

There was a clicking sound while the call was routed through the department's phone system again. I had no idea who I'd just spoken with or how to get back to him without going through the entire automation circus again. Then the system forwarded me through to Brody's voicemail, which I figured was periodically monitored by an assistant who probably never forwarded cold calls to the boss.

I left a quick and straightforward message, along with my cell number. Then I repeated my name, thanked Brody for his time, and ended the call.

* * *

Marika lived on the upper West Side, but earlier I'd agreed to meet her at Bryant Park on 42nd. It was a long haul back uptown from the US Attorney's Office, but about halfway between her place and mine. She'd volunteered to bring Sabrina all the way back down to the Village, which would have been more convenient for me, but I wanted to spend some time with Sabrina alone before I dropped her off at Janelle's place.

"What about later?" Marika asked as Sabrina chased a few pigeons across the grass. "It's pretty rare that you get a weeknight free. Like never."

"My boss threw a ton of work at me at the last minute," I said. "Taking a few days off always catches up with you."

"C'mon, Mr. K. You have to eat."

I wanted to level with her. Tell her about my chance encounter at JFK, the mysterious disappearing text, the dental X-rays—everything. I felt I owed Marika an explanation for my sudden distancing, even if I ended up sounding absolutely, positively nuts. She was the innocent party in all this and had done nothing wrong, and it was unfair to string her along, especially if it turned out that Alison was still alive.

"There's a great Italian place on Lexington," she suggested. "My treat."

"I really don't think . . ."

"Then let me do the thinking," Marika said, touching a finger to my forehead. "I promise I'll get you home at a reasonable hour. So you can do all that work."

I ran through a whole host of excuses in my mind, couldn't come up with one that sounded even close to reasonable. "Okay, sounds good," I agreed. "Except for one thing. I'm paying."

"Works for me," she replied, leaning up and kissing my brow where her fingers had just been. "I'll make reservations."

What the hell are you doing? I asked myself after Marika gave me a quick kiss and I slipped into a taxi next to my daughter.

"West Village," I told the driver. "Jane Street."

*   *   *

Sabrina had slept over at Janelle's home several times over the past year, always on weekends and never when there was anything school related planned for the next day. When my last-minute trip to LA had come up last week, she'd camped out with her friend Hannah, mostly because Janelle's mother had the same school-night rule as I did. Except, it seemed, when the next day included a trip to the zoo. I still felt a nagging guilt for forgetting my daughter's half day, but I also had an intuitive sense that I was going to need all my wits about me over the next twenty-four hours. My meetings with Elise Dillon and Dr. Cook had given just enough dimension to my far-fetched alternative universe that even the rational side of my brain was beginning to sense a glimmer of hope. Plus, my lunch with Mrs. Harding had left me feeling that even Mickey Donovan believed my suspicions weren't automatic grounds for the looney bin.

"You'll be okay tonight?" I asked Sabrina as we packed a few necessities into a small overnight bag.

"Why wouldn't I be?"

A few months back, when Sabrina had gone to a slumber party at Janelle's house, I'd received a phone call at two in the morning, telling me she'd awakened with a horrible case of nightmares. It was just a stage she'd been going through and totally understandable, considering the recent loss of her mother. Watching *Bambi* earlier in the evening hadn't helped, thank you very much. Fortunately, the episode had been an anomaly, and nothing like it had happened again. Even so, I didn't want a repeat performance.

"Never mind," I told her as I squeezed her hand. "You'll be fine."

"Of course I'll be fine," she said, giving me her best look of indignation. "I'm not a little kid, you know."

"No, you're not," I agreed. "You're growing up every day."

She beamed at my words, but I still wasn't going to let my cell phone out of my sight until I heard that she had made it to school in the morning.

* * *

"Why do I get the idea that this sleepover was at least partly your idea?" I asked Marika later as I inhaled the night air, a richly scented mix of the full urban experience.

We had just left the Italian restaurant on the East Side and had slowly strolled over to Fifth Avenue. I was having difficulty focusing on the here and now, especially the woman who had just hooked her arm through mine.

The aroma of falafel and grilled bratwurst and pretzels lingered from food carts that had been parked along the sidewalk earlier in the day. Taxi exhaust rose from the pavement as an onslaught of cabs raced downtown, and pedestrians acted like crazed squirrels as they darted through the intersections. Ghosts of steam seeped from manhole covers set in the pavement, and a faint thread of jasmine or gardenias or lilacs—or maybe it was Marika's perfume—hung sweetly in the night air.

"Sabrina and her friend cooked it up all by themselves," she insisted, shaking her head. "But I have to admit, it sounded like a fine idea."

"Just so you know, we have a rule about sleepovers on school nights."

"As you should. But Sabrina was excited about it, and I thought it would be nice to just have time to be alone with you. Besides, it's just this once."

"You're right," I said, trying to let go of my control impulse. Still, I felt a tightness in my chest and realized parent–child separation anxiety was a two-way street. "I'm just being OCD. Thank you for picking her up today. You saved my ass."

"And what a fine ass it is," she said with a giggle. "Besides, spending time with Sabrina was a lot more fun than working on sales presentations all afternoon."

"Well, anyway, I owe you one."

"My thinking exactly," Marika said, pecking me lightly on the cheek. "When do I get to collect?"

"What do you have in mind?"

"You know perfectly well what I have in mind."

"I told you, I have a mountain of work," I replied.

"You can't be a slave to your boss all night long," Marika said as she tugged on my hand to slow me down. It was then that I realized we were standing in front of Tiffany's on Fifth Avenue, the empty windows looking lonely and naked. All the expensive jewelry had been stashed in the store's safe for the night, leaving only our reflections staring back at us. It was like a scene right out of one of Alison's favorite Audrey Hepburn movies, an irony that was not lost on me for a second.

"I promise I'll make it up to you as soon as I can," I said.

We stood there facing each other, traffic racing by on one side, a dark jewelry store window on the other. Then she leaned up to kiss me, barely enough to cause a spark. The animated devil and angel sitting on opposite shoulders were engaged in a real dustup, one side arguing about decency and loyalty while the other dangled the lure of opportunity. Meanwhile, Marika pressed harder, and I felt like Adam in the Garden of Eden, succumbing to temptations of the flesh.

Please forgive me, Alison, I thought. So much for resolve.

Then my cell phone rang, and I was jolted back to reality. Sabrina was staying at Janelle's house, and I had to make sure it wasn't an emergency. Something unanticipated or like the night terrors of last time.

"I have to take this, just in case," I said.

"Of course you do," Marika said as I pulled the phone out of my pocket. The number on the screen wasn't in my contacts, but I answered it anyway.

"Quick daughter check-in," I assured her. "I'll only be a minute."

"Sure. Take your time."

I took a step away and pushed the "Talk" button. "This is Kane," I said.

"Mr. Kane—it's Mickey Donovan," the private detective said in a hurried voice. "No time to go into details, but I've come up with a few things. Can you meet me tomorrow? It looks like we may really be onto something."

We, not *you*.

"Like what?" I asked him.

"I'll tell you tomorrow."

"Where?"

"Same place, same time as before."

"I'll be there," I said.

"Come alone . . . and make sure you're not being followed."

I lowered my voice so Marika couldn't hear me. "Why would anyone be following me?"

"Just do what I say and you'll be fine," the detective told me. "And listen, make sure no one knows where you're going. And that means *no one*."

After I hung up, I stared at the phone a second, then explained to Marika that Sabrina wasn't feeling well, and

Janelle's mom had asked if I could come and get her. Just to err on the side of caution.

"I really need to go," I said, yet another rejection in a long string of them. "I promise I'll make it up to you when I know what's going on."

"What do you mean by 'what's going on?'" Marika asked. "Is this about Sabrina, or isn't it?"

"Yes," I said. "But . . . well, it's complicated."

"If there's someone else, now would be a good time to let me know."

You'd never believe me if I did, I thought. "No, it's nothing like that," I said instead. I wanted to level with her, but this was neither the time nor the place. "Rain check?"

"*Rain check*? We've been in a goddamn drought since the day we met."

"I know, and I'll explain everything as soon as I can."

"Well, call me when you're good and ready," she said. "I might pick up if I'm still in a dry spell." With that, she marched to the curb and stuck out her hand for a cab.

After her taxi drove off, I hailed one of my own and went directly home. I felt awful and had no one to blame but me. Marika didn't deserve the cold shoulder, and until last Saturday, I'd been comfortable with the idea of gradually letting her into my life. Sabrina's too. I'd tried not to think about love and all the attendant confusion that might bring. But she seemed cool with the idea of letting things progress slowly as long as they progressed.

"Andante, andante," I'd told her a few days before my trip to LA.

"No, presto," Marika had countered, with a playful giggle. "Prestissimo."

Now it seemed I'd blown all that.

23

Friday

IT FELT UNSEASONABLY cold when I let myself into the condo, a chill I attributed not only to a weather front that was moving in but also to Marika's understandably icy departure.

I poured myself a bourbon I probably didn't need, and sat down on the couch in the living room. At some point I must have fallen asleep, and that's where I was when my phone rang, long past midnight. It was on the coffee table, and as I reached out for it—worried that something actually *had* happened to Sabrina—I swept it onto the carpeted floor.

When I picked it up and answered, a woman on the other end yelled, "You bastard!"

"Who is this?" I asked, blinking the sleep out of my eyes.

"You almost got me killed, you asshole!" the woman's voice yelled at me. "I never should have met with you!"

"Please . . . calm down," I said. "Who is this?"

"*Calm down?* This is Elise Dillon, Mr. Kane! And do you have any fucking idea what you've done to me?"

"Wait . . . please, what are you talking about?"

"What I'm talking about is someone tried to kill me," she seethed. "And it's all your goddamn fault."

"You're not making sense, Mrs. Dillon." I sat upright at full attention. "What do you mean, someone tried to kill you?"

There was a long silence on the other end, and I sensed Mrs. Dillon was trying to catch her breath. "They knew I met with you," she finally said. "They must have."

"Please . . . who are *they*?" I asked her. "Just slow down and tell me what happened."

"What happened is someone followed me home tonight," Mrs. Dillon said. She was still breathing hard, but at least she had calmed down a notch. "After I met with you this morning, I pretty much wandered around the city and did nothing for the rest of the day. Tonight I caught a Broadway show, a god-awful musical that still had single seats available. After that I took the train back to Stamford. They must have been waiting in the lot or somewhere along the street, because right after I left the station, a car pulled out behind me."

What was it Detective Donovan had told me just a few hours ago? *Make sure no one is following you.*

"This car . . . it could have just been someone going in the same direction," I suggested, trying to ease her panic. "How do you know it was after you?"

"Because I made a few turns, and it stayed right there behind me. I drove around the block twice, then backtracked. They followed me the entire time, and when I turned onto Middlesex Road, that's when they tried to kill me!"

"You're still not making sense, Mrs. Dillon."

"Sense? You expect any of this to make sense? Jesus, Mr. Kane, I'm calling you from the hospital. Don't you understand? Those bastards ran me off the goddamn road!"

I heard a voice on the other end, asking her to please keep her voice down. Probably a nurse, looking out for other patients. There was a brief pause that included a few short, ragged breaths, then Elise said, "I'm telling you . . . they tried to kill me."

I stood up and walked to the back door, peered through the glass at our little backyard patio—the one Sabrina and I hardly ever used anymore. There had to be a rational explanation for what had happened to this poor woman tonight.

"What about the car?" I asked her.

"My car? Who gives a shit about my car—?"

"Not your car . . . the one that was following you."

"It drove past me, then slowed down and stopped," she explained.

"What happened after that?"

"Jesus Christ . . . is your head made of stone?"

I heard that same voice in the background again, once more warning Mrs. Dillon to lower her volume, and she said, "I'm sorry—I promise I'll keep it down." Then to me, she said, "After that is when they tried to blow me away."

I'd been downplaying her hysteria, but now alarm bells were going off inside my thick skull. "How do you mean, blow you away," I asked.

"Goddamn it, Kane, listen to me. I was still sitting behind the wheel, trapped because of the airbag. Blood was dripping from my forehead, and I was shaking all over. Then I saw this man coming toward me with a big gun in his hand. I thought he was going to kill me."

A gun? Holy shit. "But he didn't," I pointed out, unable to produce a more cogent response.

"Damn right he didn't. But only because a man who lived in a nearby house turned on a floodlight and came out into the driveway. He called out, asked if anyone was hurt. That's when the man with the gun took off."

"Did you call the police?" I asked.

"How do you think I got to the hospital?" she replied. "Look, Mr. Kane. I'm scared. Earlier today I thought . . . well, I didn't want to hear what you were telling me. I thought you were crazy. But now . . ."

Her voice trailed off, and I heard a loud thud. Then a woman in the background yelled, "Christ, she fainted. Quick—someone help me!"

24

"You're sure no one followed you?"

It was ten hours after Elise Dillon's frantic phone call, and Mickey Donovan was sitting beside me at the far end of the bar at Ryan's. Same place we'd met just forty-eight hours ago, but now he was viewing the place from a totally different perspective.

So was I.

"Absolutely positive," I said.

"How did you get to work this morning?"

"Subway, like usual. But I changed my route, since my daughter had a sleepover at a friend's house. Instead of walking her to school, I took the subway directly to my office. I stayed there until twenty minutes ago, walked a few blocks out of my way, and made a quick stop at the bank. No one was behind me the entire way. I'm sure of it."

Donovan said nothing, just grunted.

"I really didn't think you'd find anything so quickly," I continued.

"Neither did I. To be honest, I thought you were a total crackpot the other day when you told me your story."

"Yeah, I kind of figured," I replied. "What changed your mind?"

"I did a little digging, and that resource I told you about hit a couple of three-pointers."

"Looks like we got a fast break," I said, continuing the basketball analogy.

"It's going to cost me a couple of Knicks tickets next season, lower level near center court. But I've got a contact at the Garden, so you're not on the hook for 'em."

"I'm not worried about the money," I told him. "What did this resource of yours find?"

"Well, a couple things, really," Donovan said. He took a long swig of beer, then reached down to the floor and picked up a leatherette portfolio I hadn't noticed when I'd sat down. He opened it and took out a glossy black folder that had no label on it. "First, there's video from JFK. Five different angles of your guy, starting with when he comes out of the jetway."

"How were you able to do that so quick?"

"Not me, my resource. He found out that a Mr. Joseph Zaccaro was, in fact, flying on a Brazilian passport, seated in first class. "Latin America flight 8414. He preordered a gluten-free meal, if that makes any difference."

"It does," I told him, feeling an electric pulse humming through my nerves. "I remember Harding saying at one of his parties that he couldn't eat cake because he was allergic to wheat."

"You didn't put that in the file you gave me," Donovan said.

"I didn't remember until just now. Do you have any stills from the video?"

The former cop took his time opening the folder on the bar in front of him. He glanced around nervously, carefully checking out everyone in the place, then rotated the folder so I could look at it.

"The video was a little grainy, but Zemira—he's my resource—was able to get it enhanced."

"Zemira?" I asked, emphasis on the second syllable, which was pronounced *eye*. "What kind of name is that?"

Donovan shot me a tight grin and said, "One you don't want to mess with. We go way back to Desert Storm."

"You were in the military?" I asked him.

"MPs," Donovan replied. "It's what I did before I joined the NYPD. And Moon—that's Zemira's last name—was some sort of special forces later, in Afghanistan. Anyway, I want you to take a close look and tell me if this is your guy. Mr. Zaccaro."

I felt the excitement build as I looked at the photo that had been lifted from one of the videos. Then, just as quickly as the excitement had come, a new wave of disappointment hit me. I looked at the man's face again, then let out a heavy sigh.

"That's not him," I said at length, shaking my head.

"You're positive?" Donovan asked. "This isn't the man you chased outside and saw get into a cab?"

"Absolutely not," I stated, feeling discouraged and defeated. "Not even close. The guy I saw was on the thinner side, longer face, sunglasses. Silver and black in his hair. This man is heavier, with a wider head and big ears. Not the same clothing either. Harding was wearing a tailored suit, but this guy is in jeans and a sweatshirt. I can't tell how tall he is, but I'm sure it's not Zaccaro. And definitely not Harding."

Mickey Donovan tightened his lips, then lowered his head in a slight nod. "Good, because that man is not Mr. Zaccaro, and he wasn't on the flight from Rio. He was coming in from Phoenix."

I shot him a dark look and said, "What the fuck—?"

"Settle down, Kane. This picture was my one-man control group, just to make sure you're certain you saw what you thought you saw. Take a look at the next photo." Donovan flashed me a go-ahead nod, and I flipped the page to the next image.

This time there wasn't a shred of hesitation, and I said, "That's him."

"You're sure."

"Completely. What else have you got?"

"Take a look." Donovan indicated with his hand that I was free to glance through the remaining photos. "As I said, there was a lot of video of him, shot from several good angles. Including one when he brushes past you. And I have to say, he seemed like he was in one hell of a hurry."

"This Zemira Moon—how was he able to get this stuff so quickly?"

"He has his ways."

"You watched it?" I asked.

"Enough to know you weren't some gonzo nut case. In fact, in one video it looks like you called out to him, and he reacted with a distinct hesitation in his step. Then he seemed to speed up as you started to go after him."

There were six photos in the folder, all eight-by-ten color shots pulled from the airport's security cameras. "That's exactly how it happened," I said. "Did you get any video of when he does the speed-walk thing past the limo driver?"

"Mr. Zaccaro definitely slows down to take a quick look, then keeps on going," Donovan assured me. "That's a screen grab right there."

I studied the image of the Black chauffeur holding his sign, the passenger named Zaccaro appearing to eye him as he hurried by. "What about outside, when he gets to the taxi line?" I asked. "Is there any footage from out there?"

"Too many shadows to get a good shot of his face—or yours," Donovan said. "But that's not why the camera is there."

"Then what's it for?"

"Passenger security," Donovan explained. "You see, every cab that lines up in the official queue needs to be licensed to the city of New York, with an official medallion. No ride shares, no private cars. And every vehicle that stops at that taxi stand is logged on video, not only by its license plate but also by its official Taxi and Limousine Commission number."

"Then you were able to track where it went after it sped off?" I pressed him. "It had to be a hotel, maybe an office building."

"Try Wallingford, Connecticut. Ever hear of it?"

"I grew up outside Hartford," I said with a slow nod. "It's somewhere around New Haven, I think."

"A few miles north of it, in fact."

I frowned a second, trying to make sense of what I was hearing. "Why the hell would he take a cab all the way up there?" I finally asked.

"Keep in mind, he'd already booked a private town car, but you spoiled that plan," Donovan reminded me. "He had to take a taxi instead. The cab driver remembered him when I tracked him down. Apparently, Mr. Zaccaro tipped him two hundred dollars to stick around, then give him a ride back to the city."

"So, what was he doing in that part of Connecticut, especially for what I presume was a short time?"

"He paid a visit to a private boarding school up there," Donovan replied. "It seems he looked in on the boys' varsity lacrosse team."

"I'm not sure I'm following you," I said.

"The cab driver said Zaccaro demanded to be driven to the school's athletic center, where he sat and watched the team get on a bus. They were playing in a tournament up in Springfield and were loading up their equipment. Zaccaro watched them from the back seat of the cab, and when the bus pulled out of the parking lot, he asked to be driven back to Manhattan."

I thought about this for a second, and then a flashbulb went off in my brain. "Mrs. Harding told me yesterday that their son graduates from Choate next month. Headed to Princeton in the fall."

"Choate Rosemary Hall, actually," Donovan said. "Did she happen to mention that this son of theirs, name of Cyrus, is a midfielder on the lacrosse team?"

I actually let out a low whistle, then said, "You think Harding flew all the way up from Brazil to get a brief glimpse of his son?"

"It fits the scenario," he replied. "But what's the real question you should be asking?"

I said nothing for a minute as my brain went to work on what Donovan had just asked. I never liked being tested this way, someone asking me a leading question that made me feel like a dumbass for not already knowing the answer. I chewed on the question a few seconds before the answer popped into my head. "Where did the driver drop him in New York?" I said.

"Precisely," Donovan replied. "Seems the address—which the cabbie dutifully called into his dispatcher, who then provided it to me for a nice consulting fee—was a building downtown in the Financial District. On William Street, to be exact."

"Do you have the address?"

"I do, but I'm not giving it to you. The less you know at this time, the better off you are."

At that moment the bartender wandered up and asked if either of us wanted another drink or whether we'd like to see the bar menu. Donovan shook him off, then looked me in the eyes. "Without getting into specifics, Mr. Zaccaro checked himself into an apartment at a private—and, I might say, extremely exclusive—residential club."

I was still trying to soak this all in, feeling my heart race a little faster with each beat. "And he's a member of this club?"

"No," Donovan replied, shaking his head. "And neither was Harding, before the accident. But with a little assistance from Ben Franklin"—he rubbed the tips of his fingers together, the common gesture indicating a payoff—"I was able to track down who owns the place where he signed in."

"And?"

"I'll get to all that," Donovan said. His eyes roamed the bar, then blinked rapidly at something he seemed to see in the growing lunchtime crowd. "But first things first. And the first thing is, we need to get out of here."

"What are you talking about?"

"Now," he replied. "Let's walk."

I peeled a couple of bills out of my wallet and left them on the bar. "What's going on?" I asked as I tried to keep up with him, out the door, past the scaffolding, and up the sidewalk to Madison Avenue. When the light changed, we turned south and crossed the street directly in front of a box truck advertising plumbing fixtures. The entire time Donovan kept glancing around feverishly, studying the bustle of office workers who were streaming out of their buildings onto the sidewalks of Manhattan.

"Why are we walking like this?" I was struggling to keep up with Donovan, which meant I couldn't get a good fix on his eyes, to gauge how much paranoia was boiling in there. "Where are we going?"

"We were sitting ducks in that place. Far end of the bar, no way out except through the front door. Literally up against the wall."

"You picked the stools," I reminded him. "Please tell me what this is all about."

He gave me a quick flick of a glance before he said, "What this is about is the firm that owns the residence in that building I told you about."

"You're going to have to be more specific than that."

"In a minute, when we're not out here like ducks on a pond," the detective said, maintaining his rapid pace. "All you need to know is that it's enough to get us both killed."

CHAPTER

25

"CHRIST, MAN—WHO'S SOUNDING crazy now?"
"Grand Central, one block over," Donovan
abruptly ordered me as he stepped into the crosswalk. "We'll
mix with the crowd, and then I'll tell you what this is all about."

We charged along in silence, Donovan a couple steps
ahead of me. He clutched the leatherette portfolio close to
his body as he abruptly stepped off the sidewalk, waited while
a black Land Rover raced by, the rugged Defender model
usually associated with safaris in the African bush. I dodged
around a delivery van to catch up, then made up some of the
distance between us. Donovan hooked right onto Vanderbilt
Avenue, then angled toward the bank of doors that opened
into the cavernous railway station. The detective took one
last look behind him, threw the door open for me, and practically pushed me inside. Then we hurried down the marble
steps into the massive structure that served as Grand Central
Terminal.

I wove my way behind Donovan until we were immersed
in the bustling noontime crowd. Then I placed my hand on
the ex-cop's shoulder and forcibly slowed him down.

"Okay, we're here," I said, more winded than I should have been. "What gives?"

Donovan stopped near the information kiosk in the middle of the colossal structure. Once more he glanced around, then turned to face me for the first time since we'd left the bar.

"All right," Donovan said. "We should be safe here, at least for a bit."

"Safe from what?" I asked him. When he didn't immediately respond, I said, "Come on, Donovan, what's going on?"

He was momentarily distracted by a voice on the PA system announcing a train arrival, then said, "Remember back at the bar, we were talking about that apartment down near Wall Street? I did a little digging, found out it belongs to a shell company, which is a subsidiary of another shell company. That's when I first called Zemira Moon."

"You're sure it was necessary to get this guy involved?"

"He has access to people and things that I don't." Donovan hesitated a second, as if considering just how much I needed to know. Then he said, "Does the name 'Ironbridge' mean anything to you?"

"No," I replied. "Should it?"

"Not unless you subscribe to *Soldier of Fortune* magazine," he said. "It's a private security firm—founded by some ex-paramilitary thugs—that does a lot of contract work in both the public and private sector."

"What sort of contract work?"

"The official line is that they provide training support to military and law enforcement organizations, and supply security to individuals and businesses to protect their personnel and corporate secrets."

"I sense a big 'but' somewhere in there," I said.

All of a sudden Donovan grabbed my arm and turned me around. "Move. Downstairs to the food court."

"It's packed down there this time of day."

"Exactly."

We moved, Donovan physically pushing me toward the marble stairs that led into the basement. I was right; the place was jammed with tourists and office workers and train passengers on the prowl for lunch, but I suspected that was his plan all along. We pressed through the hundreds of workers scrambling to buy pizza or sandwiches or salads until Donovan came to an abrupt stop near Wexler's Deli. Then he said, "We don't have much time before we need to split up, so I'm going to tell you the basics, at least until I learn more. The fact is, unofficially, Ironbridge is a facilitator."

"What does that mean?"

"It means that if you want something done—and by something, I mean *anything*—they're the folks you call," Donovan explained, eyes darting around constantly, looking for whatever they were looking for. "They operate strictly on the dark web, so everything is done in the deepest shadows of the internet."

"Like that Silk Road website that the feds busted a few years back?"

"Worse. Fact is, the dark web is called that because it caters to the murkiest of human tendencies and depravities. Websites that sell drugs, hacking software, hijacked identities, sex trafficking—whatever your little black heart desires."

"Murder for hire?" I asked.

"For the right price. Anyway, the place where Mr. Zaccaro rested his head for two nights after his trip to Connecticut ultimately is owned by the shareholders of Ironbridge."

"What's his association with them? Does he work for them?"

"More like a customer, based on what Zemira Moon was able to discern," Donovan replied. "But what he did find, you're not going to like one bit."

I already didn't like what I was hearing, but I'd hired Donovan to come up with the truth, wherever it led. "Hit me," I said.

Donovan waited a moment before he spoke, either for emphasis or because he didn't want to be the bearer of difficult news. "Ironbridge is also your new girlfriend's employer."

"Who?"

"The woman you know as Marika."

"That's total horseshit," I told him, shaking my head rapidly in total denial. "She's a sales rep for a cable network."

"Who told you that?"

"She did."

"Have you ever seen her office?"

"She's hardly ever there. She said she mostly visits clients out in the field."

Donovan nodded. "What do you really know about her?"

"I know that she has a name," I replied, growing annoyed by where this discussion was going. "Marika, like you said. Marika Landry."

"For the record, it's Gina Collins. Her prints are in IAFIS."

"IAFIS?"

"Stands for Integrated Automated Fingerprint Identification System," the ex-cop said as he handed me another photo. "It's the largest law enforcement database in the world."

I took a quick glance at the picture—an image of her kissing a man as she got out of a black SUV—then handed it back. I said nothing for a moment, and then a feeling of utter defeat swept through me. "Okay, Donovan." I sighed. "You've got my attention. Tell me what you think you know."

Donovan took one more look around and said, "It's best if we keep moving."

We started walking again, going nowhere in particular, dodging office workers as we pretended to study the steam trays and sandwich counters. Eventually I stopped him and said, "Are you going to tell me why Marika's prints are in this database?"

"I thought you'd never ask," Donovan replied. "On the surface her story is pretty typical. Grew up in East Lansing. Attended Michigan State but didn't graduate, moved to New York four years ago. Worked for a shipping company over in Brooklyn until she got busted. Possession with intent to sell."

"Intent to sell what?" I asked.

"Cocaine. Two pounds, give or take. She claimed it was her boyfriend's, but that's what they always say. Anyway, she suddenly finds she's in one big heap of trouble, looking at serious jail time. Then along comes Ironbridge, in the form of a man named Walter Toole. He's the shithead who put her there on the escalator when her scarf got all tangled up."

"Like I said before, this is all horseshit."

"Is it?" Donovan asked. "Think back."

I did, recalled how Marika had casually stepped in front of me that day at the Deutsche Bank Center. She'd flashed me a flirty smile, and then the silk Hermes scarf dangling from her neck appeared to get snagged in the moving stairs.

"I am such an idiot," I finally said.

"You were an easy mark," Donovan countered, offering just a thread of compassion. "Grieving widower, single parent with a daughter to raise. Eleven months since your wife died.

Looking for companionship, dinners out, walks in the park. Maybe something physical."

"You make it sound like one of those personal ads in the newspaper," I said.

"Hooking up is mostly done online these days," he replied.

I rolled my eyes and felt my skin flush from embarrassment. Or was it anger? "We haven't gotten to that point yet," I said. "The hooking up part, I mean."

"Not pertinent to my investigation."

"What I don't get is why? Why all the deceit and the lies, and why now?"

"Now, that's where it really gets interesting," Donovan said as he sidestepped an elderly woman pulling a rollaboard bag through the food court. "To keep an eye on you."

"Why the fuck would they do that?"

Donovan said nothing at first, just reached into a pocket and pulled out four small objects, each of them about the size of a Tylenol capsule.

"Know what these are?" he asked.

I took one from him, turned it over in my hand. "That looks like a lens," I said. "A very small one."

"Precisely. These are cameras. And not just any camera, but high-definition color. Motion sensitive, to save energy. Each of them is equipped with a tiny transmitter capable of sending a signal up to two miles."

"Where did you find these?"

"Where do you think?"

I didn't have to think at all as I handed them back to him. "You mean they were in my home?"

"Along with no fewer than ten audio devices," Donovan told me. "The entire place was wired for sound and video. Plus, I found a keylogger installed in your computer."

"A what?"

"It's a device that captures every keystroke you make. It's an easy way to track what someone—in this case, you—has been looking at online, and good ones are almost impossible to detect."

"How do you know . . . I mean, what makes you think it was Marika?"

"Has she ever been alone in your home?"

"Damn" was all I could say.

"Does she have a key?"

"She knows where I keep a spare." I closed my eyes and shuddered at how naive I'd been. "This surveillance . . . it was twenty-four-seven?" I asked him.

"Until about two hours ago," Donovan replied. "I didn't even know about these when I called you last night, but after you cleared out of your place this morning, I slipped in. Sorry I didn't ask for permission."

Now it was my turn to feel paranoid. I ran a cautious gaze over the crowd in the food court but had no idea what I should be looking for. "What I don't get is why. Why they bugged my home and why they put Marika in my life."

He seemed as perplexed as I did. "Think back to when you met her," he pressed. "Do you remember anything peculiar happening around that time?"

I ran a mental calculation back to the escalator at the Deutsche Bank Center. That was three weeks and what . . . four, five days ago? I hadn't done anything to warrant suspicion, and my life seemed to be in a holding pattern. Although I'd sensed—hoped—I was gaining altitude.

Then it hit me. "The phone call," I said.

"The what?"

"Remember that mysterious text I told you about, the one I received this past Saturday night? When I checked my phone records, I found I'd missed a call from the same number three weeks before. Two days before I met Marika."

"Who was it?" Donovan asked.

"I don't know. It only lasted two seconds or so."

"Wrong number?"

"Damned if I know." I felt the hairs on the back of my neck prickle, that sort of crazy feeling you get when you know someone is watching you. "Do you think these bastards are responsible for what happened to my wife?"

"Look, Mr. Kane. Everything that's happened over the last year appears to be one grand deception, and somehow your wife is central to the whole thing."

"That's bullshit. You can't possibly think she's involved with these assholes."

"That's not at all what I'm saying, but one way or the other, there's a connection." Donovan cast another quick glance around, must have felt comfortable with where we were. For now.

"What kind of connection?" I asked him.

"I'm still working on that, and I hope to have solid answers soon. Meanwhile, let's back up a bit. According to Moon, Ironbridge was founded by an ex-military brute named Eagleton, who got caught smuggling shit home from Afghanistan. And by shit, I mean heroin in its purest form. He and his thugs seem to have direct ties to the intelligence community through a CIA dick named Brody—"

"Wait . . . did you say Brody?" I interrupted him.

"That's right. Long-time bureaucrat and spook. Right now he's at Homeland, but he's a career Company man. And a larcenous bastard."

This had to be the same Brody that Lew Myerson had mentioned just yesterday, the one he'd said would eat his own kids for breakfast. The same one I'd stupidly cold-called and left a message for, with my name and phone number.

"They have to have an end game," I said. "A point to all this."

"They do, and there is," Donovan replied. "I just thought I should give you an update. And a warning."

"A warning about what?"

"Tell me . . . where's your daughter, right this minute?"

As soon as the words left his lips, a massive chill raced up my spine. "She's on a school trip at the Central Park Zoo," I said. "She slept over at a friend's house last night. A girl named Janelle, and her mom was going to bring her to school this morning."

"I'm sure she's in good hands," Donovan assured me. "But you get my point: these SOBs are swine, plain and simple. You'd do well to keep your little girl close."

"Believe me, I will," I said.

"Thing is, none of this is why I called you last night. The real zinger, what Moon tracked down, is in here."

The detective handed the leatherette case to me and started to say something else, but at that instant I heard a loud crack, like a branch snapping off a tree. In the same instant Mickey Donovan was slammed backward into the hard concrete of the Grand Central food court, a red bloom the size of a large rose sprouting from his chest. A mist of warm liquid hit me on the side of my head and then—a fraction of a second later—I heard a scream. Just one scream at first, and then another and another.

I INSTINCTIVELY DROPPED TO my knees to help him. Blood was oozing from his shoulder, and fragments of flesh and bone had blown across the floor from the force of the slug that had torn through his body.

People around us shrieked and scrambled for cover. So far, the gunman had fired only once, but he was sure to do it again. I had no idea where he might be positioned, and I doubted Donovan was his primary target. Then I wondered if Donovan had been the mark at all; what if the shooter was actually aiming for me and had somehow missed?

I saw his lips move as he tried to say something, but then another slug slammed into the polished concrete just beyond where I was crouching. It ricocheted off the hard surface and struck a young man just below the knee, and he immediately tumbled to the floor. Judging by the direction from which both shots had come, the shooter was behind me, but I had no idea where. One of the food stands? The stairway at the end of the massive basement, or a service door I couldn't see? Whatever the case, he probably was lining us up again, easing his finger back on the trigger. Instinctively I rolled to my left just as another shot rang out, and I felt something nip me in my right calf.

I scurried behind the tiled counter of a pho noodle bar. The pain in my leg was hot rather than deep, and the gash in my trousers told me the slug—or shrapnel from the floor—had just grazed me. I couldn't risk glancing around to see where the gunman was, and then two more shots ripped through the food court. A chorus of panicked screams followed—people yelling for help, yelling for the police, yelling for an ambulance. I hated to leave Donovan bleeding out, especially with the shooter still somewhere nearby. But there was no way I could stick around when my brain was seized by just one thought:

Sabrina.

I pushed my way through the crowd, zigzagging the way I'd once seen a guide run from a crocodile in New Guinea. But there were no more shots. Whoever had been firing at us had either run out of ammo, patience, or a clear line of sight. One thing was clear: I'd sent Donovan into a nest of scorpions, and he'd been stung hard because of what he'd found.

I also realized the gunman couldn't have known Donovan was going to lead me to Grand Central, which meant he must have followed us into the terminal. Was he the only triggerman after us, or was there a team that had watched us as we arrived and was still watching me now?

Without looking back, I made my way up to the main concourse, then raced up the crowded incline to the doors that opened out onto 42nd Street. I pushed my way across the busy sidewalk to a taxi that was discharging a woman in a stylish blue skirt and ruffled blouse, with a black leather bag. A man in a dark suit with a red tie was poised to get in, but I pushed past him and yelled at the cabbie, "Drive!"

"Hey—that's my ride!" the man shouted, but I just pulled the door closed and jammed down the lock.

"What the hell?" the driver said.

"I've been shot, and I think they're still after me," I said as I flattened myself on the seat.

He didn't bother to ask who "they" were as his foot hit the gas and the car leaped forward.

I thought I heard another blast behind us, but there was no concurrent sound of breaking glass or lead hitting steel. I was safe, at least for now.

"Listen, man—whatever this is about, I'm not gettin' killed over it," the driver said. He was a thin Black man wearing a wool Rasta cap, with a heavy African accent. "I survived one civil war, and I'm done with that shit."

"Just go a few blocks and let me out, past the traffic," I said. There was always traffic on 42nd Street, and today was no different.

The anxious driver stomped hard on the gas, and the taxi shot forward. He made a few twists and turns as he swerved around cars and jaywalkers and bike messengers. Eventually I peered over the back seat and out the rear window to see if anyone was after us. No one, at least not that I could see. Then I glanced down at the hole where the bullet had torn through my trousers. My calf was throbbing with a dull burn where the slug had torn my flesh, but surprisingly the blood flow had eased up. I pressed my fingers around the edge of the wound, realizing I was going to live.

At least for a little while.

I took a deep breath, felt my nerves ease up a notch. Then the panic welled up again, and I said, "Change of plans— take me to the zoo. The one in Central Park!"

"I told you, I'm not dying today," the cabbie snapped.

"My daughter—she's in danger."

"I got me a wife and a little baby."

I had stopped at an ATM before I'd met with Donovan at Ryan's, partly because I needed cash and partly because he'd told me to make sure I wasn't being followed. Whole lot of good that did. Now I dug out my wallet and waved a wad of bills at the driver. "Is two hundred enough?"

The cabbie looked in his rearview and side mirrors, then said, "First sign of trouble, you're gettin' out of this car, understand?"

"Just get me there," I said as I shoved the money through the slot in the bulletproof partition. "Fast."

* * *

The Central Park Zoo is located just steps from Fifth Avenue near 64th Street. It houses everything from tamarin monkeys to Wyoming toads, thick-billed parrots to red pandas. And penguins, as Sabrina had reminded me just the other day.

The cab dropped me off on Fifth Avenue near the zoo entrance, and I scrambled out, still clutching Mickey Donovan's leatherette case. I'd tried to look through the contents on the ride uptown, but I was too shaken to do anything except peer out the glass ahead as we cut through the thick noontime traffic. My only goal was to make sure Sabrina was safe; whatever was in the file could wait.

I explained to a guard at the gate that I only was there to pick up my daughter, but he did what guards were paid to do. Rules were rules, and no one was getting in without a ticket. I had a few twenties left over, so I palmed him one to cover the cost of admission and pushed my way inside.

I had no way of knowing where Sabrina or her class might be, so I followed the signs to the popular sea lion pool, framed by vine-clad trellises and glass-roofed pergolas. I glanced around, found a group of kids swarming around a woman whom I recognized as Ms. Burton, my daughter's teacher. I also saw Janelle and her mom, who I knew was one of the chaperones for the day—but no sign of Sabrina.

"Mr. Kane, what a welcome surprise," Ms. Burton said as I approached her. "Did you sign up to be a classroom assistant?"

"Not today," I replied. "I'm here to take Sabrina home."

"She's not here," she said.

"What do you mean, she's not here?" I snapped at Sabrina's teacher. "Where the hell else would she be?"

"Please, Mr. Kane—*language*," she reprimanded me. I knew her only as Ms. Burton, and she had the shiny face of a porcelain doll and wore lipstick the color of old bricks. Glossy, like the rest of her skin. "Sabrina has already been picked up for her dentist appointment."

"Sabrina doesn't have a dentist appointment," I said. "She had an exam last month and her teeth are fine. Who picked her up?"

"Why, your delightful young friend Marika. You added her to the security sign-out sheet just the other day."

My heart suddenly felt as if someone had squeezed it from my chest up into my throat. "When was this?" I managed to ask.

"Ten, maybe fifteen minutes ago," Ms. Burton told me. "We were at the rainforest exhibit, and she just came up and said she needed to take Sabrina out of class. She had a note from you, so I let her go. Such a nice young lady."

Nice young lady, my ass, I thought. "Did you happen to see which way they went?"

"They headed that way, toward the gate," she replied, pointing toward the exit I had just come through. "My God, Mr. Kane, you have blood on your clothes and—"

I didn't respond, just made a quick pivot and raced across the zoo plaza, past the same guard I had just passed coming in. I ran as fast as the pain in my leg would allow, frantically searching for any sight of Sabrina or Marika. Gina. *Whatever the fuck her name was.*

The big question was *where*? Where were they going? And what was Marika going to do with her once they got there?

I figured our condo in the Village was low on the list of places she'd go. By now these bastards would know Donovan had found the cameras and the listening devices, and had told me about them. Whatever Marika's agenda might be, would it be worth going down to the Village to grab Sabrina's clothes or stuffed animals?

Besides, her own apartment was a lot closer. Just a few blocks on the other side of the park, and as good a place as any to reset her bearings after grabbing my daughter. I felt so damned stupid, falling for her contrived story that she worked as a sales rep for a cable news network. Or her well-played ruse with the tangled scarf on the escalator.

Midday in Manhattan is not the best time of day to hail a taxi, but I sensed the hand of fate on my shoulder. I stuck out my palm as soon as I was out of the park and caught a cab thirty seconds later. I yanked open the door and jumped in the back, told the driver to take me over to West End at 72nd Street.

"You all right, sir?" the driver asked, his voice cloaked in a thick Middle Eastern accent. "You have bleeding."

"It's why I'm in a hurry."

He said nothing more, just pulled into the flood of traffic and circled the block. He turned west on 65th Street and shot across Fifth Avenue at the light, then roared into the park. Despite the tightened traffic restrictions, he managed to make it past the runners and bicyclists and dog walkers in under two minutes, passing the restored Tavern on the Green restaurant on the right before lurching to a halt at the light at Central Park West.

"You sure you don't need to see a doctor?" the driver asked me.

"I'm fine," I said impatiently. "Just get me there."

"Yes, sir," he said, and as soon as the light turned green, he jumped on the gas and punched the cab through the intersection. "Please, no blood on seats."

I pulled out my phone and dialed Marika, but the call went straight to voicemail. I swore under my breath, figured she was avoiding me for reasons that were obvious. I remembered what Donovan had just told me about cameras and microphones and keyloggers, then weighed it against the words of affection she had purred into my ear last night. Just before she had stormed off.

I considered dialing the police, but what the hell would I tell them? That my daughter had been picked up from a school trip to the zoo by a friend who was on an approved sign-out list? That I'd been involved with the shooting of an ex-cop less than thirty minutes ago at Grand Central, and a mysterious group of black ops thugs may have staged my wife's death but actually had kidnapped her?

The next five minutes seemed like an hour. I dialed Marika again, and again got no answer. I slipped the phone back into my pocket and sat in the backseat until the driver swerved to the curb in front of her building.

I thrust another of my dwindling supply of twenties into his hand. I didn't have time for him to make change so I just said, "Keep it," as I jumped out. Then I sprinted across the sidewalk to the glass door that opened into the lobby and raced inside.

"Sir!" the doorman called out as I sped toward the bank of elevators and hit the "Up" button. "Visitors need to sign in."

"I'm going up to Marika Landry's place," I explained. "Twenty-seventh floor. I just need to get something."

"I don't know if she's in," the doorman said just as the elevator dinged and the door slid open.

"I have a key," I replied.

The doorman bought my fib and said, "Go on up."

I tried to keep calm as the elevator slowly rose to the twenty-seventh floor. I seriously doubted Marika would have brought Sabrina here, figuring this would be the first place I'd look for her. But I had to start somewhere, and this was the closest place to the zoo I could think of.

The doors finally slid open and I charged out. I hung a left and raced down the hallway to the last apartment on the right. I didn't care what I might have to do to get in, even break the damned door down if I had to. I was spared that necessity, however, when I found it unlocked and open just a crack. I pushed it open slowly and slipped inside, then gently nudged it closed again.

Marika's apartment was designed around a glaring white foyer opening onto a spacious living room with floor-to-ceiling river views directly ahead of me. A modern kitchen with a large granite island was located to my right, and her single bedroom was on the left. I slowly edged forward into the main area, ignoring the view as I gave the place a quick once-over. Marika's style was much more contemporary than mine: color-coordinated leather couch and chairs with square edges, chrome and glass cocktail table, matching chrome and glass bookcase in the corner. When I'd first seen the place, I'd chalked it up to just a difference in taste—"*degistibus non disputandem est,*" as Alison would say. "In matters of taste, there is no dispute." But now I realized all this modernist crap probably just came from a rental outfit and had been staged strictly for my benefit.

My first instinct was to call out to Sabrina, but I didn't want to tip off Marika—or anyone else—that I was there. Especially since the open door strongly suggested someone might be inside. Aside from a plate with an empty glass on the coffee table, there was no sign that either of them had been here. The balcony door was locked tight, and the air was stale and odorless. I started toward the bedroom, and that's when a flash of color on the floor caught my eye. The contrast of red on white marble was unmistakable, and my feet froze where I was standing. A horrible sense of dread engulfed me as I forced myself to take a step toward the kitchen.

I came upon the shoes first, and my heart let up when I realized they were black loafers. Men's, about size eleven, the leather scuffed and worn. Not Marika's, and certainly not Sabrina's. I slowly edged closer until the entire body was in view, sprawled face down on the polished tile. It was a man, pale skin with dark hair, black jeans and a digital-camo T-shirt. One arm was twisted underneath his lifeless torso, the other stretched out as if he'd been trying to grab something when he went down. Blood was oozing from beneath him, most likely from his chest or stomach. Gunshot or knife wound, probably.

And, by the look of it, quite recent.

But I didn't have time to consider what any of this might mean, because just then a voice behind me growled, "Don't you goddamn move, motherfucker, or I blow your head off."

CHAPTER

27

I'VE BEEN IN more hot zones around the world than I care to count. I've photographed wars, mass genocide, cartel carnage, refugee camps. I've witnessed just about every kind of atrocity humans can inflict upon other humans. Over the years I had been shot at, pistol-whipped, beaten up, thrown in jail, and left to die. And I'd lived to tell about it because not once had I tried to be a hero.

I wasn't about to start now.

"I'm not moving," I said—*very slowly*—to the man standing behind me.

"Except your hands," the voice continued. "Move 'em one at a time, where I can see 'em. Nice and slow, and lose that case."

I did as the man ordered, extending my palms outward, letting Donovan's portfolio slip to the floor. Then I raised my arms over my head and said, "I'm unarmed," waiting for a bullet to pierce my skull any second. Given the difference between the speed of sound and the speed of a bullet, I doubted I'd even hear the shot.

"Good," the voice said. "You can see there on the floor what happens if you don't follow orders."

"Got it," I replied.

"Stay put and tell me your name," the voice demanded. "And no bullshit."

"Cameron Kane. And I don't care what you do to me, just let my daughter go."

There was a brief silence, followed by a heavy sigh of relief. *"Shit,"* the voice said. "Put your arms down, Mr. Kane. I'm not going to shoot you."

I took one more glance at the dead man on the floor, then slowly lowered my hands. I turned around—again, very slowly—to face a very large Black man who held a very deadly semiautomatic in his right hand. He was dressed in crisp blue jeans and a black sports jacket that hung open enough to reveal a shoulder holster over an Army green T-shirt. A large gold ring was jammed on his left pinkie.

"Who are you?" I asked.

"My name's not important," the man said. He had Bluetooth audio buds in both ears, and I could hear the faint sound of music coming from them. One fleshy lobe was adorned with a gold yin-yang stud, and a small Navy cross was affixed to the other. "That was Mick I just heard about on the news, wasn't it?"

"The news? What are you talking about?"

The man scratched his chin, which carried a day or two of growth. "The shooting at Grand Central. Video's already been uploaded to YouTube a hundred times. I got an update on my phone."

"That's him," I confirmed. "Since it's on the news, is there any word on how he's doing?"

"No. But Mick's a tough old bastard, and this for damned sure ain't his time."

I'd been so stunned at the sight of the dead man, and then spooked by the voice behind me, that my brain had ground to a halt. But now it chugged back to life, and I realized who this guy was. "Wait a minute," I said. "He mentioned you just before he was hit. You're Zemira Moon."

"He told you that?"

"Said you were ex-military," I replied. "Special forces or something."

"And more than you need to know. Except that you've wandered into one big heap of shit, my brother."

"Looks like he did too," I said, nodding toward the dead guy on the floor.

"It was either him or me."

"Who is he?"

My question brought a minimal shrug, and Moon said, "One of *them*. And just so you know, he drew first. These assholes don't fuck around."

"I kinda figured that out when Donovan got shot." I wondered what he was doing here and how he'd gotten past the doorman, but I wasn't about to ask. He obviously had his ways. "Look . . . the woman I thought I trusted—"

"Marika Landry."

"Yeah, Marika," I said. "Except I guess that's not her real name. I thought . . . well, I don't know what I was thinking. Sixteen years younger than me, for Chrissake. And then she went and snatched my daughter from the zoo. I've got to find her."

"What's that you dropped?" Moon asked, ignoring my words as he glanced at the portfolio on the floor. Ignoring the dead dude lying just a foot or two away, as if it was the sort of thing he saw every day. Maybe it was.

"Something Donovan gave me," I told him.

"Well, pick it up. It's all in there."

"By all, you mean Ironbridge?"

"He told you about them?"

I couldn't shake the image of Donovan being blown back by the force of the bullet, blood spraying everywhere. "Just the basics," I told him. "Mostly how they coerced Marika into spying on me and my daughter. And now I need to find her. Sabrina."

"What you need to do is slow down, think this through."

"Slow down? She's got my little girl!"

"Listen to me, man," Moon said, fixing me with his dark eyes. "These motherfuckers aren't weekend paintball warriors."

"I need to call the police."

"That's the last thing you want to do. These shitheads are paramilitary thugs. Ex-SEALS, most of 'em. Hard-core pros. Led by the biggest SOB I've ever crossed paths with. Cops are only going to anger 'em."

"You're saying you know them?"

"I know the head honcho," Moon replied. "Name's Eagleton. Former army colonel. West Point, Desert Storm, Afghanistan, Iraq, back to Afghanistan. A top-grade cluster-fuck. Got three of my men killed—doesn't give a rat's ass about anyone except himself."

"What do you mean, your men?"

Moon fixed me with his cold, dark eyes. "Donovan may not have told you, but I spent a big chunk of my life in that cold and desolate corner of the planet," he said through clenched teeth. "If it wasn't for the trillions of dollars of lithium, uranium, gold, and other precious shit they've got, no one would give a damn about that dirtbag country. Anyway, back around when our president was unleashing shock and awe in Baghdad, I was running ops in Kunar Province. Surveillance and reconnaissance, mostly. One night we got caught in an ambush, and three of my men were hit. I called for a QRF—that's quick reaction force—to come in and get us all the hell out of there. Command sent a chopper, but it got shot down by a rocket-propelled grenade. My men died, and Eagleton's shit was all over it."

"You mean he was working for the Taliban?"

"Nah," Moon said, shaking his head. "Eagleton viewed himself as a red-blooded suck-up American patriot. 'Don't tread on me,' and all that bullshit. But he also was the ultimate mercenary, had his hands in a lot of shit over there. Opium, artifacts, guns, money . . . things that eventually ended up over here. If you could make a dollar off it, Eagleton was in the thick of it."

"What's his role in all this?"

"Well, as inept as the Pentagon can be, they knew Eagleton was a prime-time screwup," Moon replied as he placed his gun on the kitchen counter. "After they botched the rescue, they conducted an internal investigation and discovered he'd abandoned his post that night to meet with one of his suppliers. *Dereliction of duty* is what the top brass called it. Got a hard leather boot up his ass, so far he could tie the laces with his tongue. When he lost his stripes and his retirement, he went into business for himself. A start-up that provided private-sector operations for dignitaries and corporations—all very secure, with diplomatic protection on both ends."

"And you know all this how?"

"Like I said, Eagleton killed three of my men over there," Moon said. "I've been keeping an eye on him ever since."

"Revenge?"

"More like restraint," he replied with a tight smile.

I understood what Moon was telling me, but I was running out of time. "They snatched my daughter," I reminded him through clenched teeth, getting back to the reality of the moment, the truth about Marika ratcheting up my anger. "I need to find her."

Moon creased his brow, a mix of worry and resignation. "Don't worry . . . we'll get her back. Maybe both of 'em."

"Both of them?" I asked.

He regarded me with a distressed look, his eyes dark and impassive but still reflecting a spark of optimism. "I don't want to jump the gun," he said, "but these guys wouldn't have gone to such lengths if they weren't hiding something. This new girlfriend of yours, does she have a key to your place?"

I rolled my eyes at the thought of Marika being my girlfriend, but then I realized there was no other word for it. "No, but she knows where I keep a spare. But Marika wouldn't go there. She knows it's the first place I'd look."

"But it wasn't, was it? You came here first."

"So did you, and you killed that guy," I said, again glancing at the body on the floor.

"Like I said, he drew first. See that tattoo, there?"

My eyes followed his glance to the back of the deceased man's hand, where a scorpion with a raised stinger was inked on his skin.

"That's Eagleton's mark," Moon explained. "If I hadn't gotten here first, that could be you instead of him."

Moon had a point, but it didn't come close to satisfying my need for answers right now. Nor did I want to admit how much Marika had played me, how naive I'd been since the moment we'd met.

"Think it through, Mr. Kane," he continued. "If she's taking your daughter somewhere, she's going to need clothes."

"If this Ironbridge is as big and powerful as you say, wouldn't they have already planned ahead for this?"

"Maybe, but these guys are into guns and ammo, not dresses and teddy bears," Moon said.

I thought on this as I stared out at the Hudson River. Sabrina was out there right now, somewhere in this vast city of over eight million people—twenty million if you counted all the suburbs. She probably had no idea that her life was in danger, since she had every reason in the world to trust Marika. *Mika.* My daughter had looked forward to this trip to the zoo for weeks, but she would have left without protest if Marika had come up with a reason that sounded serious enough. The two of them had bonded over the shopping trip earlier in the week, and Mika was her friend.

I turned to Moon and said, "A minute ago you said these Ironbridge guys are hiding something. What does that mean?"

"What it means right now is I understand these fuckers," he said. "I understand how they think and how they operate. They're brutal mercenaries, not motivated by the things that drive you and me. And that means it's time to move."

"Copy that," I said, using the only phrase I knew that sounded even remotely like special ops talk. I took one last look around the apartment, realized I'd probably never be back here. Then I nodded toward the body on the floor and said, "What do we do with him?"

"We don't do shit. Look, Mr. Kane . . . time is tight and getting tighter." He dug into his wallet, took out a stylish

business card. Brushed aluminum, thick, engraved letter-
ing that listed only his name and phone number. "Take this,
keep it with you. Call me if you get in a jam."

"What about Sabrina?" I asked him.

"Start at your place, and work it out from there," he said
as he slipped his gun back into its holster. "These guys want
you weak, so you have to be strong."

"Hard to feel strong when they've got my daughter."

"Follow your instincts and trust your gut," he replied,
and then he was gone.

*　*　*

I gave Moon a thirty-second head start as I tried to figure out
what my gut was telling me. The presence of the dead guy
caused me to cut his lead to fifteen before I bolted. No telling
when the police or another one of these Ironbridge assholes
would show up.

When I was back down on the street I raced to Sherman
Square, thankful my leg injury was mostly blood and very
little pain. I flagged a taxi heading down Broadway and gave
the driver my address in the West Village, then settled into
the spongy backseat. I closed my eyes and saw Sabrina's face,
her effervescent smile and sparkling blue eyes and wisps of
blonde hair that reminded me so much of her mother.

I could have taken the subway downtown, but right now
I had no tolerance for crowds or the fetid smell of tunnels.
Besides, the thought of going underground meant I would be
leaving Sabrina behind, wherever she'd been taken.

I leaned forward on the seat and peered anxiously
through the window at the clogged artery known as Seventh
Avenue. Motivated by my last wad of twenties I'd palmed
him when I climbed in, the driver leaned on his horn at the

delivery truck ahead of us, then swerved into a small gap that opened up behind a black SUV. We lurched forward, cut wildly to the left, then punched into yet another gap and raced through a yellow light just as it was turning red.

That's when a bullet pierced the cab's rear window and struck the ceiling just inches above my right ear.

My brain shifted to lizard mode as I flattened against the seat, just as another slug tore through the shattered rear window and ripped into the driver's skull. The taxi lurched forward, the cabbie's foot pressing on the accelerator like the dead weight it was. The vehicle gathered momentum until it crashed into the rear of a white BMW that was stuck behind a FedEx truck. I heard the crack of another shot, but in the mere seconds from when the first round was fired a lot of other sounds—screams, tearing metal, shattering glass— erupted out on the street around me.

I tried to catch my breath as I pulled myself up just high enough to see the driver slumped over the steering wheel, a random smear of blood and gore on the windshield that made me think of Jackson Pollock. My primal sense of survival told me that if I remained where I was, I'd be dead in seconds. The adrenaline rush was telling me to get the hell out of there, and since I didn't have a weapon, I really didn't have a choice.

I tugged on the chrome handle and gave the door a solid push. It swung open just as another bullet took out the window. Fragments of glass rained down on the street like a handful of uncut diamonds. Whoever the shooter was, I could tell he was close. And a pro.

That's when the driver of the BMW made a mistake that took his own life but likely saved mine. He was dressed in a blue suit and a yellow tie, dark designer shades that probably cost a thousand dollars. I watched out of the corner of my eye as he got out of his car and surveyed the damage to his bumper, then marched back toward the taxi. His anger seemed so focused that he ignored the gunfire, the broken glass, and the red smear across the inside of the windshield. He stormed up to the driver's door and yanked it open just as another slug penetrated the fleshy part of his neck, where the carotid artery extends into the brain.

I hurled myself out the rear door and rolled between a delivery van and a ConEd truck. I heard two more shots as another window shattered close by. Peering under the chassis of the van, I saw a pair of feet approaching ten yards away and realized if I didn't do something, I had about five seconds to live.

CHAPTER

28

I PUSHED MY WAY up into a low crouch and scrambled out of the gutter, then made a run for a revolving door fifteen feet across the sidewalk. Again, I took short zigzag steps as I went, diving into the building's foyer as I heard another gunshot somewhere behind me.

Pebbles of glass jammed the revolving door, leaving only a small opening for me to squeeze through. I managed to claw my way inside just as I sensed the shooter coming up behind me, taking his time now. I skittered backward and rolled to my left, trying to remain a moving target.

I hadn't counted bullets and knew that was futile anyway. With all the variations of ammo magazines on the market these days, a gun could fire any number of rounds before it needed reloading. Seventeen rounds, or ten? Six shots, or only five? A line from *Dirty Harry* came to mind, and I seriously hoped Clint Eastwood wouldn't be the last image to flash before my eyes as I died.

But I guess it was not my time. Not that very instant, because that's when the shooter's head vaporized in a puff of red at the same instant a loud boom from a much bigger gun thundered in my ears.

Turns out size does matter.

I hadn't even noticed the uniformed cop out on the sidewalk, or the cannon in his hand that dropped my assailant.

My cell phone started ringing again. Despite my mad dash across the sidewalk and into the building I'd managed to hang on to it, along with Donovan's portfolio.

"Who the hell is this?" I yelled without looking at the screen.

"Settle down, Cam. It's Lillian."

Lillian Sloane? The last time we'd talked was Tuesday, when she'd called to tell me she'd arranged for me to meet with Mickey Donovan at Ryan's. I glanced back through the shattered glass at the panic unfolding out on the street. "Look, can we talk later? They shot Mickey, and now they're after me."

"Who . . . *what?*"

"Long story. Right now they've got me pinned down."

"What the hell are you talking about?"

I didn't respond right away as I glanced around the lobby I'd tumbled into. A couple of people had dropped to the floor near the security desk, and an unarmed guard seemed frozen in his tracks near the elevators. I had no idea if the dead shooter was alone or part of a team, and had no intention of finding out. I scrambled behind a marble pillar that supported the thirty or so floors above me, then gasped into the phone, "They have my daughter, Lillian. They took Sabrina."

"What are you talking about?"

"The people who shot Mickey," I replied. "I've got to get out of here."

There was a moment of silence, and I thought the call had been dropped. Then she said, "Where are you?"

"Seventh Avenue," I replied. "At 47th Street. Northwest corner."

"I think I know where you are. Here's what you're going to do."

I listened carefully to what Lillian told me, then did what she said. Except I made a critical detour along the way.

*　*　*

When I got down to Jane Street, I glanced up and down the block, looking for whatever might seem suspicious. I didn't even know what I was looking for: maybe a black SUV with tinted windows, or a man in a trench coat standing on a stoop reading a newspaper. Finding none of that, I cautiously let myself into the vestibule of my condo, then unlocked the front door and slipped inside.

I moved through the small foyer into the living room, glanced around every corner and checked behind each stick of furniture. Everything appeared just as it had earlier that morning: cluttered but tidy, no blood on the floor. The kitchen looked the same as when I'd left it six hours ago. Same dishes left over from yesterday's breakfast in the sink, same empty coffee can on the counter. I took one final glance around, then moved down the hall to Sabrina's room.

It was a mess. The dresser drawers had all been yanked open, loose pants and tops and socks had been tossed everywhere. Same thing with her closet. I couldn't tell what was missing, but Marika definitely had grabbed a few days' worth of clothes. Along with Sabrina's favorite stuffed animal, a badly soiled polar bear named Peary that I'd brought back from a college reunion a few years ago.

I sat on the edge of Sabrina's bed, overwhelmed by truths I'd never before been forced to consider. My daughter had just been kidnapped by a woman I'd trusted, and my apartment had been bugged with microphones, cameras, and that keylogger thing. I felt helpless, almost paralyzed, and had no idea what to do next. I was just one man in a city of millions, and I saw no way I could deal with this scenario by myself. Mickey Donovan was probably under a scalpel somewhere right that very moment, and even his special ops friend had ducked out on me back at Marika's condo. With a man bleeding out on the kitchen floor.

Despite what Zemira Moon had told me, the left hemisphere of my brain was telling me it was time to call the police.

The more I thought about it, the more I realized the danger Sabrina was in. Whatever—whoever—Ironbridge was, they were playing for keeps, and I was ill-equipped to go up against them on my own. I knew the cops would balk at my story, but Mickey Donovan had been one of theirs. His shooting would pique their interest, maybe cause them to take me seriously. Sure, the cops might haul me down to headquarters for a lengthy chat about my involvement in his shooting at Grand Central, but there was strength in numbers, and with a police force almost forty-thousand strong, there was a cop on just about every street corner in the city.

I took my phone out of my pocket and started to dial 911, when I noticed I'd missed a call. I recognized the number; it was the same one Mrs. Dillon had called me from last night, and she'd left me a message. She sounded a bit calmer than the last time I'd heard her voice but definitely just as terrified.

"Mr. Kane. I'm sorry for the way I sounded last night . . . but you have to understand. Whoever shot at me, I know he had something to do with my husband. Anyway, I'm getting rid of this phone, 'cause it has GPS. So don't call me back, 'cause you can't. And don't try to track me down, since I'm going someplace no one will ever find me."

End of message.

I thought about what the poor woman must be going through right now. Two days ago she had been sitting up there in New Canaan, probably dreading the first anniversary of her husband's disappearance. Now she was on the run, and it was all my fault.

Well, no it wasn't—not really. Sure, I'd called her and set things in motion, but this had all been started by Ironbridge and the ex-Army pirate named Eagleton that Mickey Donovan and Zemira Moon had told me about.

The person I really wanted to talk to was Marika. A bunch of nasty adjectives came to mind, and my blood was boiling just thinking about what she had done to Sabrina. I felt so totally foolish at how easily I let her drift into our lives as if she were part of our long-term future, and then invited her into my home so she could install microphones and cameras all over the place.

For what purpose?

I again started to dial 911, but then I heard Moon's words in my head: *"No cops."* At the same instant, my phone rang, causing my heart to almost jump out of my chest.

I checked the screen, saw it was Dr. Nguyen's office calling. I wondered if Dr. Cook had already called him as I hit the "Talk" icon.

"Mr. Kane, this is Dr. Nguyen," the voice on the other end said in that distinct Asian accent. "I want to tell you . . . I was unnecessarily short with you the other day."

"No worries, Doc. I know I was a bit pushy. And I'm in the middle of something right now."

"Then I'll be brief," the dentist said. "Remember how I told you I'd go through our records, see what courier we used to send your wife's X-rays?"

"Right, but—"

"Well, you see, Mr. Kane . . . my receptionist, Annika, overheard our conversation, and she reminded me of something."

"Go on," I said, detecting a sense of urgency in Dr. Nguyen's voice.

"Well, I hadn't made the connection, but the day before your wife died, we had a break-in here. Some drugs were taken. Novocain and painkillers, mostly. The police investigated but came up with nothing. But after thinking about it . . . well, it seems that could have just been a ruse."

"Someone could have switched the X-rays at the same time," I said, feeling that familiar icy tingle.

"Possibly. Anyway, I want to apologize for how I must have sounded."

"Thank you, Doc," I said. "I really appreciate it."

I slipped the phone back into my pocket before temptation struck again.

I got up from the bed and took one last look at my daughter's room, wondering when I'd be back here. Tucking Sabrina into bed, reading her a chapter or two of *Stuart Little*, listening as she told me her stories about squirrels. Kissing her on her forehead, switching off the light, and telling her, "Good night, sugar."

I checked my watch, realized I had fifteen minutes until I was supposed to meet up with Lillian. I hurried into my bedroom and ducked into the en suite bathroom Alison had insisted we needed when we were condo shopping. Some gauze and adhesive tape fixed the nicked skin on my leg, and

I pulled on a fresh pair of jeans. Then I opened the closet door and flicked on the light. A high wooden shelf ran around the upper perimeter of the closet, and a pile of old sweaters and other junk clogged my allocated sector. Even after Alison died, I'd confined my stuff to only my third of the space. I rummaged through the pile, and my fingers finally found the old Colt .380 pistol I'd stashed in the back. A Mustang Pocketlite, actually, with a barrel just under three inches and a weight of just slightly more than a pound, fully loaded.

I never thought I would come to own a gun, until someone tried to mug me in Hell's Kitchen a few months before Alison and I had gotten married. I'd made the unwise choice to walk to Times Square from the Jacob Javits Convention Center on the West Side, and a man in a red hoodie approached me near the old horse barns and demanded my wallet. I'd made it seem as if I were going to comply with his demand, then stomped on his foot and took off running. I'd expected to feel gunshots in my back, but nothing happened, and I'd made it home in one piece.

A week later I purchased the pistol. I learned how to shoot it, and when we'd moved into the condo, I'd hidden the empty weapon—along with a box of ammo—where neither my wife nor daughter would ever find it. I think it's the only secret I ever kept from her, which didn't make me feel very good. But now it might just turn out to be a lifesaver. Or not.

In any event, I found the bullets and loaded six rounds into the magazine. I wanted to be ready for whatever came next.

29

"YOU'RE CERTAIN NO one followed you?" Lillian Sloane asked me.

"Absolutely, but that's the same thing Mickey Donovan asked me, and look what happened to him." My heart felt ready to seize up from all the running and the adrenaline, and I wiped a bead of moisture from my brow. "I took all sorts of precautions and detours getting here. And by the way, thanks for the tip about the underground connector from that building into the subway."

Sloane exhaled a deep breath and said, "There's public passages all over this town most people don't know about."

"I hate to be rude, but I need to get out there and find my daughter," I replied. I was still gripped by the tightening tentacles of panic, and my mind was everywhere but here.

Here was Nelson Rockefeller Park on the Hudson River, a two-block walk from the Chambers Street subway stop and just a stone's throw from the new World Trade Center. I'd initially balked when she'd suggested we meet in such an open area, but she finally convinced me she'd chosen it because we would see anyone approaching across the grass or from the water. On the phone I'd summarized what had happened to Donovan and Sabrina, and I was at a total loss about what to do next.

"You think something Mickey found might lead to an answer?" she asked.

"What he found got him shot," I reminded her. "I don't want to think what they might do to Sabrina."

"Please . . . just tell me what he learned."

The distant, painful look in Lillian's eyes suggested Donovan was more than just a friend to her. I quickly filled her in, beginning with what he'd mentioned about Ironbridge, the defrocked and disgraced colonel named Eagleton, and a career spook named Brody. Plus, Marika Landry, aka Gina Collins, and the recording devices hidden throughout my apartment.

"This building down near Wall Street, where the cab dropped Harding off," she said. "Did Mickey mention where it was?"

"He made a point not to. You think maybe they took Sabrina there?"

"It's as good a place to start as any. Maybe it's in that file he gave you."

I reached inside my jacket and took out a manila envelope that had been in Donovan's leatherette case, which I'd ditched back at the condo.

"With all that's happened I haven't had more than a second to glance at it," I replied as I unfastened the clasp and slid out several sheets of paper. They were stapled together at the corner and contained a handwritten outline Donovan had put together. I read through it, unable to take my mind off my daughter, and more questions came to mind as others were answered. Much of it was a detailed report of what he'd already summarized for me—background info on Harding/Zaccaro, the private residence on Williams Street, a mercenary group known as Ironbridge. Even a detailed bio on Marika, aka Gina Collins. When I finished, I handed the pages to Lillian, who quickly scanned them before handing them back.

"I didn't see a street address for the place downtown," she said.

"Me neither," I said, shaking my head.

Lillian started chewing her lip, as if that would help her digest what we both had just read. "If Mickey was correct in what he dug up, the US wasn't the only country that was going after Harding." She stabbed her finger at a bullet point halfway down the top page. "Germany, France, Italy, the UK, Luxembourg—even the Russians were drawing up indictments against the bastard. Securities fraud, wire fraud, mail fraud, money laundering, perjury, tax evasion, currency theft. He was looking at spending the rest of his life behind bars."

"Being dead is a good way to get away from all that," I pointed out.

"You really think that's what this is all about?"

I scanned the park while I thought back to what Myerson had told me the other day at the US Attorney's Office. "That, and absconding with billions of dollars in cash."

"You can't possibly think Alison could have been in on that," Lillian said.

"My wife was a mathematician, not a criminal," I replied. "She dealt with approximation algorithms and rare prime numbers. I guarantee you she wasn't a part of this scheme."

That's when I heard Lady Gaga in my pocket, and a sudden rage swept through me. I grabbed my cell phone and screamed, "Where's my daughter, you lying, double-crossing—"

"Settle down, Kane," a male voice said. Definitely not Marika. "First things first. I'm texting you a photograph. You have five seconds to look at it."

"Where's Sabrina?"

But the call had already ended, and I just sat there on the bench staring at my phone. Lillian asked me what was going on, but just then it pinged again, indicating that a text had arrived. It was a color image, and when I realized what it was, I felt the blood drain from my brain.

The screen had cracked during the shootout earlier, but I still recognized the face of my daughter. Sitting in a chair at a glass table, a hotdog in her hand and a smear of ketchup—not blood—on her face. She seemed to be oblivious to her sur- roundings, and the fact that she'd been snatched by a band of treacherous cretins. Which told me Marika was somewhere nearby, and all was good with her world.

My phone rang again, and the same voice—maddeningly calm and controlled—said, "You see, Mr. Kane. Your daugh- ter is in excellent hands. Marika's going to make a great mother, don't you think?"

"You fucking bastard . . . let her go."

The man on the other end offered a self-satisfied chuckle and said, "As long as you do what I tell you, nothing happens to her. You have my word."

"Your word? I don't even know who the fuck you are."

"Immaterial to this conversation," the man said. "Look . . . I'm sending you another photo. Your friend seems very nice, which makes it such a pity."

"*I want my daughter,*" I yelled, but the connection had already gone dead.

Just as I knew Sabrina would be if I didn't find her soon, despite the ketchup and hotdog.

My phone pinged again and another photo appeared, this one depicting me sitting with Lillian on a park bench. Not just any park bench, either, but *this* bench we were occupying *right now*. And she was at the center of the photograph, the crosshairs of a rifle scope fixed directly over her face.

How did they find time to photoshop it? I wondered. Then I glanced over at her and spotted the pale red laser dot hovering over her heart like a ruby pendant.

"Down," I screamed as I reflexively thrust out my hands to push her out of the line of fire.

But I was too late. The shot was a clean one and the spiraling lead bullet released a massive spray of blood and tissue as it tore through her chest and lodged in the back of the park bench.

CHAPTER

30

INSTINCTIVELY I DIVED sideways toward a concrete trash bin just as another gunshot filled the air.

I was certain the same rifle scope that had found Lillian Sloane was tracking my movement. Which didn't make any sense, as they already had my undivided attention as well as my daughter. Yet here I was, pinned down by a sniper a good distance away, who had telegraphed his intention by texting me that last photo.

As I collected my thoughts, I wondered where the shooter might be holed up. From the placement of the red dot over Lillian's heart and the way she'd been blown back, I had a vague sense that the bullet had come from the parking garage at the edge of the greenbelt. Low down, no more than the second or third level. For the moment I was safe where I was, but as soon as I made a run for it, I'd become a target again.

Which caused me to wonder why—for the second time in just as many hours—the person I'd been with had drawn first fire. Mickey Donovan and now Lillian Sloane.

Maybe I still held some value to these Ironbridge fuckers.

I needed to regain a sense of control and not keep glancing over at where Lillian's body lay sprawled on the bench. I'd dropped both the manila envelope and my phone during the shooting, and there was no way I could risk going back to get them. That meant these bastards had no way to contact me, or for me to make sure Sabrina was still alive. I didn't know if they knew this, however, and might just assume I wasn't answering. Either way, they'd lost some of their power and would have to regroup, find another way to get me under their control and do what they wanted. I mentally weighed that balance for a second, figured I could get a prepaid burner as soon as I managed to get out of there, and call Marika back when I was good and ready.

Another thought crept into my mind, and when it did, I was surprised it had taken this long to take root. How had they known I was in the food court at Grand Central? Or the cab on Seventh Avenue, or here at Rockefeller Park? I'd covered my tracks, and I was certain I had not been followed. Still, they knew where I was, and that only meant one thing: they'd been tracking my movement through my cell phone. Maybe Donovan had already figured on this but hadn't had a chance to let me know.

Well, good luck with that now.

I crouched behind the concrete garbage bin, tried to reduce my body mass and become a smaller target. The Hudson River was fifty yards behind me; no cover that way. A few people were lounging on the grass or strolling by on the esplanade, but none of them seemed to have heard the shot. Or if they had, maybe they thought it was a truck backfiring over on the West Side Highway. Even Lillian's lifeless body on the bench wouldn't seem that out of place, just another office worker soaking in the sun. Until they got close.

I'd once spent four days in the desert with a Marine sniper, and he'd explained the basics of his craft to me. Whoever had his finger on the trigger was waiting for me to make a break for it, and then I would be out in the open. As soon as he took his shot, a powered bullet would be traveling close to a thousand miles an hour in my direction. That would be after he'd calculated wind speed, and added the effect of gravity and humidity into his computation. Also, he must have been pissed that his shot that had killed Lillian also had destroyed my phone.

In the end I had no choice. I planted my toes on the pavement where I was crouched, then launched myself like a sprinter coming off the blocks at the sound of the starter's gun. I heard a shot somewhere in the distance, but I ran like hell, once again striking a zigzag pattern to make it harder for the gunman to track my movement. I hated to leave Lillian where she was, just as I'd abandoned Mickey Donovan in Grand Central. But I knew a runner or roller skater would find her soon enough, and by then I hoped to be long gone.

I raced around the Irish Hunger Memorial and thirty seconds later took the steps into Brookfield Place three at a time. Only after I pushed my way inside and fell in with the crowd did I slow down and collect my breath. I leaned forward with my hands on my knees until I stopped shaking, then slowly straightened my body. My lungs burned from my mad sprint, and the raw jangle of panic rattled every nerve ending in my body.

Brookfield Place is a cluster of buildings in the shadow of the resurrected World Trade Center. Originally known as the World Financial Center, it covers several city blocks and houses dozens of high-end shops that range from Gucci to Hermes, Lululemon to Ferragamo. The place was crowded for a Friday afternoon, largely tourists interested in viewing the memorial pools and One WTC, the steel and glass tower that rises like a mighty phoenix from the ashes of Ground Zero.

I edged my way through the shopping concourse, remaining close to the wall, keeping an eye open for everyone and everything. From what I could see, no one was running up the steps behind me, no one was talking into a Bluetooth device dripping from an ear. I took a few more ragged breaths, then glanced around the glass-enclosed mall. At the far end of the concourse I spotted an Old Navy clothing store, and I tried to remain inconspicuous as I made my way toward it. Giving one last glance behind me, I slipped inside, doing my best to blend in with the other customers.

Hard to do with my face and clothes covered with Lillian's blood.

Now was not the time to be picky. All I needed was a new shirt and a pair of jeans that wouldn't attract attention, plus a lightweight jacket with an ample pocket for my gun. I quickly found what I was looking for, then used the men's room to scrub the flesh and gore from my face and hands. I told the clerk at the register that I wanted to wear my purchases home and had left my old clothes in the trash bin. She regarded me curiously but gave me a friendly "no problem" as she scanned the bar codes from the loose tags I'd given her. While the cash register beeped, I studied the other shoppers with a wary eye. No one seemed to be lurking on the other side of the clothes racks, keeping me in their sight, and the cashier just wanted me to move on so she could get to the next customer.

I checked my watch as I left the store. Fourteen minutes had passed since the shooting, meaning Ironbridge had had

fourteen minutes to set a new plan in motion. I tried to figure
out what their end game was, but my brain was still trying
to process the information Mickey Donovan had given me a
couple hours ago. These assholes clearly were reacting to his
discovery of the bugs Marika had planted in my home, but I
couldn't figure out what they intended to achieve by snatching Sabrina. Except to use her as leverage because they knew
I was onto them.

* * *

After I left Brookfield Place, I took the 1, 2, 3 line uptown,
getting off at 14th Street just half a block from where I knew
a Duane Reade drugstore would be. Inside I purchased a prepaid phone that came with sixty minutes of untraceable talk
time. As I walked out of the store, I wrestled it out of its
plastic packaging and dialed a toll-free number to activate
the network service. Next, I punched in Marika's number,
waited for someone to answer.

"Who the fuck is this?"

"Who the fuck do you think?" I replied.

"You are becoming one massive pain in the ass, Kane,"
the man on the other end snapped. "One more fuck-up and
your little girl is as good as dead."

Which told me she wasn't, not yet. But I also knew I
didn't have any cards to play. "Let me trade places with her."

"That's not how this works, asshole. You don't have a lot
of room to bargain in this."

"I haven't even figured out what this is," I said.

"Then you are one real dumb fuck. Do you play chess?"

"Fuck that," I replied. "Where's my daughter?"

"Ever heard of the Ilundain variation?" he asked, ignoring my response.

"Goddamn it! Where's Sabrina?" I screamed into the phone.

"Take it easy, Kane. Fact is, you're trapped. We've got your little girl, and that means we've got you. Checkmate."

"I can go to the police," I threatened him.

He laughed at my words, and said, "They all say that, sooner or later. Never works out well, I'm afraid."

They all say that. How many times had they done this sort of thing? I wondered. "How do I even know she's alive?"

"You don't. But you have my word, she's watching *Shrek*."

"Show me."

"No can do, pardner," he said in a voice that made me want to strangle him through the phone.

"Then we have nothing to talk about," I told him, and hung up. I fought every instinct not to answer when it rang, and rang again, and then again. That would hand the end game back to them and, extending his own analogy, result in certain checkmate.

I had no leverage here except to make these fuckers come to me.

Problem was, I had no plan. My only objective was to save Sabrina, even if it meant giving up my life in exchange for hers. Not something they seemed interested in at all. She was an innocent party to all that had happened today, but I had no doubt these fucks saw her as nothing more than eventual collateral damage. And there was no way I could trust them to let her go if I gave myself up. Still, I had to do something to keep them off-center. I collected my bearings, figured out I was only a few blocks from the old meatpacking district, which, like many run-down areas of Manhattan, was going through a process of regentrification. Old warehouses and slaughterhouses and abandoned factories at one point had given way to crack houses and cheap bars, and now the area was transforming into a neighborhood of trendy bars, galleries, restaurants.

I knew the area because an old friend from college had been interested in renovating one of the dilapidated brick shells, and was pitching a scheme to turn it into an upscale nightclub to anyone who would listen. The building was close to several chic hotels that were giving the area a badly needed cultural infusion, and there was talk that the neighborhood was fast becoming one of the swankiest destinations in lower Manhattan. Plus, it was located less than three blocks from the NYPD's Sixth Precinct house, which might come in handy if things started to spiral down the drain.

I crossed Hudson Street against the light, dodging cabs and service vans and delivery trucks. A bike messenger raced around the corner and practically ran me over, and I stumbled on the curb as I tied to catch my balance. I turned to curse at the guy, but he was already well past me, weaving his way through traffic. Without losing my stride, I speed-walked up the sidewalk, checking every doorway for street numbers or any familiar sign from the last time I was here. I recognized almost nothing and found it hard to believe the neighborhood could change that fast in only a few months. I was certain the structure my buddy was planning to gut was along here somewhere, but I felt completely lost.

I stopped at the next corner to get a sense of direction, and that's when I turned and saw a black Land Rover Defender bearing down on me a half block back. Same sort of vehicle I'd seen earlier when I was running after Donovan toward Grand Central. Instinct and paranoia seized me at the same moment, and I kicked into high gear and bolted through the intersection. I heard horns and a crunch of metal behind me as I veered across two lanes of cars, then made a mad dash up the sidewalk on the other side of the street. As I darted around a dog walker, I happened to glance up and spotted a railroad bridge spanning the street a half block ahead of me, a set of brick stairs leading up from the sidewalk.

Holy shit . . . the High Line, I said to myself.

The elevated park where Alison and I used to take Sabrina on weekends was directly ahead, and I took the steps one at a time. I swerved around a group of girls in private school uniforms, licking ice cream cones and giggling, which only caused me to think of my daughter. Where was she, and what were these shitheads doing to her at that very moment? I doubted these Ironbridge scumbags would harm her physically before they had me under wraps, which told me I had to stay at least a step ahead of them until I could come up with a workable offense.

On the street below a door slammed, and I heard the slap of footsteps on pavement. I had no idea how many men had been inside the Land Rover, and when I hit the top step, I glanced both ways, then quickly made my way north. I zigzagged in and around the crowd of pedestrians—old and young, men and women, tourists and locals, all of them out for a quiet stroll in the spring sun. I stole a glance over my shoulder, caught a flash of movement back at the stairs I'd just climbed up from the street. Someone was close, and getting closer.

The guy was about thirty yards back, dressed in black jeans and a T-shirt with a red logo that looked like the Rolling Stones lips. I wondered if the prick would try to shoot me with all these people around, not giving a damn who else might get hit. That seemed to be the way they worked, and I didn't expect them to stop now.

I veered around an elderly couple that had stopped to admire the view down 14th Street toward the river, then raced past some children who were cooling their feet in a fountain. It was an unusually warm spring afternoon, and people were dressed in shorts or skirts, reading books and listening to music and playing video games on their phones—all of them totally oblivious to what was going on around them.

That changed an instant later at the sound of the first shot. A bullet ricocheted off the metal railing in front of me, where a young man was taking a selfie with his girlfriend. They both froze for a second before the man—I figured him for early twenties, with a frizzy soul patch—cranked his head around to see what had caused the noise.

"What the hell?" he cursed.

The gunman squeezed off another shot, this one missing me but striking the young woman in the arm. The force of impact spun her around, and she dropped to the pavement, a red pucker forming where the slug pounded into a tattoo just below her shoulder.

She screamed. So did her boyfriend. Then others joined in, and a swarm of people ran. They scattered to the north and south because on the High Line there was nowhere else to go. The gunman seemed undeterred by the commotion; he just kept advancing on me, his gun extended outward as people dived to the pathway.

But he wasn't there for them. This was no random attack, no lunatic with an arsenal of weapons trying to shoot up a school or a theater. Or even the narrowest park in New York City. He had one mission, and that seemed to be to take out the son of a bitch named Cameron Kane.

I kept running. The screams of panic receded in both directions, including the man with his injured girlfriend.

That meant the two of us now were alone on this section of the High Line.

By now someone had called 911, and in the distance I heard a siren. One way or another, this was going to end soon. I casually made my way through the Chelsea Market transverse, past the ice-cream cart where Sabrina habitually ordered her chocolate cone every weekend. I only had a few seconds to get out of there before someone realized I'd been involved with this active shooting incident, but I figured a running man attracts more attention than someone on a leisurely stroll, taking in the sights.

As I neared 18th Street, I spotted an exit to the sidewalk, figured this was the easiest way off the elevated track. I took the steps two at a time and was breathing hard by the time I hit the street. I bent over to catch my breath, when I heard a squeal of tires directly behind me and the black Defender jerked to a halt alongside me.

A different man in black jeans and matching T-shirt jumped out and moved toward me. I barely had time to react, definitely did not see the device he was holding when he pulled the trigger and two electrodes pierced my light jacket. They embedded themselves in my chest, and shock was immediate and excruciating as fifty thousand volts shot through me, rattling my entire core as I fell to the concrete in a massive seizure of pain and terror.

The next few seconds were a blur. I remember being lifted—dragged, more like it—into the rear of the Defender and a black hood being jammed over my head. At some point the electroshock ceased, but the barbs remained fixed in my skin. The implied message: give us any trouble, and you go through hell again. I was still shaking from the first convulsions and wasn't eager for more, so I lay on the floor where they dumped me, trying my best not to piss my pants.

At some point I heard some mumbling, and someone lifted up the corner of my hood. I felt something sharp prick me in the neck, like the stinger of an angry wasp. A few seconds after that, my brain fogged up, and then I blacked out.

CHAPTER

31

Saturday

WHEN I WOKE up, it was night.

I could see the sparkle of city lights reaching way out into the distance, like fresh-cut diamonds and rubies scattered in a jeweler's tray. My eyes were still a bit fuzzy, so I blinked a few times to reset my vision. Not much help, just enough to make out the terminus of the Brooklyn Bridge and some of the midtown towers. And a string of pinpricks that I determined was traffic hustling up FDR Drive.

This meant my hood was gone, which was both a good thing and a bad thing. Good because I was still alive, and my captors most likely were done transporting me. Bad because it appeared they weren't concerned that I might get a look at them when they returned to whatever place this was. I felt an itch in my neck—possibly a residual effect of the taser jolt—but when I tried to scratch it, I realized my wrists were constrained with zip cuffs. So were my ankles. I was bound to a chair with layers of duct tape, same kind as I assumed was affixed over my mouth.

As consciousness began to return, I glanced around the room. It was large, about fifteen by twenty, and a single mattress lay on the hardwood floor in one corner. A cheap desk from a warehouse supply outlet was positioned in another, and I was imprisoned in what I figured was the accompanying chair, with the wheels removed so it couldn't move. One wall was floor-to-ceiling glass, with the expansive view that told me I was on a top floor of a high-rise building. And, judging from the landmarks I was able to discern, somewhere downtown on the eastern edge of the Financial District.

The only other object I was able to see was a camera in the corner of the far ceiling, its lens angled at where I was bound and gagged.

Instinctively I tried to wrestle my hands free from the self-locking nylon ties, but whoever had zipped them up had given me no room to maneuver. Same with my feet. The only movement I was able to manage was to turn my neck a few degrees from right to left, and it was clear I wasn't going anywhere.

I was still dressed in the jeans and T-shirt I'd purchased at Old Navy, but my jacket was gone, as were my Colt .380 Mustang Pocketlite and my prepaid phone, along with virtually any hope for survival.

I recalled what Mickey Donovan had said about Zaccaro/ Harding's cab driver dropping him off at a residential tower on William Street, at an address he refused to give me. A residence owned by a subsidiary of a shell company that was owned by the mercenary group known as Ironbridge. Was that where I'd been transported, drugged to the world and a black bag pulled over my head?

More important, could it also mean Sabrina was in this place too, maybe in the room next to mine?

Any answers to my questions would have to wait. Whoever was watching the security monitor must have known I was awake, because a few minutes later I heard a key turning in a lock. Three of them, in fact, and then the door to my right swung open. A man in black jeans and armored vest over a matching black T-shirt entered, a threatening handgun and extra magazines strapped to a belt at his side.

"You are one stubborn son of a bitch," he said as he came over to where I was seated and rapidly yanked the tape from my mouth.

"And you are one heartless motherfucker," I replied, recognizing his voice from earlier. "And by the way, Bobby Fischer crushed the Ilundain variation. I thought you'd want to know."

"What?"

"You mentioned it on the phone earlier. I photographed Fischer once, at his home in Iceland. Not long before he died. Told me he destroyed some chess master Robask, or something like that."

"Karl Robatsch." The guy with all the armament glared at me with a sneer that would have made Elvis proud, then nudged the door closed with his foot. "None of that matters, now that we've got you and your daughter."

"So what now? You're just going to kill us?"

He shook his head, said, "Not here. Too much trouble getting you down to the garage if you're already dead. You're going to go for a ride."

"Where?"

"Does it really matter?"

It did to me, but it clearly was only a rhetorical question. "You must be Toole," I said. "Great American soldier and patriot."

"You don't have a clue."

"At least I was able to look in the mirror this morning with pride."

The man who didn't deny his name touched the butt of his gun but didn't draw. "You've been a lot more trouble than you're worth, Kane," he said. "Time's up."

"I don't care about me, but you're just going to shoot a seven-year-old girl in cold blood?"

That brought an evil grin to his face. "Well, I've been thinking about that, Mr. Father of the Year. You're right— you are of no use to us, so yes . . . we're going to take you off the board, to continue the chess metaphors. But your daughter—well, I made a quick call to an associate of mine in Panama, and he tells me there's a healthy market for pretty little girls down there. For the right price, of course. Seems your sweet little Sabrina has an interesting life ahead of her."

I couldn't tell if he was simply taunting me or just baring his vile soul. I had no idea what these people were fully capable of, although Donovan had given me a good idea. Zemira Moon too. If Toole was looking for a reaction, however, I wasn't about to give him the pleasure, so instead I released a torrent of swear words in my brain without letting one of them get past my lips.

After a few seconds, he shrugged and said, "Well, time to get this show on the road."

"Do I at least get to see my daughter one last time, Toole?"

Again, he neither confirmed nor denied the name. Instead, he pulled an object from his gun belt and flicked a switch with his thumb. Instantly a blade popped out, four inches of serrated steel with a nasty hooked tip.

"As long as you don't give me a reason to relieve you of your eyesight," he said with a snarl. The blade sliced through the zip cuffs binding my ankles, but he kept the bonds tight around my wrists. He hauled me out of the chair, shoved the knife up under my chin. "One move, this goes straight up through your palate into your brain. Got it?"

"Ten-four."

"Then move."

I moved. Not as if I had a choice. I felt a trickle of blood from where Toole was pressing the blade into my skin, and he guided me out the door into a hallway. From the illumination of a dim overhead light, I could see two more doors to my left—most likely bedrooms, similar to the one I'd just left—and an open area a few yards down the corridor to my right. He pushed me in that direction, and I slowly trudged toward what I assumed was the living room of this downtown penthouse. If I were a betting man, I'd wager my life that this was where Harding had checked in last Saturday after spying on his son at Choate. But I had no chips with which to gamble, since my entire life already seemed to be in the pile in the center of the table.

"Is he still here?" I asked anyway.

"Who the fuck are you talking about?"

"Harding. Or did the motherfucker already bug out, back to Rio?"

"Last warning I'm giving you, Kane," he said. "And you might want to check your language at the door. There's a young lady present."

By then we were walking into the living room, and I felt a tsunami of relief wash through me. Sitting on a leather chair near another wall of glass was Sabrina, a very large man also dressed in black holding her in place with a massive arm. I caught the scorpion tattoo, decided not to mention it. A look of absolute terror was on my daughter's face, but her eyes brightened when she saw me come into the room.

"Daddy!" She tried to jump up and run to me, but the man sitting next to her tightened his grip and held her back.

At the same time a pit bull tethered to the leg of a couch sprang up with a nasty snarl and lunged at her.

"Meet Spartacus," Toole said. "And I should warn you, his bite is just as bad as his bark."

I ignored both him and the slobbering dog, not an easy thing to do. "Sugar," I said to Sabrina, "have they hurt you?"

She seemed too terrified to speak and simply shook her head. The man gripped her even harder, causing her to wince. And causing me to decide to do horrific things to him if I ever got even a remote chance.

"Such a heart-warming sight," Toole said. "Father–daughter reunion. Makes me feel warm and fuzzy all over."

At that point a door off the marble foyer opened, and Marika walked in. Our eyes met for just a second, but then she quickly turned away and refused to look at me again. Nor did she dare venture a glance at Sabrina. Instead, she moved to her right and wandered down the same hallway that led to my brief holding cell, and I heard another door close. I thought of a dozen things I wanted to say to her, followed by a dozen more. None of them was suitable for mentioning within earshot of my daughter, however, so I kept my observations to myself.

"All right," Toole continued. "Time to hit the road. You first."

He meant me. This time he dug the curved tip of his knife into the fleshy part of my back near my kidneys and gave me a thrust into the foyer toward a massive mahogany door. There was no knob like a normal entry, just a button on the wall to the right.

Toole touched it with the blade, and a second later it slid open, revealing a private elevator about six feet square. I'd been correct about that part, and I was convinced I was right about this being the place where Harding had holed up after his trip to Connecticut. Toole prodded me again and pushed me inside; we were followed by Sabrina and the man who had been restraining the dog named Spartacus. Instead of a knife, he had his massive hand tightly wrapped around her upper arm.

We rode down in silence, me pressed into one corner and Sabrina in the opposite corner. No chance for a hug, or even a light touch of her hair. Neither of us dared say a word.

There were three lighted buttons inside the door—P, L, and G—which told me this elevator serviced only one residential unit. The penthouse. Perfect for privacy, security, and protection. Toole pushed the button for the garage, and when the doors slid open on silent runners twenty seconds later, two banks of recessed overhead illumination flickered on. He pushed me out first, and I saw we were in a private, walled area separated from the rest of the underground parking. Mirrors on one side, a roll-up door opposite it, walls painted bright white, and a rubberized floor without a scratch or a speck of oil to be seen.

Two vehicles were parked in this private area: the black Land Rover Defender that had chased me earlier in the day, and a black-over-gold Rolls Royce Spectre plugged into a wall charger. Identical to the luxury car I'd seen parked just down the street from my condo in the Village, same as the one I'd seen when I left the Indian restaurant yesterday with Mrs. Harding—and probably had missed a dozen other times over the last few days.

"Looks like torture and treason are profitable," I said.

"Shut the fuck up," Toole said. "You're lucky I don't open you up now."

Another man—again in black jeans and T-shirt—was standing in front of the Land Rover. Arms were folded across his chest, gun strapped to his waist, trying to look like a tough guy. I figured him for the driver.

Toole pushed me toward the rear of the Defender, then opened the door and thrust me inside. My head collided with the roof and sent a round of searing pain shooting through my skull, but I kept it to myself. The more agony Toole could inflict, the more power he felt he had.

"I wish I could do the honors myself," he said in my ear, "but unfortunately, pressing matters demand that I remain behind."

"Till we meet again, then," I replied.

"Keep dreaming, Kane."

The thug who had been guarding Sabrina strapped her into the front seat, then climbed in back next to me. He pressed a gun into my ribs, probably figuring Sabrina wasn't about to make a move on these bastards. Neither was I, but I clearly was more of a threat than she was.

Eventually the driver slid in behind the wheel and started the engine. He hit a button in the ceiling, and the door ahead of us began to roll up while Toole stood by the elevator and waited until we were gone.

32

Private as the exclusive garage was, it used the same
ramp to the street as the rest of the underground parking. Money can only buy so much, even in the heart of Wall
Street.

When we got to the top of the incline, the driver hesitated a second as he checked for traffic, then began to make
a right turn. At that moment a large dark sedan swerved in
front of us and braked to a halt. My attention was focused
one hundred percent on Sabrina in the front seat, so I didn't
see all that happened for the next few seconds. The driver in
front of me leaned on the horn and cussed at the car blocking
our path, and out of the corner of my eye I saw a flurry of
sudden movement. Then the side window of the Land Rover
exploded in a galaxy of stars that cascaded in on him, followed immediately by a massive hand—Black with a large
gold pinkie ring—that reached in and slammed his forehead
against the steering wheel, hard.

The driver slumped sideways in the seat, toward Sabrina,
who would have screamed had she been able. The thug next
to me raised his gun to shoot but, before his finger could

squeeze the trigger, he found himself staring down the barrel of a larger gun—and the large, dark eyes behind it.

"Drop it," the stranger ordered.

"Who the fuck are you?" the guy next to me snapped.

"I'd say 'your worst nightmare,' but that's too cliché," Zemira Moon snarled. Despite the chaos of the moment, I recognized his voice and thought, *What the fuck?* "But for the sake of conversation, let's just say I'm your papa. And Papa's got a brand-new bag."

"You don't know what the fuck you're doing."

Moon seemed to be of a different opinion, however, and said, "Give me your weapon."

"Like hell—"

"Sucks to be you," Moon said, and shot him in the shoulder.

The man beside me wailed in sudden pain as the force of the shot blew him sideways. His gun dropped from his hand to the floor, but my zip cuffs prevented me from grabbing it. Sabrina screamed. Moon tried opening my door, but a few tugs on the handle did nothing, so he reached through the broken front window and hit the "Unlock" toggle. The entire time he kept his gun trained on the man beside me, who was rocking back and forth in agony.

"Get out," Moon said.

"Can't," I told him, showing him my wrists. "Zip ties."

"Shit." He dug into a pocket, pulled out a folding knife that seemed smaller than Toole's, but just as sharp. A few quick flicks of the blade, and I was free. I slipped out of the backseat and stood up. He pressed the knife into my hand. "Get your daughter. Be quick."

I pivoted around the rear of the car and yanked the front passenger door open. The look in Sabrina's eyes was one of sheer terror, and all I wanted to do was hold her in my arms and squeeze as hard as I could. I gave her a hard hug, then said, "You're going to be just fine, sugar."

I sliced through her cuffs and then pulled the tape from her mouth as gently as I could. As soon as she was able to speak, she said, "What's going on, Daddy?"

"I'll explain later. Come with me."

"Where?"

Good question, and I didn't know the answer. I glanced over at Moon, who was collecting guns and phones from the scumbags in the Defender. He cocked his head toward the car he'd used to block the garage ramp, a dark blue Jaguar with a chrome cat poised on the hood. One of the older luxury models that still possessed a look of elegance and grace.

I bundled Sabrina up in my arms and carried her to where the Jag was parked, engine still running. I pulled open the door and gently placed her on the soft, springy rear seat. She had wrapped her arms around me and was clinging with all her might, and I clung back. Then I slid in beside her and closed the door, just as two more gunshots cracked the night. I glanced over at the Defender, but Moon was already lumbering toward us. He pivoted around the back of the car and dropped his large frame into the driver's seat. As he slammed the door, he glanced over his shoulder at Sabrina and said, "Pleased to meet you, young lady."

"Are you from Wakanda?" she asked him, her eyes wide with wonder. She must have watched the *Black Panther* movie at one of her sleepovers, since I was pretty sure she'd never seen it at ours.

He made the crossed-arms salute and said, "At your service."

A second later he shifted into drive, and we were barreling down the street. What street, I did not know, nor did it matter. All I knew was we were out of there, away from these bastards who had snatched my daughter and threatened to kill us both. Or, in Sabrina's case, possibly worse.

This time of night—or early morning—traffic was light. I stared out the window as my brain processed thousands of bits of information. Intuition told me everything was going to be all right, but some distant reptilian instinct felt exposed and vulnerable. A twinge of dread rattled my nerves, an untethered reaction to all that had gone down over the past twenty-four hours. I was still fueled by an adrenaline rush, and as Moon hung a sharp right, I stole a glance behind us.

"No sign of them," he said, as if reading my mind.

My daughter was quaking with fear on the seat next to me. My arms were still wrapped tightly around her, and she began to whimper. Zemira Moon made another turn, took another look in the mirror, then quickly glanced back at us again.

"You must be Sabrina," he said. "That's a very pretty name."

His deep voice and honest tone served to lessen her quivering, and she said, "It came from a person in a movie. You're really from Wakanda?"

"I've been all over the world," the hulking man told her. "And I'm a friend."

"It's okay, sugar," I assured her in as soothing a voice as I could muster. "I know this man, and he's on our side."

"Which side is that?" Sabrina wanted to know.

"The good side."

She considered this, seemed to accept what I was saying.

"Your father's right," Moon told her with a warm, broad smile.

"Where are we going?" Sabrina asked.

"That depends on your father." He glanced at me in the rearview mirror.

"Me?" I asked.

"We can't go to your place—not yet," he said. "Any suggestions?"

"A hotel?"

"Too public."

I gave the question some serious thought and eventually said, "My brother, up on 88th Street."

Moon considered this for a few seconds, then offered a slight shrug. "That works."

"How did you find us?" I wanted to know.

"I don't have time to explain. Not here."

I nodded, then squeezed Sabrina closer and said, "If we can trust anyone, we can trust this man."

"Darn tootin'," she replied, squeezing back. "He's a warrior."

I gazed out the tinted window and studied the empty storefronts and parked cars and ghosts of steam rising from subway grates. My mind ricocheted from Marika to Harding, Donovan to Toole. Terminal 8 at JFK, dental records, prime numbers, and blockchain programs. And, most important, Alison. The events of the last week had been set in motion by a chance airport encounter with a man who shouldn't be alive, but very clearly was. I had absolutely no doubt in my mind who he was, and my instinct was on the mark.

"Business coming through. Money on the move."

33

SEVERAL RIGHTS AND lefts later, we were heading north on the FDR. There was almost no traffic this time of night, and we had all three lanes almost all to ourselves. Every five seconds Moon checked his mirrors to see if we were being followed, and seemed to breathe easier as the heartbeats ticked by. A movement from a string concerto was coming from the British car's high-end speakers, and I said, "What are you listening to?"

"A ritornello," he replied. "From Vivaldi's Concerto for Four Violins in B Minor."

I sat up and tentatively peered over the windowsill to my right, then craned my neck and glanced up at the moon in the western sky. Waxing gibbous, as the meteorologist on the radio had explained earlier this morning. *Yesterday morning.* A tightness gripped my chest as if I were having a mild heart attack, and I took a deep breath. I had to hold Sabrina close in order to keep my hands from shaking with uncertainty. The rest of me too.

"How did you know where we were?" I asked him.

"Do you still have that card I gave you?"

"They took everything," I said, shaking my head.

Moon held up a device about the shape and size of a cell phone, and said, "But not until after they brought you to that building."

"You mean . . . it was a tracking device?"

"There's a chip embedded in it," Moon admitted. "Range is five miles, give or take. And it was expensive, so I'm going to want it back when this is all over."

"Yeah, along with my wallet and gun." I glanced at Sabrina, who didn't seem to hear me.

"I didn't figure you for a gun type of guy," he said. "What kind?"

"A Colt .380 Pocketlite, short barrel."

"Good weapon for protection. Did you fire it?"

"Never got the chance," I said.

"Chance to do what?" my daughter asked, wriggling in my arms. Had she really been listening all this time?

"Kiss you goodbye this morning," I replied, the lie coming to me almost too quickly.

At that she reached up and gave me a peck on the cheek, then said, "I love you, Daddy."

I returned her kiss and told her, "I love you too."

"I don't think we'll be seeing Mika again."

"Probably not," I agreed.

"I don't think she's a very good person," Sabrina went on.

You got that right, sugar, I thought. Then I leaned forward and said to Zemira Moon, "How did you know I'd need that card, anyway?"

"Because I know how these people work," he replied. "But there's another question you should be asking yourself."

"I'm too tired to think," I told him.

"Then I'll help you out. How do you think these motherfu—" His eyes slipped to Sabrina in his rearview mirror, and he corrected himself: "these creeps knew where to find you?"

"They were tracking my phone."

As soon as I said it, I realized the fallacy in my reasoning. I'd left my phone in Rockefeller Park after they'd killed Lillian Sloane, and had bought a burner at Duane Reade. Yet they still had found me just a minute after I'd crossed Hudson Street, and had apprehended me right after I'd descended the stairs from the High Line. How would they possibly have known where I was?

"My phone got busted earlier," I finally said. "It couldn't have been that."

"It wasn't," Moon agreed. "While you were busy running all over Manhattan this afternoon, I dropped by your place on Jane Street again and took a closer look around. Care to guess what I found?"

"I'm tired of guessing . . . just tell me."

"What I found was you have eleven pairs of shoes," he said. "Twelve, if you count the ones you've got on your feet. And what do you suppose I found in the soles of every one of them?"

This time there was no surprise. "Tracking devices," I said, letting out a weary sigh, suddenly feeling defeated.

"Two of them, one each in the right and left," Moon confirmed. "These guys don't play around. Go ahead—take them off and check where the sole meets the heel in the back."

Moon switched on the rear dome light so I could see what I was doing. I took off my right shoe and looked where he'd suggested: sure enough, there was a tiny separation where the leather had been partially pried away from the heel. And there, inside the gap, was a small object that looked to be about an eighth of an inch thick and an inch wide.

"Christ on a cracker," I said.

"Who's having crackers?" Sabrina murmured next to me as she stirred against my left shoulder.

"No crackers," I told her. "But we'll get you something when we get to Uncle Elliot's."

"Not ice cream," she said. "Mika bought me some after she picked me up at the zoo, before she took me to *that place*."

"No, not ice cream. Maybe some hot cocoa with marshmallows."

She nodded and made a sort of purring sound, then rested her head on my arm again.

Moon glanced at me in his rearview mirror and said, "Use that knife I gave you to dig 'em out, then toss them out the window. Both at the same time. Same with your daughter's shoes."

I did as he instructed, and thirty seconds later I was holding four flat GPS chips in my hand. "Damn," I swore under my breath as I looked at them. Total state of the art, not that I had the vaguest idea what the art of tracking devices was these days. I hit the window switch and waited for the glass to roll down. "Right here?" I asked Moon up in the front seat.

"Do it quick," he said with a nod. "I'm taking the next exit up ahead."

I took one last look at the four transmitter chips, then flung them out the window into the night. "What happens when we get to my brother's house?" I asked. "It's pretty early in the morning. I'm sure no one is up."

"Too many questions, man," Moon replied. "Let me handle the ops, and you take care of your little girl, there."

I felt the panic tighten in my throat, not liking the sound of this. None of it.

"These guys are relentless," I told him. "You saw what they did to Mickey."

"Mickey Mouse?" Sabrina asked, stirring beside me.

"That's right, sugar," I replied. I hated to lie to her, but she'd already been through enough today.

"What did they do to him?"

"You know those big white buttons he has on his pants?" I said to her in the most soothing voice I could muster. "Well, someone took them."

"Did his pants fall down?" she asked with a giggle.

"Something like that," I told her, kissing her on the top of the head.

She sighed and snuggled up against my shoulder again. I stroked her hair and felt her relax, even if she didn't go to sleep.

"Don't worry, man," Moon assured me from the darkness of the front seat. "You and your brother—everyone— will be fine."

We were on York Avenue now, having taken the 91st Street turn off the FDR. It was still several hours before daybreak, not even a crease of dawn in the eastern sky. I could hear the sounds of New York City waking up: garbage trucks emptying trash from dumpsters, delivery vans barreling toward the shops and restaurants of midtown Manhattan. Somewhere a dog barked and a car door slammed. I leaned back in my seat and closed my eyes for just a second, realizing that just twenty-four hours ago I'd received the panicked phone call from a terrified Elise Dillon, and my life had begun to spin out of its orbit.

Two minutes later we pulled up in front of Elliot's apartment building. It was an old prewar walk-up, no elevator, just a set of stairs that had been painted and sanded and painted again over the decades. An ancient fire escape was bolted to the facade, its platforms and ladders zigzagging all the way up to the roof. A single tree of undetermined species grew from a hole near the curb, a favorite target of neighborhood dogs. Across the street, a lamppost cast grotesque shadows that reminded me of an avant-garde film I'd seen in a film class in college: *The Cabinet of Dr. Caligari*. Funny the weird shit you remember when your brain is in total overdrive.

Elliot's wife, Janet, was a psychiatric nurse specialist in the mental health unit at Mount Sinai Hospital, and their combined salaries barely afforded the pricey two bedrooms and two baths on the third floor, with just enough left over to save for Julia's college education. If she went to a state school, and if they didn't have any more children. Those were two big ifs. Elliot confided in me once that his wife wanted at least one more child, preferably a boy to balance out their daughter. The all-American, perfect family; all that was missing was a picket fence. My brother, on the other hand, was content to keep things just the way they were, which in his mind meant barely staying above the East Side's low-water financial mark. Now that Julia was eight, the prospect of having another child to feed and clothe was growing slimmer by the day.

"What now?" I asked Zemira Moon from the backseat.

"Now you go inside."

"Hold on . . . I can't just knock on the door at"—I stole a glance at my watch, which I'd forgotten was busted—"whatever ungodly hour it is. We'll wake them up."

"They'll take you in," Moon said. "You're family."

I glanced up at the dark windows, saw the custom drapes that had set them back almost two grand were drawn tightly across the glass. "My brother already thinks I'm nuts," I replied. "What am I going to tell them?"

"Enough, but not too much."

I'm sure Moon didn't see me roll my eyes, which was just as well. I'd had it with his nonanswers, but who was I to quarrel with him? He'd gotten us out of a seriously deep mess, and for that I owed him.

"You're sure we can't just go home?" I asked. "You already took care of those two guys in the Defender."

"The tsunami often is far more devastating than the earthquake," Moon explained. "Like you said, these guys are relentless."

"What if they followed us here?"

"That's why you need to get inside."

"I still don't like this," I objected again. "We could be leading these guys right to us. Right *here*. For all I know, you could be one of them."

"If that were the case, you'd already be dead. Your daughter too."

I considered that logic, realized it made some sort of convoluted sense. "So, if I trust you, what are we supposed to do?"

"Ask your brother to fix some coffee," Moon said. "And some hot chocolate for your daughter, like you said. Visit a while, like family does, and leave the heavy lifting to me."

"And what are you planning to do?"

"Settle a score I should have dealt with a long time ago."

I didn't like the sound of that either, but I felt a layer of the panic begin to ease. Whatever this former special ops guy had in mind, it was bound to be messy. And ugly.

"And you promise my brother and his family—all of us—will be okay?"

"I'll do everything I can to make sure nothing happens to any of you," he assured me. "But only if you move—*now!*"

I hesitated another second, then pushed the door open and gently lifted Sabrina out of the car. "Where will you be?" I asked him.

"Close by."

I nodded at his vagueness as I began to close the door. Then I stopped and poked my head inside as far as I could so Sabrina couldn't hear me. "I was right about Harding, wasn't I?"

"Ten-four," Moon replied, his voice barely above a whisper. "And there's something else you need to know."

"What's that?"

Moon dipped his head in the slightest of nods, then said, "I believe your wife is alive."

I fought the rush of hope that surged through me. "Alive? Where—?"

"Executable bite-sized chunks."

"What's that supposed to mean?"

"It means you get your daughter upstairs, now. If Ironbridge is as good as I think they are, they're probably only minutes out now. You need to be safe."

CHAPTER

34

MY BROTHER SEEMED delighted to see Sabrina and me,
even if it was just barely after four in the morning.
He greeted us with open arms and lifted his niece into the
air and spun her around. Then he steered us into the living
room, where he waved us onto the oversized couch that had
taken us almost a full hour to get up the switchback staircase
the day they'd moved it in.

His wife—my sister-in-law—was far less effusive and
welcoming. I didn't blame her, since we'd shown up in the
middle of the night, totally unannounced, no explanation.
Still, she brought a mug of hot chocolate piled high with
miniature marshmallows to Sabrina, who sighed a contented
"thank you" as she took it in both hands.

"You're welcome, sweetie," Janet said, giving her a kiss on
the forehead and retreating to the kitchen doorway, arms
tucked tightly across her chest.

An uncomfortable silence followed. I felt two very curious pair of eyes on me, wondering what the hell was going on
here. I didn't have an easy answer for that unspoken question, so I simply said, "Is Julia asleep?"

"Yes," Janet said. "And I aim to keep it that way."

Her husband shot her a look that said *"please don't start,"* but she didn't seem to notice. "What's this all about, Cam?" he asked. "I mean, we're always pleased to see you and Sabrina, but this early on a Saturday morning?"

"I didn't know where else to go," I said.

"Did your house burn down or something?" Janet inquired.

"No, nothing like that."

Sabrina's eyes began to droop, and the mug in her hands began to tilt. I rescued it from certain calamity and set it on the coffee table, then gently helped her stretch out on the sofa cushions. My sister-in-law pushed off the wall where she had not stopped staring at me, and stepped forward.

"Let me put her in with Julia," she offered.

"Thank you," I replied as she lifted Sabrina into her arms. "She's totally exhausted after everything that's happened today."

Once they were out of the room, Elliot came over and sat down next to me. "You'll have to forgive Janet, but . . . well, please tell me what the hell is going on." He didn't exactly seem angry, not like his wife. Just anxious, and definitely a little scared. "What's this all about?"

"Did you watch the local news tonight?"

"Some of it. Yankees won, Knicks lost in overtime."

"Did you see anything about a shooting at Grand Central around lunchtime?"

"Yeah. Some lunatic opened fire and shot an ex-cop in the food court. He's lucky to be alive."

"He pulled through?" I asked, relieved by what my brother was saying.

"Critical but stable, was what they said. A couple others were wounded, and witnesses said they saw someone run away from the scene."

I nodded slowly and said, "That was me."

He stared at me a moment, both eyes open as wide as they could possibly go. "Have you totally lost your mind? You shot a cop?"

"No. I was there with him. He was doing some work for me, and it looks like he found out way too much."

"Wait . . . what the fuck." He shot a glance toward the bedroom hallway and lowered his voice. "What the hell are you talking about?"

I didn't say anything for a second or two as I let the gravity of the situation sink in. Eventually, I said, "Remember what I told you last weekend when we were at the Garden?"

"You mean that bullshit about Alison's dead boss?"

"That's right. Maxwell Harding. I told you how I was certain he'd bumped into me in the terminal when I landed at JFK—"

"And I said you were nuts," Elliot finished for me.

"Turns out I'm pretty fucking sane." I gave a quick glance to the hall that led to the bedrooms and added, "Sorry."

Elliot sat very still, his writer's mind working on all the disparate pieces of a twisted puzzle. "You're telling me . . ." His voice trailed off.

"I found out more than I should have," I said, completing his sentence. "Harding's still alive."

"Holy shit, bro. If you're right about this—"

"I *am* right about this. There's no ifs anymore. Which brings me to why we're here. Sabrina and me."

"Yes, please elaborate on that," Janet said, keeping her voice low. She'd quietly emerged from the dark hallway that led to her daughter's room, and was looking at something on her cell phone. Probably a nanny cam app. She didn't seem quite as agitated as when we'd arrived, but there was still a quiver of tension in her tight forehead. Which I totally understood—the protective mother guarding her nest, and all that. "I mean, we're always happy to see you, Cam. But at four in the morning?"

I mentally put myself in her shoes—*both their shoes*—and imagined what I'd be feeling if they'd shown up at my place in the middle of the night. Not just the off-hours imposition, but the worry and fear about what might be going on. I had no easy response to Janet's question. There was no quick journey from point A to point Z, or whatever letter of the alphabet we might be on. I hadn't had time to decide how much—or how little—to tell them about the events of yesterday. To buy some time, I got up from the couch and walked over to the front door, which I'd noticed my brother had not bothered to latch when Sabrina and I had arrived just a few minutes ago.

There were three steel locks, and I threw all of them in rapid order before turning to look at my brother and sister-in-law. The last bolt clicked into place with a heavy thud, as if to convey the gravity connected to what I was about to tell them. There was a moment of silence, and then I started to speak.

"What I'm about to tell you is a long story, but we don't have the luxury of time," I began. "Let me start with the last hour and work my way backward, until you understand what's going on."

"That would be really helpful," Janet replied. She looked at her husband, who nodded in agreement.

I took another second to gather my thoughts, then said, "Today I learned a deep, dark secret I wasn't supposed to know, and people are trying to silence me because of it. Sabrina too."

"Cam, if this is another one of your paranoid stories."

Elliot put a hand on his wife's shoulder, which caused her to stop mid-sentence. "I've known my brother a lot longer than you have, Jan, and we both know that he's a logical, rational guy. Hear him out."

Mrs. Kane clearly did not like to be mansplained by her husband, but she fell silent anyway. She locked her lips with an imaginary key, then folded her hands in her lap and offered an obedient handmaid's smile.

I interpreted the silence as an invitation to continue my story. "Yesterday I was with a friend when he was shot at Grand Central Station. Not long after that, Sabrina was snatched from the zoo in Central Park, and later I was sitting with another friend in a park near Ground Zero when she was killed."

"Oh, dear God," Janet said, her eyes flashing equal parts fear and anger. "And you . . . you led these people here?"

"No . . . I mean, obviously we're here, but I didn't lead them here. In fact, I'm sure they don't even know that I have a brother or that any of you exist." Lie number one, the reality being that I was certain Ironbridge knew every damned thing about me, including my extended family. "My real concern is that Sabrina has had a particularly traumatic day, and this is the best place for her to get away from all that."

Janet Kane didn't appear to be listening, and I didn't blame her. All she seemed to hear were the words *shot*, *snatched*, and *killed*, none of which provided her any comfort that the refuge she had built for her family wasn't about to come under siege. Or subject to some imminent bloodbath.

"Cam, don't take this the wrong way, but I don't want you here," she told me through clenched teeth. She had balled her knuckles into tight fists, although I was pretty sure she wasn't intending to use them on me. Or her husband. "I know we're all family, but you will not jeopardize Julie by bringing your troubles into my home."

I hated to put my brother and sister-in-law in danger, or at odds with each other. "Okay," I said. "I'll leave, right this minute. All I ask is you take care of Sabrina until all this is over."

"But you just said these people are after her too."

"I'm a much bigger threat than she is," I assured her.

Janet obviously didn't like the sound, sight, smell, or feel of this, and the look on her face was one of subdued fury. Again, I didn't blame her.

"Fair enough," she said. "Sabrina can stay. But if all this happened the way you said it did, you need to go somewhere else. Now."

"Honey—" Elliot started to object.

"A mother has to protect her own," Janet said.

"Sabrina doesn't have a mother," her husband pointed out.

"Which is why she can stay. But we're sitting ducks with your brother here."

"No problem," I told her. "It's my juju, and I'll take it with me."

"Cam—" my brother said to me.

"No, Janet is right," I insisted. "The last thing I want to do is place any of you in danger. I'll let you know when the coast is clear."

I turned to go, twisting the locks one by one to open them. But before I got to the last one, there was an unmistakable sound of gunfire out on the street: two short automatic bursts followed by a brief silence, then two more. There was a muffled yelp of some kind down below, and then the apartment was plunged into darkness.

35

M Y SISTER-IN-LAW LET out a scream, a sudden release
of fear that she softened by covering her mouth with
her hand. Not a good time to wake the girls up, even if she
believed her home was under assault. At the same time Elliot
uttered a single curse word under his breath, and then I heard
something tumble to the floor. That led to a longer string of
four-letter words, and a few seconds later the lights flickered
back on.

The thud I'd heard was a hand-carved onyx statue that
was a memento from their vacation to Tulum several years
ago. Elliot had complained that it doubled the weight of his
suitcase to fifty-four pounds, and he'd had to pay an extra
twenty-five dollars to check it through to New York. When
the lights blinked out, he'd jumped, hit his knee on the end
table, and knocked it off. The damned thing had fallen on
his foot, and now he looked as if he wanted to hurl it across
the room.

"Fucking Mayan curse," he swore to himself, then hefted
the heavy object back onto the table.

"Please, honey," his wife said. "The girls."

"Sorry. Goddamned thing could moor a boat."

I wasn't sure if I should stay or go. The brief blackout and gunfire down below on the street clearly indicated that Ironbridge had arrived. Zemira Moon had seemed confident they were on their way, and I hoped he'd taken measures to get the drop on them. But I had no idea what that involved, especially now that the lights were back on and the shooting seemed to have stopped. Had the old special forces operative succeeded in taking out the sons of bitches, or was he bleeding out in a gutter somewhere?

"Close by," as he'd assured me.

I glanced at Elliot, who only offered the slightest of shrugs before looking to his wife for guidance. Janet hadn't moved an inch since the first sound of gunfire, and it didn't look as if she was going to start anytime soon. The raw fear in her eyes was unmistakable, and her hands were trembling.

"You'd better lock up after I go," I told both of them as I turned the last bolt and pulled the door open.

"Are you crazy?" she said, almost spitting the words out. "Close that."

"I need to leave," I replied. "You were right—you're all in danger as long as I'm here."

But Elliot was shaking his head now, his senses coming back to him. "Nonsense," he said, waving me away from the door. "You go out there, you'll get shot."

"Same thing might happen to all of us if I stay here. I'll take my chances."

"I don't like this."

"You've got to let him go, dear," Janet encouraged her husband. "Like he said, it's him they're after, not us."

"But—"

"But nothing," I said. "Lock up tight the second I'm gone. I'll call you later."

"When?" My brother wanted to know.

"When this is all over, I'll be back to pick up Sabrina," I replied. Then I slipped out into the hallway, pulling the door tight behind me. I was still standing at the top of the stairs when I heard the muffled scurrying of feet behind me in the apartment, then a trio of locks clicking into place.

I stole a quick glance down the stairwell to the ground level, then started descending one cautious step at a time. The stairs had the telltale creak of old prewar wood, and there was no use thinking I could make it to the foyer undetected. Still, it had been several minutes since I'd heard gunfire, and I took that as a good sign.

I made it down to the main floor vestibule, which, as with my own building, was locked from the outside by a heavy wood door with obscured glass. The walls were a stylish, muted cream, and the trim around the front entrance and the first-floor apartment doors was painted a chocolate brown, to match the stairs. Because it was still dark, I couldn't see what was going on out on the street, and it would be foolish to just walk out and see what the sitrep was. I had no key to my brother's place, so once I was outside, there was no coming back in. Nor did I have a weapon, a grim reality that spoke for itself.

But right then, in that moment, I wasn't thinking about myself. I was thinking about Sabrina, who I kept telling myself was safe upstairs with my brother and his family. None of them had any direct connection to what had gone down today—*yesterday*—and if Ironbridge was out for revenge or retribution, I was their prime target.

I cupped my hands around my eyes and tried to peer through the glass, as if that would give me a better view of what lay beyond. I chewed my lip a second, then decided to go all in. I gripped the old brass latch and started to thumb it down, and that's when I caught a brief flash of movement behind me, reflected in the glass.

Acting purely on instinct, I whirled around at the same time I balled my right hand into a fist. But a massive hand grabbed it before it could even begin to do any damage, squeezed until my fingers went limp like sausages.

"What the fuck do you think you're doing?" Zemira Moon demanded as he gripped my hand tight. Tighter than tight.

"I heard gunshots," I told him.

"And because of that you decided to come down and see what was going on? Unarmed?"

"I told you, they took my gun," I said, as if that explained everything.

"That's no excuse for stupidity," Moon said, releasing my hand. "Good thing I've got everything under control."

"Where were you?" I wanted to know.

"Taking care of business."

"I mean just now. I didn't see you until you snuck up right behind me."

"*Snuck* isn't a real word," Moon said as he gave a quick jerk of his head toward the middle of the three doors behind them. "Service entry, opens onto the alley out back. Which is where we're going now."

"What about Ironbridge?" I asked him.

"Incapacitated."

"What does that mean? Is my daughter safe?"

"As long as she stays here," Moon replied. "But you and me, we've got one more thing to take care of."

"What kind of thing?"

Zemira pulled open the service entry door, and I noticed that the lock had been busted right through the wooden jamb. "After you," Moon said.

"Where are we going?"

"Like I told you before, executable bite-sized chunks."

*   *   *

Ten minutes later we were speeding down Seventh Avenue. A different concerto was playing on the stereo, this one Vivaldi's Concerto in B minor for violin. At least, that's what Moon told me as he cranked the volume up and gripped the wheel at ten and two.

This time I was sitting in the front seat of Moon's Jaguar, staring through the windshield at the street. Lighted storefronts and neon signs and darkened theater marquees slid by, the glitz and glamour of the city that never sleeps reflecting off the car's ultra-waxed hood. I paid no attention to the last stragglers of the night, skulking about in the streets, instead focusing on the gun I'd been told to retrieve from the glove box. Moon had told me it was a SIG Sauer P226—originally designed for the US military and carried by elite forces— widely considered to be the premier combat pistol.

"Nine-millimeter with an X-Five undercut at the trigger guard, which allows for a higher grip and greater shooting control," he'd explained patiently. "Plus, there's front-cocking serrations, giving it greater purchase for cycling the action and clearing it. That one there holds ten rounds, although you can get it with a twenty extended. And there's no safety, so be careful with it."

Safety or not, the last thing I wanted right now was a gun. Or a reason to shoot one. I just wanted all this to be over, my life back to whatever semblance of normal I could expect. Some of my fear had been eased when Moon assured me that Sabrina would be safe at my brother's place, but the P226 had caused my panic to reboot.

"Now can you tell me where we're going?" I asked again as Moon hooked a right onto West 41st.

"Lincoln Tunnel."

"We're going to New Jersey? What the fuck is out in New Jersey?"

"They don't call it the Garden State for nothing."

"C'mon, man. Give me *something*."

"I gave you that gun, didn't I?"

"Yeah, but you didn't say why."

"Sometimes it's better to appreciate life's unsolved questions than to be burdened with the reality of the answers."

"What, now you're some kind of armchair philosopher or something?"

"No . . . just a pragmatist," Moon said as he stared through the windshield. "A pragmatist who wants to live to see another sunrise, and the one after that."

"And answering one goddamned question will keep that from happening?"

"It could," Moon told me. "Look, Kane . . . just relax. Let your mind unwind, and leave the driving to me."

"Easy for you to say," I grunted. "You know where we're going."

"The night's still young."

"Not really," I said, nodding toward the glow of a new day that was just starting to infuse the eastern horizon with a bittersweet glow. Then, realizing I wasn't getting anywhere with my current line of questioning, I asked, "Any update on Donovan?"

Moon turned down the volume and said, "Punctured lung, shattered clavicle, major blood loss. Hanging by a thread. But like I said, he's one tough dog. If anyone can make it, he can."

That was the best news I'd heard since all this began yesterday, and I told him so. Then I said, "How'd you meet him, anyway?"

Moon seemed to think about this, realizing there was no reason not to divulge a bit. "He was working a case. A double homicide, couple years back. It involved someone I knew, another special forces guy. Mick came around, asking questions. He was a stand-up guy, smart, very intuitive. I've met a few investigators in my life, cops and MPs, and Mick is one of the best. I don't know if what I told him helped any, but he solved the case. Perp is doing life up in Attica, no parole."

"Yesterday he mentioned a man named Eagleton," I said. "So did you."

"Motherfucker," was all Moon said.

"He's in charge of this whole thing, right?"

"Not anymore."

I studied Moon's profile in the predawn darkness and asked, "What are you saying?"

Moon shook his head. "I've already said too much."

He started to turn the volume up again, but I swatted his hand away. He shot me a dark glare, but I'd had it with his "executable bite-sized" shit.

"C'mon, man," I told him, not quite pleading. "Just level with me: What do you know about my wife?"

"Just enough to get your hopes up," he said. "Thing is, the last time I tried that, it didn't end well. Just trust me."

* * *

An hour later we exited the New Jersey Turnpike and made our way into a rundown industrial ghetto just south of Elizabeth. The Jaguar was too old to have built-in GPS, but Moon seemed to know where he was going. We made good time, mostly because of the early hour and the fact that this now was Saturday, so the millions of commuters who filled the roads were still home in their beds.

Moon made several left turns and a right, then pulled up in front of a dilapidated warehouse that seemed to have been abandoned for a very long time. The first floor consisted mostly of an empty loading dock with about a dozen bays, but there were no tractor trailers or forklifts in sight. No vehicles of any kind, in fact. Just mounds of trash, rusted equipment that had seen much better years, and the obligatory graffiti sprayed on the old brick walls. At one time there had been glass windows higher up, but those that hadn't been boarded over had been busted out.

The structure was surrounded by a ten-foot-high hurricane fence topped with spooled razor wire. Shreds of paper and plastic grocery bags had been snagged by the sharp barbs, and weathered signs warned of the dangers of trespassing. The whole place looked like a Garden State version of Dachau.

Moon stopped the car in front of a rolling gate that had been fastened tight with a chain and padlock. He cut the engine and stared at the dark building, saying nothing as the gears went to work in his head. Eventually he opened his door and climbed out, then grabbed from the floor a very menacing rapid-fire weapon, tucked close to the front of his seat. Curved bottom-loading magazine, carbon shoulder stock, and screw-on sound suppressor.

"SIG MPX," he said, as if that explained everything.

"What is this place?" I asked as I climbed out the passenger side. I had a tight grip on my own SIG, which looked like a toy compared to Moon's.

"The end game," Moon said.

"What does that mean?"

"It means you may have to use that thing, so watch out for the trigger. Pull it too hard, it fires, on account of the lack of a safety I told you about."

"Fantastic," I replied, my voice a mix of sarcasm and anticipation.

Moon circled back to the rear of the car and used his key fob to pop the trunk. There was a *thunk*, and then the lid bumped up an inch. He used his unarmed hand to raise it the rest of the way, then peered inside.

So did I. For some reason I'd expected to see a huge stash of automatic weapons and rocket launchers. *Thank you, Hollywood.* Instead, I took a step back and said, "Holy shit . . . who the hell is that?"

Zemira Moon didn't answer right away as he studied the hog-tied man lying on his side. His hands and feet were tightly bound together with duct tape, another length of which was wrapped tightly over his mouth. His nose was left unblocked, just enough so he could breathe the stale air inside the trunk.

The prisoner twisted and turned, trying to free his hands, his eyes burning with fear and anger. Contempt too. He was mumbling something, but the tape on his lips caused his words to be lost in translation.

"Cameron Kane, meet Colonel Eagleton," Moon said, aiming his SIG MPX at him.

"The dickhead who got your men killed?"

"Motherfucker," Moon said with a slow, resolute nod.

I studied the former Army officer, who looked like a wild boar being readied for a spit at a luau. "Jesus," I finally said. "Where did you . . . I mean, how long has he been in there?"

"Found him in the street." Moon's words came out all matter-of-fact, no compassion or contrition. And definitely no remorse. "He was with some buddies who weren't as lucky as he was. Son of a bitch is our get-out-of-jail-free card."

"Who's in jail?" I asked.

"Your wife," the ex-special forces operative said. "And we're going to use this scumbag to bust her out."

36

*B*UST HER OUT?

My brain jumped to warp speed as I realized that all the crazy shit I'd set in motion last Saturday at JFK had not been the work of an unhinged man. Or maybe it had been, and it took an irrational, unbalanced mind to color so far outside the lines. If I'd ever had any question that Alison might still be alive, now I was certain beyond all doubt.

"You mean . . . she's in there?" I jerked my head toward the dilapidated building ringed with fencing and razor wire.

"We're about to find out," Moon told me. "And this fat fuck is going to be our insurance policy."

"But what—?"

"No time for questions." Moon glanced at the pistol in my hand and said, "Think you could fire that gun if you had to?"

"Whatever it takes," I replied. "Just lead the way."

Moon dipped his head in the affirmative and handed me the larger SIG MPX. "Hold this for a second," he said, then turned his attention back to the trunk. There was an audible crack as he slowly rolled both massive shoulders, then leaned in and hauled Eagleton out. Without ceremony, he dumped the man on the pavement, then pulled another knife I hadn't seen before and crudely hacked through the tape that bound the defrocked colonel's trussed wrists to his ankles.

"Get up," Moon ordered him.

But Eagleton didn't budge, just glared at him in defiance. "Go to hell," he snarled. Even though the duct tape was still firmly stretched across his mouth, the meaning was loud and clear.

Zemira Moon clearly lacked the patience to play games. He snatched his machine pistol from my hand, pivoted, and promptly shot the man in the elbow. Eagleton bucked with pain, writhing in agony while the tape covering his lips prevented the tormented scream from echoing through the abandoned industrial slum. Moon then hauled him to his feet and shoved him toward the locked gate.

"Move," he said.

Despite the raw pain and flow of blood, Eagleton still hesitated in a continued display of senseless bravado and defiance. Moon ignored the show of bluster; instead, he pressed the barrel of his gun against the man's other elbow and said, "You really don't want to push me. There's lots of places in the human body where a bullet can maim but not kill."

That got Eagleton moving. Moon shot the padlock off the rusted chain that held the rolling gate in place, then heaved it open just wide enough for all three of us to edge through. Once we were inside the compound, Moon swept the gun around and pressed it into Eagleton's lower back.

"One bullet can sever the spinal cord neat and clean," he said. "Keep that in mind."

"Up yours," Eagleton mumbled through the duct tape. His arm was oozing blood, and his eyes reflected the pain in his shattered elbow, but he was trying his damnedest not to let the agony show.

At one time in the distant industrial past, semitrailers would pull into the large lot, then back up to the roll-up doors so forklifts could drop loaded pallets inside. Now the place had gone to shit, trash and glass and old tires and rusted equipment scattered around the corrugated asphalt perimeter. By all appearances the place had been abandoned for years.

Fresh tire tracks betrayed the lie, however. Around the corner of the building was a red Dodge Challenger Hellcat, matching red brake calipers, and carbon black aluminum wheels. Opening into the warehouse was a steel fire door, with a shattered lightbulb overhead, and an electronic keypad with ten push buttons.

"Combination," Moon ordered, crudely ripping the tape off Eagleton's mouth. "You know what happens if you make a mistake."

Eagleton didn't respond right away, taking the time to weigh his options. But it didn't take him very long to figure out there weren't any, because eventually he spat out six numbers.

Moon nodded at me, and I carefully punched the digits into the lock. When I finished, there was a resounding click, and when I gave the fixed handle a firm yank, the door creaked open. I pulled it just far enough for us to slip inside, then gently closed it again. My hand instinctively went for the light switch that should have been to the right of the door, but Moon caught me by the wrist.

"No," he warned in a low voice. Then he dug into yet another pocket and pulled out a flashlight. "Just this."

He flicked a button and a narrow beam cut through the darkness. He played it across the floor, then angled it up to the ceiling a good twenty feet above us. It was caked with old spray-on insulation and cobwebs and grime, and water dripped from pipes that ran from one side of the massive structure to the other. Moon drew the shaft of light across the plumbing until it fell upon a wall about twenty feet away.

The flashlight was one of those rechargeable high-lumen models I'd seen advertised on the Web as the most powerful beam you can buy. Moon painted it across the wall in front of us, which looked like an average American living room: front door, windows, couch and chairs, even a fireplace embedded in the corner. It seemed more like a movie set than a home, and I found myself whispering, "What is this place?"

"Shooting range," Moon said, more of a guess than fact. He dug the gun further into Eagleton's back and said, "Isn't that right, asshole?"

Eagleton said nothing, but to me it made sense. In fact, now that I really looked at the living room setup, I could see a random spray of holes where bullets had torn into the drywall. "Ironbridge owns this place?" I asked,

"Actually, it's owned by a holding company that was set up through a shell company that hides behind a parent company," Moon explained. "Still connected to Ironbridge, but hard to connect the dots if you don't know what you're looking for."

Eagleton still said nothing, his mind most likely preoccupied with finding a way to get out of this. Or at least send a warning to whoever owned the red Hellcat outside.

"There's got to be surveillance cameras," I said.

"With the latest night vision technology," Moon agreed.

"Won't they see us coming?"

"That's why we've got to be quick and coercive."

"So, what happens next?" I asked.

"That's up to our friend, here." Moon twisted the gun into Eagleton's kidney and said, "Where is she?"

She? I wondered. *Moon had already suggested Alison might be in here, but could it really be true?*

"Fuck you."

Moon let out a breath that really was more of a disappointed sigh. "Let me tell you something, you filthy shit. When I was going through special ops training, we were given a crash course on human anatomy," he observed. "Just in case something happened in the field. And, I guess, if we happened to meet up with a particularly stubborn enemy combatant. One day in particular, one of the doctors was lecturing about the mayhem inflicted by a bullet as it tears through the human body. In most cases, a direct hit, such as through the heart or a major artery, is an instant death warrant. But what I found particularly interesting is that if you get shot in the area surrounding your kidney and don't suffer any vascular damage to the organ itself, you have a good chance at survival. Given the proper dressing and medical care, of course. On the other hand, kidneys receive around twenty percent of the body's average blood volume at any given time, so if you actually happen to get shot in one of them, you have about five minutes before you bleed out. Things like adrenaline and vascular retraction response can affect survival time, but only for a couple minutes. After that you die."

The grim lesson in physiology was not lost on Eagleton who, with great reluctance, told him, "Basement."

"Show us," Moon said.

"It's rigged," the former colonel warned him.

"The life you save may be your own."

37

THE ENTRANCE TO the basement beneath the old brick
warehouse was at the far end of the building. Moon
prodded Eagleton through a maze of shooting sets that
expanded on the living room theme. There was an office
setup complete with a glass-enclosed boardroom and cube
farm, and a convenience store complete with beer coolers in
back and a cash register in front. Even a generic bank lobby
with a row of teller windows. All of them were pocked with
craters where bullets had struck the walls, all part of some
training program for the Ironbridge team.

We moved through the warehouse in almost total darkness, except for the piercing beam of Moon's flashlight.
The cavernous space was musty and carried a faint damp-
ness that had seeped into the masonry walls and concrete
floor. Eagleton eventually led us to yet another steel door,
again fitted with a keypad. Since his elbow was shattered
and bleeding, and his hands were still bound with tape, I
punched in the numbers as he recited them from memory.
When I finished, I pulled on the handle, but this time the
door did not budge.

"Don't screw with me," Moon warned him, twisting his injured arm behind his back.

"I'm not," the ex-colonel said. He winced from the throbbing pain, then recited the numbers one more time.

I entered them again, but still the door did not yield.

"You have one more shot to get this right," Moon told him. "Then I get to take one at you."

"I swear—that's the combination," Eagleton said, panic surging in his eyes. "On my mother's grave."

"How 'bout the graves of Hendricks, Beale, and Park?"

Eagleton looked at Moon with a blank stare; the names meant nothing to him.

"Those are the men on my team you killed," Moon said. "Swear on them instead, and the torture they went through because of your greed."

Eagleton started to utter some kind of retort, then thought better of it. He closed his eyes and tried to concentrate, then shook his head.

"That's the only combo I know."

Moon's finger tightened on the trigger, and he was a fraction of a second away from pulling it completely when a tinny voice came from a small speaker set on the wall.

"Who's up there," it said, fuzzy with static like a fast-food drive-up window.

Eagleton hesitated, but Moon bent down and whispered one word in his ear: "Kidneys."

The former colonel glowered at him, then said into the speaker, "Is that you, Toole? It's me. Eagleton."

Toole?

"What's up?"

"Asset security check, given everything that happened today," Eagleton grunted. "What the fuck's up with the combination?"

"Brody said to change it," the voice named Toole said. "Enter the same numbers backward, last to first."

A look of relief washed across Eagleton's pained face, and he took a big gulp of air. Then he slowly ran through the numbers in reverse order, while I punched them in as he went.

"Who are you talking to?" the voice asked.

"Myself," Eagleton replied. "Anyone down there with you?"

"Just me and the Prime Queen. Give me a second to deactivate the mousetraps."

Prime Queen?

Eagleton appeared torn on how to respond. The traps clearly were the protection he'd mentioned earlier, and shutting them down would make entry to the basement easier. But he also appeared to believe Moon would not hesitate to use the gun again.

"Do it quick," he said. "I'm coming down."

I entered the last of the six digits and the lock clicked. This time the door opened easily, revealing a flight of wooden stairs that led down to a lower level. There was a soft glow at the bottom, off to the left, which suggested a light was on somewhere in the dingy bowels of this decaying building.

"You first," Moon told Eagleton, with another jab in his spine.

"The duct tape will be a dead giveaway," Eagleton replied, holding up his bound wrists. "They're all trained to shoot first, ask questions later."

"Your problem, not mine. Go!"

He went, Moon right behind him while I brought up the rear. The stairs were creaky and old, the bowed wood sagging between the risers. I wondered if they were strong enough to support the weight of three good-sized men. There was a strong smell of mildew and wet concrete and, oddly enough, freshly microwaved popcorn. That caused me to remember that I hadn't eaten anything since the poppyseed muffin I'd wolfed down while buying coffee yesterday morning.

At the bottom there was no way to go but left, toward the dim light. Something liquid that did not appear to be water oozed from the ceiling, and rodent droppings littered the concrete floor. Strands of spiderwebs dangled from an overhead light that was covered with what looked like a hamster cage, and old paint was peeling from the walls in long curls. Moon pushed Eagleton in front of him, using him as a human shield. There was an open door at the end of a corridor about ten yards away, but no sign of the man whose voice Eagleton had identified as Toole's.

When we arrived at the doorway, Zemira Moon prodded Eagleton in the kidney and forced him inside a sterile room that was decidedly high-tech. The walls were a stark white, and the drop ceiling was water-stained acoustic tile, illuminated by bright halogen lighting. The man I recognized as Toole was seated at a cheap table with his back to the door, staring at a bank of flat computer monitors. He had changed into a red and black plaid L.L. Bean shirt and a Yankees cap, with the bill and logo facing backward. A cluster of hard drives was set in a steel rack next to the table, colored lights and LEDs glowing steady or blinking rapidly as the man tapped his keyboard.

Our movement must have reflected off one of the screens, because he spun around in his chair as he reflexively grabbed a gun that had been on the table in front of him.

"Put it down," Moon told him. "Or you owe the colonel, here, a kidney."

"Who the hell are you?"

"Do as he says," Eagleton said through his duct tape.

Toole didn't respond, didn't say a word. Didn't lower his weapon either. He just fixed his gaze on Eagleton, then shifted it a few inches to where Moon was boring his eyes into him. Then Toole glanced at me, standing behind both of them, my SIG Sauer leveled at his head.

"How the fuck—?"

"Ever hear of fool's mate?" I asked.

"This is nonnegotiable," Moon said, cutting us both off. "I won't hesitate to kill this sack of shit, and then there's nothing between you and me. Put it down."

Toole looked back at Eagleton, who gave the subtlest of nods. He hesitated again, a few seconds longer than necessary, then finally lowered the gun.

Zemira looked disappointed, as if he'd really been looking forward to putting another bullet into the colonel.

"On the floor, then kick it this way."

Toole did as he was told, scuffing what turned out to be a Glock halfway across the floor to the doorway. He shot a dark glare of contempt at Moon, who didn't seem to notice. Or care.

"On your knees."

Eagleton again indicated for him to follow Moon's command, so Toole slid out of the chair and lowered himself to the floor.

"Now—hands behind your back."

Toole did as he was told. Moon roughly pushed his way past Eagleton, then bent down and snapped a pair of forged steel cuffs on Toole's wrists. The colonel appeared to be contemplating an ill-advised move, so I touched the SIG against the base of his skull and said, "You too. On the floor."

Eagleton's elbow was growing worse, not better, and he appeared on the edge of shock. I could tell he wasn't accustomed to taking orders, and evidently didn't like doing so now. But the odds were stacked against him, so he had no choice. Down he went.

Zemira Moon swept his SIG SPX from one captive to the other, using the element of time to defuse any chance that one of these two men might try to do something stupid. Then he said, "Where is she?"

The two prisoners looked at each other, maybe trying to send coded signals. Neither said a word, so Moon said to Toole, "Talk now or you lose your foot."

Toole winced just at the thought of the pain, then glanced at Eagleton, who gave a firm shake of his head. *No.* "Brody gave strict orders—"

The wail of agony almost muted the blast as a gas-powered slug exited the SIG's barrel and tore through muscle and metatarsal. Blood spattered the concrete floor and walls, and Toole writhed in agony as he gaped at the crimson hole that had been blown through one of his Converse high-tops. He howled as he rocked with pain, his cuffed hands unable to provide any false comfort to his damaged foot.

"Your knee is next," Moon warned him.

"Don't say a word," Eagleton said.

"Three seconds. Choose wisely."

"I'm warning you, Toole," the colonel hissed.

Zemira Moon had not survived thirty-eight sorties into the mountains of Afghanistan and Pakistan by being a patient man, especially when the lives of his special ops teammates were at stake and quick action was vital. Eagleton was responsible for the deaths of three of them, and that knowledge weighed heavily in the events that came next.

Moon blithely swept his gun from the man he had just shot to the colonel and said, "Have you prepared yourself for the answer?"

"What's the fucking question?" Eagleton growled.

"It goes something like this: Of all the times, in all the places on this amazing and beautiful planet, when and where am I going to die?"

"What the—?"

The single shot caught the colonel in the left ear, his body knocked over by the force of the bullet as a wash of red sprayed on the moldy concrete wall. Blood pooled on the floor where his pulverized head had come to rest, and I stared at him with what I know was an anesthetized daze. All the death and dying of the last twenty hours had inured me to the reality of what I had just experienced.

"That one's for Hendricks," Moon said as he drew his gun back to Toole. "Let's try this again. Where is she?"

There was no hesitation this time, no searching for subtle indications of how to respond. Instead, Toole said, "Through that door, there." He was almost weeping from the pain screaming in his foot, but managed to add, "At the end of the hallway there's another door."

"And another combination?"

"Six digits, like the others," he winced. "One-three-one-zero-seven-one."

Moon glanced over at Kane and said, "You got that?"

"Got it." Kane nodded. "Who picked those numbers?"

"Damned bitch did," Toole snarled. "She said it's one of only two six-digit Mersenne primes—whatever those are."

"You go," Zemira Moon told me, cocking his head in the direction of the door. "I'll keep our friend company."

38

THE PASSAGEWAY WAS short, ten yards at best. Filthy and damp, just like the other one. As Toole had promised, there was a door at the end, more steel plate with three massive hinges fastening it to the wall. A fixed handle was welded to it, and a keypad was embedded in the concrete beside it. Lighting was minimal, but I could see enough to carefully punch in the numbers I'd been given.

When I pressed the final *1*, I heard a loud click, like the tumblers of a safe falling into place. My hand froze, just for a second, while a biting chill rolled from the base of my skull all the way down to the tips of my toes. Then I grabbed the door handle and gave it a slow pull.

Exactly one year ago my life had disintegrated at the sound of the police officer's voice on the phone. The first days following the accident had been both terrifying and tortuous, the bottom falling out from under me like an elevator plunging fifty stories to the ground. But over the past year I'd somehow managed to reassemble the shattered pieces of my world, although I'd never fully accepted that Alison was gone. It was a persistent denial stage of grief, and I'd been unable to forget all the dreams of the past and let go of all the promises I believed our future would hold.

Now I had no idea what I might find as I gave the door a gentle tug. The room was dark and smelled slightly of lavender, or maybe gardenias. A dim light was glowing somewhere within, but I could hardly see where it was coming from as I waited for my eyes to adjust to the blackness.

Then something hit me on the side of the head.

The sudden impact took me by surprise, but it was neither hard nor painful. In fact, whatever had hit me fell at my feet like a rolled-up ball of socks.

"Go away, you bastard," a voice called from within. "I told you, you're not getting one more thing out of me."

The voice sent another chill through my entire body, as if I'd jumped into a snowbank after stepping out of a sauna. *Impossible,* a disbelieving whisper in my head was telling me, but there it was. Real and indisputable.

"Alison?" I said.

"I've told you assholes before: to you, I'm Dr. Kane—"

"Alison?" I ventured again. "It's me. Cam."

A long silence followed. I didn't know what more to say, what else to do. My wife was somewhere in the dark room, or whatever was on the other side of the door. I still had not dared to pull it open all the way. Then she said, "Don't you mess with me."

"No one's messing—not anymore," I replied. "It's me. May I come in?"

"Stay there." Alison's voice was cold and hard and cautious. Distrustful. I could almost hear her beautiful brain working through the calculations, and then she replied, "*My* Cam?"

Fearful and skeptical. Understandable.

"Yes," I told her. "I've come to get you."

"But how—?"

"Please . . . may I come in?"

Another silence, more indecision and doubt. Then she said, her voice hesitant and quavering, "Tell me where we met."

"Charleston," I replied without thinking. "Jake's on the Creek, to be specific. We danced."

"What song?"

"Lots of songs. But the first one was 'Be Young, Be Foolish, Be Happy.' We danced all night, every song the band played."

"I was better than you," Alison said.

"At just about everything under the sun and the moon," I couldn't help but agree.

"Not everything," she responded with a giggle.

"I did say *just about*."

Just then, down the hall, came a noise that sounded suspiciously like a gunshot. Just one, and I hoped it was Moon who had pulled the trigger.

"My God, I've missed you," she said, her voice barely a whimper.

"Tell me about it," I replied. "So, may I come in?"

"Right this very second," Alison said, her words coming out like the cooing of a dove. "But keep the light off. I look like shit."

CHAPTER

39

Z EMIRA MOON HAD given me about five minutes to go
look for my wife, then came to check on us.

He found us both on a single bed that looked as if it had
come out of a military barracks, with a lumpy mattress and an
old Army blanket and a rock-hard pillow. We were sitting side
by side, holding hands, stunned expressions etched on both our
faces. I used my arm to wipe away a stream of moisture from
my eyes while Alison allowed hers to flow. Except for a dim
nightlight in one corner, the room was dark, and in the beam
of Moon's flashlight I could see why. One of Alison's eyes was
blackened and her cheek was bruised and swollen. Hair that a
year ago had been professionally styled every few weeks looked
as if it had been hacked with a pair of garden shears. She was
pale, her eyes seemed sunken, and she appeared exhausted.

"We have to go," Moon urged us. "Now."

"But you just got here," Alison protested. Even in the
beam of the high-powered flashlight she seemed confused
and dazed. "You can't leave me—"

"No one's leaving you," he said. "But we have to move
this very second."

She stared at him, then squeezed my hand. "You mean . . . this is over?"

"Only if we go right now," I replied.

"But . . . my work." She glanced over at a modest wooden desk set in a dark corner of the already dark room. "It's on my MacBook, there."

"Leave it," Moon said. "We really need to go. Now."

"No . . . I need it. It took a year to solve."

Once again Alison looked bewildered, almost scared, as if none of this made sense. One year in solitary captivity can really screw with a person's mind. Acting on impulse, I grabbed the computer off the desk, then helped my confused wife to her feet.

"Can you walk?"

"As long as I go slow," she said as she shuffled along beside me.

Slow was not an option, not right then. Without a second's thought, Zemira Moon scooped her into his massive arms and carried her out into the hallway.

"We have to go out the same way we came in," he told me with a sudden urgency. "And it's going to be tight."

"What do you mean, 'tight'?" she wanted to know.

"Timing is everything."

We reentered the room that held the racks of computers and the array of terminals. Eagleton's lifeless body lay crumpled against the cement wall where he had fallen, and Toole had struck a similar pose on the floor. A pool of blood was starting to form under his head.

"He sent out a silent alert, so I shot him," Moon said as he gently set Alison down. "Reinforcements are on their way, and we don't know where they'll be coming from."

"What's he talking about, honey?" Alison asked as she stood on wobbly legs.

"It means we're going to get you out of here," I replied. Then I glanced at Moon and said, "Right?"

"Right as rain."

Alison glared at Tootle's lifeless body as she sidestepped around him, then spat on him. "Bastard," she cursed.

It took us just under a minute to navigate our way back up the stairs and across the expansive warehouse to the small door that opened out on the windswept parking lot. Another fifteen seconds and we were through the rusted gate, and then Moon was helping my wife into the rear seat of the Jag.

"You ride in back with her," he told me. "And, ma'am . . . take off your shoes."

"My what?"

"Your shoes. Leave them. You'll get new ones when we get to where we're going."

"And where is that?" I asked. Alison slipped off the dusty slippers she'd been wearing and let them drop in the dirt.

"Somewhere safe," Moon said. "Meanwhile, keep your heads down."

I wasn't about to argue. I still couldn't believe I was here with Alison. My mind was still having difficulty grasping the fact that the entire accident had been staged by a cadre of cut-throat fucks just so Harding could escape a life behind bars. And my wife had been held against her will, a prisoner toiling away on a laptop to achieve . . . well, to achieve exactly what?

All of it caused me to think: What if I hadn't taken the red-eye after the job interview in LA? What if I hadn't brushed past Maxwell Harding in the terminal, hadn't chased after him to the taxi line and watched him drive off in a yellow cab?

Zemira Moon keyed the engine to life, and we sped off in a sizzle of gravel. He retraced his route back to the Turnpike,

merging into the weekend traffic that was getting thick even
at this early morning hour. No one followed us, shot at us,
or tried to run us off the road. The car sped through the spa-
ghetti maze of overpasses until we cruised through the toll
booth and were heading toward Delaware and other parts
south.

"Why are we going this way?" I asked from the back seat.
I was cradling Alison in my arms, holding her close to my
chest, trying to keep her from trembling. "New York's the
other direction."

"Like I said earlier, you can't go home," Moon told me,
his voice dull and impassive. "Not yet."

"But we have to," Alison objected. "I need to hold my
daughter."

I swept a string of hair out of her face and tucked it
behind her ear. "You will, sweetie," I assured her. Then to
Moon, I asked, "Now can you say where you're taking us?"

"You'll know when we get there. Right now, just focus on
your wife and leave the driving to me." More Vivaldi then,
and before I could ask, Moon announced, "Concerto for gui-
tar and strings in D major. Second movement."

*   *   *

There turned out to be a small cottage right on a stretch of
sand known as Seaside Park. The town was just one of many
overcrowded clusters of summer homes jammed together
along the shore of a narrow barrier island on the Atlantic
side of Barnegat Bay, a haven for summer refugees from New
York and Philadelphia. Tourist season was still more than
a month away, which meant that most of the homes were
empty, some of them boarded up against the winter storms
and local miscreants with criminal mischief on their minds.

"This place belongs to my sister's husband's cousin," Moon explained when we pulled up in front of it.

"Is someone expecting us?"

"No one's coming for a few more weeks," Moon replied, lifting a shoulder in a shrug. "But I know where they keep the key."

"Where's Sabrina?" Alison asked as the Jaguar's engine died. "I need to see her."

"She's safe and on her way. Now, let's get you inside."

*   *   *

I only learned later that my brother had refused to turn Sabrina over to the skinny Ethiopian who had shown up at his door. Wiry beard, dark glasses, and tricolored knit cap in red, green, and gold. A heated discussion had ensued, Elliot standing firm in his living room with his arms locked around Sabrina, insisting that wherever she went, he went. Janet Kane had remained in the hallway, terrified by this turn of events, worried that the actions of the last few hours surely would lead to their collective deaths. The thin Rasta tried to explain to my brother that he was on a mission to reunite Sabrina with her parents. Yes, both of them.

Elliot, the eternal skeptic, insisted that Sabrina had endured enough for one day, going on two, and he was not turning her over to a complete stranger. The gaunt Ethiopian eventually called Moon, who handed the phone off to me. I'd assured my brother that the guy was there to bring Sabrina to me, that I was fine and the events of the past twenty-four hours were over. Still, my brother was not convinced.

"What did we do last Sunday?" he asked me.

"Disney on Ice," I told him. "Julia dressed up as Elsa, and Sabrina was Belle."

He ran a few more safety questions by me, about our childhood and our parents and my first girlfriend. Just to make sure I was who I said I was.

Eventually he relented but still demanded to go with her, wherever the guy was taking her.

"Also, can she borrow a pair of Julia's shoes?" I asked him.

"Shoes? What for?"

"Long story." I'd already chiseled the GPS chips out and tossed them from the car, but my rough handwork had kind of trashed the sneakers she'd worn to the zoo.

"Whatever, bro," he said.

Did I mention that I really love my brother?

The hand-off ninety minutes later had been quick, the driver pulling up in front of the beach cottage just long enough for Zemira Moon to whisk Sabrina out of the car. Then he thumped his fist on the roof, signaling for his friend to take off. My brother began to protest from the back seat, but there was no use. They were gone in a cloud of sand, and not even a drone in the sky would have caught the exchange. Besides, I'm pretty sure Elliot saw Alison and me standing in the plate glass window, because I detected a look of total disbelief etched on his face.

40

"I STILL CAN'T BELIEVE you're here," I told Alison, both arms wrapped tightly around her. I nuzzled her neck and kissed her, tasting the salt from her tears. "It's been like living in a black hole since . . . well, for every second of the past year."

Alison said nothing, just held me as if she would never let go again. That was with her left arm; with her right arm, she clasped Sabrina just as tightly. Then she said, "I am so sorry about all of this."

"You're *sorry*?" I said, giving her an even tighter squeeze. "What do you have to be sorry for? Those men were total bastards." I felt my wife stiffen as Sabrina shot me an alarming glance. "I mean . . . *monsters*."

We were sitting on the weathered trunk of an old tree that had washed up on the sand. Initials circled by hearts had been carved in the parched wood, and little holes had been bored in it by woodpeckers and other critters hunting for beach grubs. The tide had slipped far out, and a gentle onshore breeze was drifting up on the expansive beach while plovers and sanderlings darted through the foam at the lip of the surf. The clear morning sky was a light powder blue, not a single cloud anywhere to be seen. Zemira Moon said he would be close by, keeping an eye open for *irregulars*, whatever they were. He didn't say, and I didn't ask. And true to his word, a pair of canvas topsiders had been waiting for Alison, almost a perfect fit.

I clung to Alison as tightly as possible, our daughter sandwiched between us. Each of us afraid to let go of the other, ever again.

* * *

The reunion went on for hours, and oceans of tears were involved. Not too many words, not until the disbelief and crying and near-paralysis had worn our souls bare. That's when the questions began to arise, Sabrina wondering aloud where her mother had been and why she'd left her and her daddy for so long. Alison had no easy answer for her daughter, just kissed her on the top of her head, her nose, her neck, and just about everywhere else.

Mid-morning, I caught a few hours of television and saw that last night's gunfight near my brother's apartment had made the news. Three heavily armed men had been shot on East 88th Street just a few blocks from Central Park. Two of them were pronounced dead at the scene, and the third was in grave condition at Lenox Hill Hospital. New York's finest had not provided identification of any of the victims, and they were looking into whether the incident was at all related to the shooting death of a woman in Nelson Rockefeller Park earlier in the day. And possibly the wounding of Mickey Donovan, a former NYPD detective who remained in critical condition after surgery.

Or the death of a young woman who apparently had jumped from the twenty-seventh-floor balcony of her apartment on 72nd Street, near the river.

Another loose end?

My questions were numerous and complex, and I knew enough to leave them for a later time. Alison had just as many, since she'd been locked in a hole for the last twelve months, where she'd had almost no outside contact. No internet, no cell phone, just stray bits of news that had been spoon-fed to her. Neither of us could imagine the pain and suffering the other had endured, not knowing what had happened to each other after that night just one year ago. I figured all three of us had months of personal anguish and family counseling ahead as we came to grips with the roller coaster that our lives had become. So many ups and downs, twists and turns on that corkscrew ride through hell and back.

"It was all about greed," Alison finally said, her voice just above a whisper.

"One of the deadliest of sins," I replied. "Harding was a cheat and a fraud and a scumbag."

"And I was naive. It never occurred to me the lengths he'd go to when he discovered what I'd done."

"Maybe because you never wanted to believe he could scheme up what he did."

"You never liked him, and I should have listened to you. Should have seen him for what he really was."

"But eventually you did," I said, trying to convince her that in no way should she feel guilty for the scam Harding had tried to pull. "When he tried to drain his accounts, your program froze him out of the system."

"You know about that?" she asked me.

"I talked to a lawyer from the US Attorney's Office—"

"Let me guess . . . a smarmy pencil pusher named Hartoonian?"

"Not quite. I was handed off to one of his underlings, a guy by the name of Myerson."

She ran the name through her cranial processor until it lined up with the right brain cells. "I remember him," she said. "He was there a lot of those nights I had to work late, but didn't have a whole lot to say. Or do."

"Well, for what it's worth, the feds are still trying to unlock what you did," I told her. "Myerson wasn't very forthcoming at the start, but eventually he told me how you were cooperating with the government to bring that bastard"—I caught myself again and looked at Sabrina, who was listening intently to what the two of us were saying—"that *monster* down."

"People died because of what I did," she said, keeping her voice to a whisper.

"You can't blame yourself for trying to do the right thing," I said. My mind briefly flashed on Elise Dillon, as I wondered where she might be.

"Maybe someday I'll believe that." She sighed. "Right now, all I want is to enjoy this moment, and the next one."

I nodded at what she was saying, and she gently rested her head on my shoulder. She kept running her fingers through Sabrina's hair as we fell into a silence balanced by the rhythmic purling of the waves on the sand. But my mind was awash with thoughts, and eventually I said, "One of these *somedays* I'd like to know how they did it."

"How they did what?"

"Got you into the car that night, then staged the accident," I told her. "That operation took some serious planning."

"It's what these *monsters* do. And they're *darned* good at it."

"But how—?"

"Shh." She kissed me on the cheek for the thousandth time. "We'll have time for all that later."

CHAPTER

41

*L*ATER CAME LONG after the sun touched the horizon in the west, casting a violet afterglow across the clouds that towered over the beach and the pewter sea beyond.

Alison and I were sitting on a wicker loveseat out on the screened porch that faced the dunes and the ocean in the distance. Sabrina was inside the house, sleeping on a foldout couch in the living room, right on the other side of the wall. We'd left the door open so we could hear any traces of the night terrors I was afraid might come, but so far our daughter was deep in dreamland. The evening was warm, the air was still, and for a few minutes we watched a frenzied colony of bats as they emerged from a drainage culvert and flapped and squeaked through the dusky sky.

Zemira Moon had dropped by a couple hours before, bearing two pizzas: a loaded veggie pie for Alison and me, and a Hawaiian one with ham and pineapple for Sabrina. *How did he know about that?* I wondered.

"You need some time as a family," he'd explained as he keyed the Jaguar engine to life.

"Are we safe here?" Alison asked him.

"I've seen to it," Moon assured her. "No traces, no bugs. No one knows where you are. The kitchen is stocked, and the cable is pretty good. Wi-Fi too. Just don't make any phone calls or use your credit cards, and you'll be fine."

"We can't hide out forever," I pointed out. "This is a nice place to hang for a few days, and I thank you for all you've done. But we have a home."

"And you'll be back in it before you know it," he replied. "I'll let you know when the coast is clear."

"How?" Alison asked.

"You'll know," he said, directing his answer to both of us. Then he looked away evasively as he rolled up the window and drove off. True to his nature, he didn't divulge where he was going, and by now I'd learned not to ask.

Although his words *close by* kept echoing in my ears.

*　*　*

After dinner Alison had slowly soaped and scrubbed Sabrina during a long bath that involved many months of catching up and an almost constant flood of tears. This was followed by three chapters of a well-worn book Sabrina had found in the back bedroom about a girl named Keena, who kept a secret journal. Eventually her eyes drooped, and Alison tucked a warm blanket under her chin.

Alison had clutched my hand almost nonstop since morning, but she let go to pick up a glass of merlot—also courtesy of Mr. Moon—that she'd carried out from the kitchen. She took a sip and continued to stare out at the last remnants of the day, not finding the words she wanted to say. I'd opted for a splash of bourbon in an old jelly glass, and now let the taste wash over my tongue.

I gently squeezed her knee through the tired jeans she'd been wearing when I'd found her that morning. I asked her about that, and she told me her captors brought her new clothes about once a month, mostly thrift shop castoffs and drug store necessities.

"You don't need to talk about it if you don't want to," I told her.

"I owe you an explanation," she whispered.

"You owe me nothing. In fact, there's something I need to tell you. Something that happened while you were gone."

She gripped my hand and said, "I know all about that woman, if that's what you're getting at."

"How did you know about that?"

"My captors made sure I was well informed," Alison explained. I could think of a lot more vicious and expressive words for them than *captors*, but I kept them to myself. "I think they figured it was some sort of motivational thing, telling me that my husband had found love again and was getting on with his life. My daughter too."

"How was that supposed to motivate you?" I asked.

"They were all dumb as rocks. They had no idea what makes my brain tick."

"No one does," I reminded her with a grin. "I just want you to know that if I'd had any idea you were still alive, I never—"

"Shh," Alison hushed me. "You thought I was dead. It was all over the news, and they made sure I knew what they'd done. Those poor people who died in that car . . . so horrible."

"I thought one of those poor people was you," I told her. "There was surveillance video of you in Harding's car, driving out of the parking garage."

"I know," she replied. "I remember calling you that night and telling you I'd be working late. All those government lawyers, going through mounds of printouts and sorting through Maxwell's blockchain. We wrapped up earlier than I'd thought, and I told them I was going home instead of grabbing dinner. I made a pit stop at the ladies' room, and that's when these two thugs attacked me. They actually forced themselves into the stall and jabbed a needle into my neck. The next thing I remember was waking up from whatever they injected me with. Afterward, they showed me newspapers full of details about the car crash, two people burned beyond recognition. All I could think about was what you were going through. You and Sabrina."

"What about Harding? Where was he?"

Alison shook her head and said, "I have no idea. After they made the switch that night, they took me to this swanky place downtown, way up on about the hundredth floor. I was locked up twenty-four-seven for the last fucking year—nothing but a bed, a computer, and a view of the river. The only exercise I got was walking tiny laps around the room."

Instinctively I knew she was talking about the same penthouse where they'd held Sabrina and me yesterday. Which begged a question: "When did they move you to the dungeon in the warehouse?"

"About a week ago. I managed to get hold of a cell phone that belonged to one of my guards and tried to send you a text."

"My dearest huckleberry friend," I said.

"Oh my God . . . you did get it."

"For about five seconds. Then it disappeared from my phone."

"I'm not surprised," she said. "They had some pretty decent programmers working for them."

"Not good enough to get past your firewall."

"That's why I wrote the code the way I did," Alison explained. "Anyway, when they found out what I'd done, they moved me to that rat-infested hole. As they were leading me to the elevator, I ran into Harding, smug grin on his face. He told me if I didn't finish up soon, both you and Sabrina would be dead. All I wanted to do was punch him through that plate glass window."

I wanted to ask her *finish up what?* but I knew she'd get to it in her own time. Instead, I whispered, "Shh. That was all a bad dream."

She nodded, as if trying to convince herself she actually was sitting here in this screened-in porch on the Jersey shore, with her husband beside her and her daughter just a few feet away in the living room. Finally, she said, "She's beautiful. The woman you started seeing."

I cringed at the lengths to which Ironbridge had gone to screw with our lives. "I was an idiot, a grieving widower trying to get on with my life," I told her. "I didn't know it was a setup. Once she squirmed her way into my life, she tapped my phone, put cameras and microphones all over the house, and God knows what else. I just can't figure out why."

"Desperate times called for desperate measures," Alison said.

"What do you mean?"

"You know that phone I used to send you that text? Well, about a month before that I managed to steal the same cell from the same guard. I thought if I could call you this would all be over. I got caught, but they had no idea whether I'd gotten through to you or not. Just as a safety precaution, they started watching you night and day, and arranged it so you would meet your new girlfriend."

"That would have been just around the time they put Marika on that escalator," I said.

"That was her name?"

"That's what she told me, but her real name was Gina. I got played."

"We all did," Alison replied. "When Eagleton found out that I'd almost made contact with you, he was furious. Something he explained with his fists."

That explained the bruises and the black eye. "Bastard got what he deserved," I told her, knowing my words did nothing to ease the pain she had suffered.

"But not before he went code red."

"What does that mean?"

She squeezed my hand tightly and said, "The day before yesterday, he gave the order to kill you both."

I squeezed back and pulled her close. "Well, that didn't work," I replied.

"No, but he was capable of anything. Remember, he killed two innocent people just to make you—*everyone*—believe Max and I had died."

I nodded at what Alison was saying, but then something Myerson had mentioned came to mind. I figured I already knew the answer, but wanted to hear Alison tell it in her own words. "Myerson said Harding had you create a trapdoor for him in case there was some kind of emergency," I said. "But it slammed shut on him after he posted bail."

"Essentially that's right," Alison said. "The thing is, when you're looking down at the forest from above, you often don't see the trees below."

"Meaning?

"Meaning, in this case there's a man named Brody."

"I know. Myerson told me about him, how he was part of the investigation. I even called him earlier this week, left him a message."

"Dear God, Cam." Alison gasped. "You think Max is a bastard? It was Brody who had his ear from the beginning."

"That's probably what triggered everything that happened yesterday," I replied.

"Maybe, but it really started when you ran into Max at JFK last weekend. After they'd been so meticulous in planning everything down to the last detail and having a contingency plan for everything, that was not supposed to happen."

"I had an employment interview in LA and didn't tell a soul except Hannah's mom."

"Who's Hannah?"

"One of Sabrina's friends. You'll love her. Thing is, I didn't even tell Marika about it."

"You didn't have to," Alison replied. "Toole and Eagleton set that up."

"What are you talking about?"

"The job thing. They wanted to move you a continent away so you wouldn't be a threat."

I suddenly felt more stupid than ever. And embarrassed that I'd thought for some reason the Bradley Museum would seek me out for a high-level curator job. Now I didn't feel quite so bad for not getting back to Claire Beckett. I also wondered who might have pressured her to make me an offer I could hardly refuse, since I'm sure other candidates were far better qualified for the job than a rights procurement agent at a photography licensing firm.

"Their reach is far and wide," she said. "Anyway, you were talking about your friend Moon?"

"Right." I told Alison how my old friend Lillian Sloane had hooked me up with a former New York detective named Mickey Donovan, but deliberately left out the part about how she'd been shot and killed. I explained that Donovan had turned to an old special forces guy from Afghanistan, who tracked everything back to an organization called Ironbridge and Colonel Eagleton.

"I met him that first day after the crash. Him and Brody. Arrogant lying bastards, and both of them were behind all this."

I heard what she was saying but was having trouble making sense of what she was telling me. I also wondered who the unfortunate woman was who'd been snatched—much the same way Jason Dillon had been snatched—and strapped into the passenger seat of Harding's Lamborghini.

"You're going to have to tell me what 'all this' was," I said at length.

"Do you want the short version or the long version?" Alison asked.

"The version with the least amount of math."

She giggled as she pecked me on the cheek, and it felt good. "All right—I'll spare you the pain." She grinned. "Like Myerson probably told you, a couple years ago Harding asked me to create a firewall that would prevent anyone from hacking into the company's servers and accessing his clients' accounts. He said he was worried about ransomware, and it also was supposed to protect his cryptocurrency transactions. At least that's what he told me at the time, so I went ahead and created a program that would add a layer of security."

"Based on prime numbers."

"Max insisted," she confirmed. "But I wasn't very far into it when I began to suspect he really was building a failsafe system to protect his own larcenous interests."

"Then you did have your suspicions about him."

"I was a little slow on the draw, but yes, I started to have some misgivings. I'd begun to hear things internally, rumors that he was committing fraud and the company was on shaky ground. I figured if the feds started to close in on Max, his plan was to just disappear."

"Along with a boatload of money."

"An entire flotilla of it," Alison said. "Anyway, without his knowledge, I developed a worm designed to lock down the corporate servers as soon as anyone tried to access those accounts. And sure enough, when Harding bonded out after being arrested, the first thing he did was try to bypass the firewall and divert all of the company's assets as well as those of his clients. All of which automatically triggered my digital deadbolt. Shut it down tight, and holy crap, was he royally pissed when he figured out what I'd done. Kicked and screamed and swore he was going to kill me."

I'd been swallowing a sip of bourbon and almost choked on it as I launched into a coughing fit. When my throat finally settled down, I said, "I thought he had."

"And that's what I thought was happening when they grabbed me out of the ladies' room the night of the accident. Until I woke up, and Eagleton and Brody told me what they were really after."

I took another long sip from my glass, waited until this one had safely gone down my throat before speaking. "He kidnapped you to pop the lock."

"Exactly. The problem was, I didn't have a key."

"That's what Myerson said," I replied. "I don't think he believed you."

"None of the feds did. They were all red-tape, type-A bureaucrats who couldn't conceive how I could create a security system that didn't include a failsafe way to override it."

"They may have had a point."

"Not at all," Alison said with a dismissive wave of her hand. "They were just so totally focused on ransomware and cryptovirology that they completely missed the exercise itself. The program I wrote was based on theoretical mathematics and advanced approximations, and they couldn't believe that an actual key was only hypothetical. At least at that point."

I leaned over and kissed her on the cheek. "If you're trying to lose me, you're doing a good job."

"Sorry . . . I can't help it," she replied as she kissed me back. She fell silent for a moment, snuggling against me as the first star of the evening blinked on. Was this a sign that she was returning to a point of normalcy, or just a side-effect of the merlot? "Math is what drives me."

"I know," I said. "One of so many things I love about you. But maybe we can skip ahead to the car chase?"

That drew another laugh, and she said, "I'll try. Do you remember my doctoral thesis?"

"Yeah," I replied. I flashed back to that very first spin around the dance floor with her in South Carolina years ago as I followed her wherever she led me. I hadn't felt intimidated by what everyone called her superhuman brain then, nor afterward. "I tried to read it, but all I remember is that French monk who was into prime numbers."

"That's right. Marin Mersenne was a seventeenth-century scholar who compiled a list of a certain kind of prime number, those that are one less than two raised to the power of another prime. Since the beginning of time only fifty-one Mersenne prime numbers have been identified, and the most recent one that was discovered is almost twenty-five million digits long."

"That's a damned big number," I said, trying my best not to sound impatient. "But what does this have to do with Harding?"

"I'm getting to that," she assured me. "You see, to create the failsafe system, I used an approximation algorithm to create a program based on the theoretical existence of the next unsolved Mersenne prime."

I swirled the last trickle of bourbon in my glass before bidding it farewell down my throat. "I don't have a clue what you're talking about," I confessed.

"No one did," Alison replied. "Not the feds, not Harding, not Brody. And the fact is, I wrote it mostly as more of a challenge to myself, since I never once thought I might actually have to solve it."

"Not until they kidnapped you."

"To put it in very simple terms, yes," Alison replied. "To solve the impossibly complex equation I set for myself."

"So, for the past year you've been working on a *math problem?*"

"It's more than just a math problem," she said, just a hint of indignation in her voice. "I've been trying to find the next Mersenne prime."

"Jesus." I sighed. "That could have taken forever."

"Unless you just happen to be sitting around a sterile high-rise condo with nothing but time on your hands. Plus, I'd already started working on it before."

"Before what?"

"Before . . . all this. My preliminary research was on my old MacBook."

"You're telling me . . ." My voice trailed off as I thought back to the burglary, and suddenly it all made sense. "They robbed our condo during your memorial service so they could get it for you."

Alison shook her head rapidly. "*Damn*—I had no idea that's how they'd gotten it. After Eagleton told me why they'd grabbed me, I happened to mention that the root of the solution was on my old computer. Then a couple days later there it was, on a table in that empty room. I didn't know how they'd gotten it. Anyway, with nothing else to do, it didn't take long."

That's when her face broke into a big grin.

I flashed her a suspicious look and said, "What are you trying to tell me?"

"I'm telling you that I actually solved it last December. Without any distractions it really wasn't that hard."

"You mean you figured it out? This new Mersenne prime?"

The grin evolved into a satisfied smile. "I'd come close before, back in college," Alison said. "But I knew if I gave it to those greedy pricks—Harding and Brody and Eagleton—they'd use it to open the lock and empty the accounts. And then they'd have no more use for me."

I nodded at that. Everything was starting to come together now. "And since the world already thought you were dead, they'd have to eliminate you for real."

"Precisely," Alison agreed. "And you and Sabrina, most likely. They were really big on tying up loose ends."

Like Marika, whom I now was sure had been pushed from her West Side balcony.

"You tricked them," I said.

"I bought some time, is all," she replied. "I didn't have a lot of leverage, but I kept telling them I was closing in on the solution, and just to let me work. That's when they started giving me photos of you and Sabrina, showing how you were getting on with your lives. Both of you."

"That had to be difficult."

"It was, but I knew you were dealing with much worse. I knew you and she were alive, but you both believed I was dead."

"How long do you think you could have kept stringing them along?" I asked.

Alison inhaled a deep breath and let it out slowly. "That's the thing," she said. "The day before yesterday, a European math journal reported that someone else had, in fact, discovered the next Mersenne. A physicist in Switzerland. That meant they no longer needed me, and I was expendable. As soon as they were able to get their hands on the number, they'd be able to unlock the code. At least that's what they thought."

I'd wondered why Ironbridge had chosen yesterday to gun down Mickey Donovan, snatch Sabrina, and try to kill both of us.

"What do you mean, 'that's what they thought'?" I asked.

"When I wrote the original security protocol, the next Mersenne prime was entirely theoretical," she explained. "No one had a clue what it might be, and at that point the firewall was impossible to crack. Which was a good thing, since the only reason to do so would be to steal what was behind it. Now, I'd also written into the program a complex equation that's widely used in math circles to determine if a number is, in fact, a valid Mersenne, and then I set it to reject any of those that had already been discovered. Just to keep one step ahead of anyone who got wise to my strategy."

"Please, Math, can we try to keep it simple?" I begged, using my nickname for her.

Alison giggled and took a sip of her merlot, then cradled the glass in her hands. "Sorry . . . once the brain kicks into gear, inertia takes over," she said. "The thing is, I knew someone eventually would find that next prime. In fact, I was well on my way to doing just that when Harding's goons snatched me and interrupted my work. But to answer your question, the entry code actually was the theoretical Mersenne prime I'd been working on, minus the last one that was found a couple years ago."

"You mean they were looking for the wrong number all along?"

Alison nodded and said, "It was just a simple precaution I took in case Max found some hacker smart enough to figure it out."

I did my best to digest what she was telling me, realized that it made some sort of sense, at least on a higher level of theoretical mathematics. But there was something that was still bothering me, and I mentioned it to her.

"Just because Eagleton's dead doesn't mean we're beyond the reach of Ironbridge."

"Decapitated worms can regenerate their brains," she agreed. "Eagleton and Toole are gone, but Max is still out there. So is Brody. How long do you think we'll have to stay here, living like outlaws on the run?"

"Moon seemed pretty optimistic about that," I said. "Couple of days, no more than a week. He'll let us know."

"And what if he doesn't?" she pressed me. It wasn't like Alison to be all negative and gloomy, but she had good reason. We all did. "What if something happens to him, and we never hear from him again?"

"Executable bite-size chunks," I heard myself say.

"Meaning what, exactly?"

"Meaning we take things one step at a time. Right now, I'm just enjoying the lapping of the waves on the sand, feeling the warmth of you next to me, and knowing that our daughter is sleeping safely in the next room."

Alison didn't say anything right away, and I used the silence to think about where Harding might be. Was he still in New York, holed up in the apartment on William Street? I doubted he'd hang around the city after the events of the past few days, his plan unraveling and everything he'd worked toward spiraling down the john. If I were him, I would have booked the next flight back to Rio or some country that didn't have an extradition deal with the US. But then, if I were Harding, I never would have pulled any of this shit in the first place.

As if she were reading my mind, Alison looked at me and said, "As long as that SOB is out there, we're in the crosshairs. Despite what Mr. Moon says or does, we all know too much. And Max has too much to lose."

For the last week all I'd cared about was finding my wife, getting her back into our lives. Going home to our Jane Street condo, eating ice cream on the High Line. Playing board games with Sabrina on the living room floor. Wrapping my arms around her, making love as if it were the very first time. But she was right: none of that was going to be possible, not for the foreseeable future.

"I don't see that we can do much about it," I told her. "As Moon said, we need to stay here, off the grid."

"No phone calls, no plastic," Alison replied. "But he didn't say anything about the internet."

She had a look in her eyes, one that I'd first seen years ago when she'd first whispered "Your place or mine?" in my ear. I flashed her a wary but intrigued look and said, "What are you talking about?"

"Just now you mentioned something about bite-sized chunks, right?"

"I did."

"Well, I took the first nibble a couple hours ago," she said, a mischievous hitch in her voice. She snuggled closer and nestled her head on my shoulder. "Part of a backup plan just in case we need to disappear for a while."

"What are you telling me?"

She ignored my question and asked me one of her own. "Do you have any idea how much money is actually in those accounts Max and his cronies have been trying to get to?"

"Myerson said something about four billion dollars."

"Four-point-two-six billion," she corrected me. "That's four billion, two hundred sixty million. Give or take a few. No one besides me—not even Max—knows for sure what the exact amount is, because they haven't been able to touch it for over a year."

"Okay . . ." I said, wondering what Alison was getting at.

"The reason I wanted to bring my MacBook when we left that hellhole this morning was because it contained all my work, including the next Mersenne prime. And I needed it to run my approximation algorithm, so I could pop the lock. To use your words for it."

Alison and I were together again for the first time in a year, she wasn't dead, and Sabrina was sleeping on the other side of the wall. I understood that her entire world for the last twelve months had revolved around discovering this elusive prime number, but why was she obsessing so much about it now?

"Do you think this can wait?" I asked.

"Just hear me out, and you'll see the whole picture," she replied with a wink. "The thing is, I couldn't wait to see if my theoretical key actually fit the deadbolt."

"Are you telling me you broke through the firewall?"

She said nothing, just gave me a big, innocent look with those beautiful blue eyes. Then the faint lines of a smile crept into her lips.

"Alison," I said. "When did you find the time—"

"Earlier, when you thought I was in the bedroom taking a nap. After I logged in, it didn't take very long."

"Holy shit—you know they can trace that computer."

"Don't fret, Mr. Worrywart," she assured me, giving me a kiss on the cheek. "I know my way around cyberspace, and I'm pretty good at covering my tracks. Risk management and all that. Anyway, do you know what half of one percent of 4.26 billion is?" she asked me.

"You know I can't do that kind of math in my head."

"A little over twenty-one million," Alison told me, drawing invisible numbers in the night air. "A minuscule fraction of the whole. No one is ever going to miss it."

She stopped talking, let it hang there until I figured out what she was implying. It took a few seconds for her words to sink in, but eventually the reality hit me.

"What have you done?"

She squeezed my hand, then lightly kissed my cheek. "Don't worry, honey. No one's going to miss it. Not a penny. The feds have no idea how much is in Max's accounts, and they're going to wet their pants when they eventually get access to it all."

I'd only partially been listening before when she'd asked me about percentages, still basking in the knowledge that Alison was here, snuggled up beside me on a love seat in a screened porch on the Jersey shore. But now I replayed her words in my head, until I got to the figure she had mentioned.

Twenty-one million? I mouthed, without actually saying the number.

"It's below the government's threshold of error," she said. "An infinitesimal fraction of the total. Consider it a finder's fee."

"But twenty-one million . . ." This time I actually said the amount out loud, and I had to admit it sounded pretty good. And damned worth all the hell we'd been put through over the past twelve months.

"If nothing else, it's the start of a good college fund," she said quickly. "And it affords us a little wiggle room, if we have to wiggle."

"We really need to think this through."

"Too late," she said, touching a finger to my lips. "I already moved it to an offshore account I set up this afternoon."

"I don't have any say in this?"

"You do if you say yes."

END GAME

Ethan Brody had a good bead on both targets. Always a hands-on man when push came to shove, he'd decided to end this business himself, once and for all. Even though he ostensibly worked for the government, he was private sector through and through.

He'd parked the stolen Toyota Camry six blocks from the tiny beach house, then hung in the darkness while he walked back. Without hesitating, he stealthily climbed onto the raised deck of a two-story house across the sandy road, two doors down. The windows were covered by roll-down hurricane shutters, which told him no one was going to be showing up anytime soon. He took up position in the shadows of an outdoor stone fireplace with a massive gas grill and wet bar, all locked down for the season.

He figured the two shots would be easy. It was only thirty yards to where Cameron and Alison Kane were sitting on the screened porch, a distance he'd mastered when he was still a boy, shooting rats at the town dump.

He heard them talking about something in hushed tones, all giggles and lovey-dovey words, making up for lost time.

He almost felt sorry for them—*almost*—given all the shit they'd gone through this past year. Well, at least they'd had a few good hours together before he blew their brains out.

On the other hand, Brody had given up on the little girl. Despite the fact that everything had gone to hell over the past thirty-six hours, he decided she really didn't know enough to be a threat. Or a liability. Besides, it would be far too difficult to hit her inside the house and make a clean escape. Too many variables, too much that could go wrong. He could live with that, and she would too. Brody really wasn't that much of a heartless bastard after all.

He decided to keep the laser sight off. In the growing darkness, the bright red dot would give him away, and he had no margin for error. Besides, the overhead lamp in the screened porch provided more than enough light to take care of this, once and for all.

He fixed the sight's horizontal and vertical lines right over Kane's chest, then gently tightened his index finger on the trigger.

There was a muffled pop, followed almost instantly by a final breath of life taking flight in the evening air.

*　*　*

Deep in the shadow of a carport two doors down, Zemira Moon lowered his SIG Sauer MPX gas-operated semiautomatic and unscrewed the hand-crafted silencer.

"That one's for Beale," he whispered to the night.

He stood in the darkness, watched as Mr. and Mrs. Kane slowly kissed in the dim light of the screened-in porch. For a moment he recalled how good that had felt, many years ago in a time when his own life seemed young and new and alive with hope and possibility. He waited until he saw them step inside the living room, then slipped the gun firmly into its leather holster. He flexed his shoulders in a circular motion, working out a kink that had set in while waiting in the growing night. He briefly considered whether he should move Brody's body from where it had fallen, but decided it wasn't worth the effort.

Nor did he have the time. He'd accomplished everything he'd come here to do, and he wanted to put this business to rest, once and for all. In the morning a courier would deliver a package to Mr. Kane, the contents of which would provide everything he and his family would need to go back to their condo on Jane Street and get on with their lives. The New York District Attorney suddenly was taking a profound interest in a clandestine outfit known as Ironbridge, which had tried to kill a former NYPD detective and allegedly was responsible for a half-dozen other bodies scattered across Manhattan and New Jersey.

Meanwhile, Moon had one last item to cross off what he called his "fuck-it list."

He inhaled the fresh scent of the sea into his lungs, felt the cell phone in his pocket begin to vibrate. He'd silenced the device until he'd finished his business with Brody, but now, as he glanced at the screen, he recognized the number and the international phone code. It was Travis Leon, who would have just touched down in Casablanca after a two-hour flight from Gibraltar.

"Status report," Moon said when the call connected.

"Target arrived thirty minutes ago," Leon replied. "Took a limo to the Four Seasons on Boulevard de la Corniche, where he has a suite reserved for a week."

Maxwell Harding no doubt figured he would be safe hiding out in Morocco. Unlike Brazil, the country had no official extradition treaty with the US, even though the government had returned a few suspected criminals over the years. He'd been forced to change his escape route after the events of yesterday, but—like most narcissists—he was possessed of a cocky false confidence that he was smarter than everyone else, and therefore his movements could not be traced.

Moon was one step ahead of him, however. He'd been tipped off by an E-ring Pentagon source who had told him that a Mr. Joseph Zaccaro from Rio had booked a nonstop earlier in the day from JFK on Royal Air Maroc.

"You want me to keep an eye on him?" Travis Leon asked.

"Please," Moon confirmed. "Find out where he's having dinner tomorrow."

"I'm on it."

"And make sure there's a full tool kit in my room."

"It'll be waiting for you."

The call ended, and he slipped the phone back into his pocket. He nodded to himself in cold satisfaction, then said, "This last one's for you, Park," his voice barely a wisp of a breeze as a nearly full moon emerged from behind a passing cloud.

ACKNOWLEDGMENTS

N O NOVEL IS completed in a vacuum, even if it starts out that way. Once the first words are affixed firmly to the page, other people are invited to weigh in with their thoughts and insights. Such is the case with *Beyond All Doubt*, which went through well more than a dozen drafts before I felt confident enough to share it with my agent.

That would be Kimberley Cameron, a great friend and colleague, whom I thank not only for believing in this book from the beginning but for finding such a good home for it so quickly. You always seem to make the impossible possible, and I am eternally grateful to have you in my corner. Merci beaucoup.

Heartfelt thanks and appreciation to my editor, Marcia Markland, at Crooked Lane Books, whose boundless enthusiasm and accolades made me feel like a king, and whose invaluable suggestions then brought me back down to earth again. Same thing for everyone else at Crooked Lane who worked to bring this book to fruition: Madeline Rathle, Dulce Botello, and Rebecca Nelson, who expertly steered everything through the publishing and marketing maze;

Nebojsa Zoric for an awesome cover; and Thaisheemarie Fantauzzi Pérez and Yezanira Venecia for early edits.

I extend my most sincere gratitude to all my beta readers, who provided brutally honest criticism and advice that, while sometimes painful, was always most welcome. The same goes for multiple editors—you know who you are—whose red ink served to make this a much tighter book. It truly does take a village.

Andrew Guest: I owe you lunch. A big one.

Last—and by no means least—there's my wife, Diana. For better or worse, I couldn't do this without you, your support and belief, and your love. Bold and dashing, baby. Bold and dashing.